Pawns in the Shadows

Pawns in the Shadows

The Game Was Never Fair

A Will Anderson & Casey Murphy Thriller

W Mark Harrington

Disclaimer

This is a work of fiction. While the streets, towns, and landmarks of the Carolinas and surrounding areas may feel real, the people who walk them in these pages are creations of the author's imagination. Any resemblance to actual persons, living or dead, or to actual events is purely coincidental.

Content Warning

This story pulls no punches. It contains graphic depictions of violence, sexual assault, abduction, and murder, along with strong language and themes that may be disturbing. It's intended for mature readers who can handle the darker corners of human nature.

Dead End Ink

ISBN 979-8-9998766-4-5
ISBN: 979-8-9945440-1-3

This Book is the third book in the
Will Anderson and Casey Murphy Thriller Series.
You can find them fighting for survival in the books,

Demon of Oakhaven

Devil at Rocky Pointe

along with

Will Anderson Origin: Blood and Silence

available at your local book retailer, online
at Amazon.com, and other online outlets.

DEDICATION

To the overlooked. To the underestimated. To those placed where the fire burned hottest, and told it was an honor.

This is for every pawn sacrificed without ceremony, whose story ends where someone else's power begins.

For those who learned the rules were fixed, the board was tilted, and winning was never the point—
Obedience was.

You moved anyway.
And that frightened them.

This story is for you.

Table of Contents

Prologue: Opening Move 1
The Watcher Sees All 8
The Intern 14
The Rook's New Message 25
Day Drinking 32
Ravenwood University Security 44
Ryan Cho 49
Watcher Observes 57
Kristen's Courtroom Failure 60
Second Pawn Off the Board 64
Sheri Langley 68
Cool in the Pool 77
Twins in Danger 86
Casey's Discovery 96
Rachel's Research 105
Sorority Sister Interviews 111
Frustration of Office 129
Watcher Journal – Corrections to be Made 134
Dark Webs 139
Carter Vance 145
Enter Agent Rivers 151
The Pawn Dared, The Pawn Captured 157
Dark Web Discovery 163
Second Summer 171
Breadcrumbs 175
Another Pawn 182
Atlanta 187
Home Cooked Meal 194
Targeting the Tower 204

Shadows in the Dark....217
Pawns Under Siege....219
Close Enough....228
Rachel Delivers....236
The Phone Call....239
Confession....253
Getting Back Home....257
The Watcher Observes....266
Family Dinner....268
Shadows Intent....286
Pieces in Play....297
Breakthrough....300
The Date....307
Check....315
Checkmate....322
The Fallen Piece....331
Hard Day for Carter....333
Aftermath....341
Epilogue: Hellbound....347

"Every pawn carries the hope of reaching the other side, even when the board is designed to break them."

— Mark

"Those who deny freedom to others deserve it not for themselves."

— Abraham Lincoln

Prologue: Opening Move

The body lay sprawled beneath the looming clock tower of Ravenwood University, its hands frozen at 10:04 p.m., casting a long, accusing shadow across the quad. The yellow wash of campus floodlights turned the stonework a sickly gold, the blood beneath him darkening to a sticky black against the cobblestones.

A crowd pressed against the perimeter of police tape, students jostling for a better view. The August heat clung heavily, dampening shirts and plastering hair to foreheads. The air buzzed with murmurs—the faint hum of phones recording, the stuttering click-click of phone shutters, tinny echoes of a bygone mechanic—until a low whisper began to repeat, over and over, like a chant.

"Justice. Justice. Justice."

The victim was nineteen. Brock Prescott. He lay half-curled on the damp grass, one arm thrown awkwardly above his head, as if he'd tried to shield himself at the last second. Floodlights bleached the color from his skin, leaving it waxy—too pale for someone who should have been sweating in the August heat. A gold chain glinted at his throat, resting against the stretched collar of a fraternity T-shirt stamped with the faded letters of Sigma Epsilon Rho—The Serpents. His sneakers were spotless white, the kind worn to be seen, not scuffed, not worked in.

Up close, the features that had probably read as cocky in life looked slack, unfinished—an upper lip slightly curled, as though the smirk had finally slid off and left nothing behind. His hair, dark blond and gel-stiff, was matted now where it pressed into the grass. Insects had already begun to hum near his ear.

Brock Prescott. Pledge. Eager brother-in-the-making for the Serpents, the fraternity that boasted more scandals than championships. Months ago, his name had surfaced in whispers—ugly ones. A freshman girl, a party, a drink gone wrong. Charges filed. Evidence "inconclusive." Case dismissed. He'd walked away untouched, shielded by the thinnest of technicalities.

Now he lay in the open, nothing left to shield him. Tonight, his story ended under the clock tower.

Detective Casey Murphy slipped under the tape, flashing her badge at the campus security guards, who strained to hold the line. She wasn't tall, but the way she moved—measured, unhurried, utterly confident—made people step aside before they even realized they'd done it. Her blazer and slacks hung loose enough to pass as standard-issue uniform, yet the cut couldn't quite disguise what was underneath: a body sharpened by discipline, built for long hours and sudden bursts of action. There was an athletic grace to her, something that might have belonged on a different stage entirely, concealed beneath the blunt edges of her bulldog attitude. The August humidity clung to her copper hair, twisted into a knot at the nape of her neck, but was already loosening, strands curling damply against her skin. Floodlights caught the faint spray of freckles across her cheeks, softening the hard lines of focus in her face. Her eyes—bright green, restless—swept the quad with the quick cuts of a camera pan: left, right, center, every detail locked and cataloged.

Around the precinct, Murphy's reputation was shorthand: relentless, unflappable, with a taste for *Star Wars* quips that could break tension or needle suspects until they cracked. More than one perp had found himself wilting under her steady stare and a quiet, pointed: *I find your lack of honesty disturbing.*

Now the scene seemed to close in as she dropped into a crouch beside the body, black latex gloves snapping tight with the precision of ritual. Her gaze fixed on the dead man's hand, slack fingers curled around a lone white pawn, its pale plastic gleaming beneath the lights like a signal waiting to be read.

"Well," she muttered, voice dry, "somebody thinks they're the Emperor pulling strings. Spoiler alert—the Emperor gets tossed down a shaft."

Bootsteps crunched on the cobblestones behind her—measured, deliberate, each one carrying the weight of a man who didn't hurry for anyone.

Will Anderson stepped into the yellow wash of the floodlights, tall and broad, shoulders set like they'd been carved to carry burdens. His suit was plain, functional, cut for long nights rather than style, but it couldn't disguise the solid build beneath—strength held in reserve, never flaunted. He moved like a man who expected resistance and had learned to push through it, quietly, without wasted effort.

His face carried the kind of gravity that made people lower their voices without knowing why. Dark hair trimmed close, the first threads of gray at the temples, and eyes that seemed to measure everything at once: not hurried, not harsh, just relentless.

Will lived by three rules: *trust no one, the truth is out there, and everyone matters.* A contradiction on paper, but not in him. The distrust kept him alive. The truth kept him working. And the belief that every life counted—that was the part that still made him human.

Where Casey burned brightly, Will was all quiet storms, holding pressure tight. He studied crime scenes like puzzles—patient, careful, fitting chaos into order piece by piece, locking everything in place in his mind.

He caught the tail end of her remark, one brow lifting. "Really? Star Wars already?" His voice was low and steady, almost flat, but there was the faintest tug of humor at the corner of his mouth, a rare crack in the stone.

Casey shot him a sidelong glance. "What? I cope with humor. You brood with bourbon. We've all got our methods."

Will's gaze lowered to the object in the victim's hand. "Just don't start calling me Skywalker."

"Relax," she said, sliding out an evidence bag. "You're more Obi-Wan on a bad day."

His jaw tightened, but his eyes stayed on the body. "Obi-Wan got blindsided, remember."

Casey stood, grabbed the camera, and snapped a photo. "Then let's make sure we don't."

"Chess piece?" His voice was low, even, but his eyes narrowed the way they always did when a puzzle lay in front of him.

"Pawn." Casey raised it so he could see, her tone clipped. "Someone left it for us."

Will's jaw worked, a muscle ticking hard beneath his cheek. He studied the pawn, the stark white shining under the floodlights, before flicking his gaze to Casey. His eyes held something unreadable—something that tightened the space between them.

"Or for you," he said quietly.

Casey stiffened, just for a second. Then the mask slid back into place, and she dropped the piece into an evidence bag, ripping off the sticky closure seal. Her eyes cut sideways at him, sharp. "What's that supposed to mean?" Checking the time and noting it on the bag.

Before he could answer, the atmosphere shifted. The crowd beyond the tape seemed to breathe as one, hundreds of murmurs swelling into a wave that rolled across the quad. Phones rose higher, glowing rectangles in the dark, capturing every angle like a constellation of unblinking eyes. The lenses didn't blink. The kids behind them did. Some chanted *justice,* voices rhythmic, rising and falling like a litany. Others whispered eagerly, the excitement of the spectacle tightening their voices into harsh little laughs.

The word kept surfacing in the noise—*justice*—but here, under the yellow glare of the floodlights, it sounded less like principle and more like hunger. The crowd's chant gnawed at the night, sharp-edged, insistent, teeth in the dark.

Casey peeled off her gloves, the latex snapping like a starter's pistol against the hush. She scanned the mass of faces beyond the tape, copper hair damp at her temples, sweat slicking the hollow of her neck. "Jesus. Half the damn campus is out here."

"Half of them think this is justice," Will said, his gaze never wavering from the mob. His voice was granite—flat, heavy, unmovable. "The other half just want to watch someone burn."

The sea of students swelled again, the buzz of their voices prickling at Casey's skin. She felt it in her chest, the heat of their eyes, the charge of attention pulling toward her—not just toward the body, not just toward the pawn, but toward *her*, as though she were part of the show.

Through the August haze, a bulkier figure pressed forward, Chief Pete Manning, head of campus security. His shirt clung damp to his back, collar stained dark, a limp handkerchief crushed in one fist. He looked more like a man drowning in the heat than one in charge of it, but his eyes were locked on the evidence bag in Casey's grip.

"Looks staged," Manning muttered, the words shaky, his breath shallow. "Not just a killing—" He swallowed, Adam's apple bobbing, voice shrinking as though naming it made it real. "—a performance."

Will's eyes swept the scene again. He saw it too: the body wasn't simply placed; it was posed, that's for sure. Not like the Julien Cain victims, but deliberate. Brock Prescott's limbs bent in deliberate angles, with every line intentional. His upturned hand resembled an offering, fingers curled in unnatural repose around the gleaming white pawn. The piece rested there with surgical precision, perfectly centered beneath the looming clock tower—as if time itself had been drafted into the script.

No signs of panic. No wild struggle. Just... precision.

Will exhaled slowly, the sound almost lost under the chant of the crowd. His voice dropped, meant only for Casey. "Not chaos," he said. "Intent."

Casey folded the bag, the crisp rattle of plastic loud in the thick night air. Inside, the pawn gleamed cold and pale, a secret wrapped in reflection. Her gut twisted hard. A clue. A warning. A taunt. Maybe all three.

And beneath the weight of the floodlights, beneath the endless murmur of the crowd, she felt it—a current running against the noise.

Eyes.

Somewhere out there—beyond the tape, beyond the phones, maybe even inside the circle itself—someone was watching. Not as a bystander. Not as a student. Watching her. Studying.

Whoever had left that pawn knew her. Knew exactly how she'd react.

Exactly who she was.

The Watcher Sees All

From the edge of the crowd, unseen behind the masks of a hundred other faces, the Watcher stood still.

Phones buzzed. Voices hissed. But all the noise blurred into nothing. The only thing that mattered was the board.

The pawn was placed. The opening move had been made.

The rook had arrived, just as expected. Strong. Predictable. But even rooks could be toppled.

The king stood beside her, steady but slow. Kings always hesitated. That was their weakness.

And the pawns? The pawns were still blind, stumbling forward, unaware of the traps that waited to swallow them whole.

The Watcher's fingers brushed the outline of another pawn tucked safely away in a pocket. Smooth. Cold. A promise of what was to come.

Justice isn't blind, the Watcher thought. *Justice plays the game.*

Precinct – Two Hours Later

The fluorescent lights of Oakhaven PD hummed overhead, buzzing faintly like a nest of wasps. Too bright. Too sterile. After the yellow haze of the Ravenwood quad, the place smelled wrong, with burnt coffee in the pot that had been cooking all day, floor polish, old paper files, and the bite of air conditioning that ran too cold, even in August. Goosebumps rose on her arms, a ridiculous reaction when her shirt was still damp with the night's humid heat.

Casey dropped into her chair with a low groan, peeling her jacket off her shoulders. The fabric was still damp from the swampy night air, clinging to her skin like the crime scene itself had followed her inside. Her copper hair stuck to the back of her neck, sweat long since dried into salt.

She opened her laptop, the glow of the screen washing pale across her face. Fingers moved automatically, typing out the bones of the report:

Nineteen-year-old male. Ravenwood University student. Fraternity pledge, Sigma Epsilon Rho, "The Serpents." Cause of death: blunt force trauma to the head. Evidence recovered: one white pawn.

Her hands paused. The cursor blinked in the empty space after those words, as if mocking her. *Evidence recovered: one white pawn.*

A flicker of memory tremored through her—an email from three weeks back, one she'd dismissed as spam. No subject line. No sender name she recognized. Just a single attached photo of a white pawn sitting on a clean black background. Under it, four words: *The pawn knows.*

She'd rolled her eyes, deleted it after showing it to no one. Probably a phishing attempt, or some edgy frat boy playing at mystery. She hadn't thought about it again. Not until tonight. Not until the pawn she'd bagged from Brock Prescott's hand had caught the floodlight just so—white plastic gleaming like an accusation.

Now she couldn't get the earlier email out of her head. The two images overlapped in her mind, impossibly aligned. A coincidence.

She tried to believe that.

But she didn't.

Will says there are no such things as coincidences in murders.

Her inbox pinged.

Casey frowned. Midnight emails weren't unusual in their line of work—tips from students, press inquiries digging for soundbites, the occasional angry parent demanding answers. But this one was different. Unknown sender. No subject line. Just the timestamp glowing at the top of the screen, as if it had appeared out of the ether.

She clicked.

The email was bare. Empty except for two sentences, black letters stark against the screen's white glow:

The board is set. You are the Rook.

Play your part, or more pawns will fall.

Casey froze. The words seemed to pulse on the screen, each one carrying more weight than it should. Her breath caught, shoulders tightening. She reread it. And again. The letters didn't change. Two sentences that somehow shifted the ground under her feet. The hair stood on her neck.

Her hand hovered over the mouse, suddenly heavy. Her pulse thudded in her ears, too loud for the silence of the bullpen. The goosebumps returned, crawling up her arms as if the precinct's chill had followed her inside her skin.

"What?"

Will's voice came from behind her, cutting through the hum of the fluorescents. Steady, but sharper than usual—his cop's instinct always caught the shift in a room before anyone else.

Casey's jaw clenched. She tilted the laptop so he could see. "You need to see this."

Will leaned in, his shadow falling across the desk. His eyes narrowed as he scanned the lines, his frown deepening with each word. The muscles in his jaw worked.

"They're calling you the Rook," he said finally, voice flat but grim.

Casey swallowed, her throat gone dry. The word clung to her, foreign and personal all at once. "Which means what?" she asked, low. "They've been watching me? Is somebody studying me?"

Will didn't answer right away. He shut the laptop with a firm, deliberate click, as if closing the message might smother the threat inside. His gaze locked on hers, steady as stone.

"It means this isn't random," he said, his voice carrying the weight of certainty. "Whoever's behind this already knows you."

The words sank into her like a blade. Casey leaned back, her pulse hammering, blood rushing in her ears until the whole room seemed to shrink to just the sound of it.

She'd worked homicides before. She'd seen copycats, obsessive freaks, killers who wanted to turn their crimes into theater. But this felt different. The pawn in Brock Prescott's hand hadn't just been evidence. It was a message—a move.

And now this email—this taunt, this challenge—meant she was on the board too.

For the first time in months, the case felt like more than just a body cooling on the quad.

It felt like a game.

A game with rules she didn't yet know.

And she couldn't shake the sick certainty that she'd already been lured into playing.

Watcher's Journal

They thought the pawn was nothing, a sacrifice, forgettable.
But pawns are the soul of the game.
Tonight, one pawn fell. Not mine. Theirs.
The rook will see the truth now.
She will learn that protection has a price, and if she fails, the board will drink more blood.
The game has begun.

The Intern

The bullpen smelled of coffee grounds and copier toner when Chief Robert Mason pushed open the glass door. Conversations dimmed as he entered, flanked by Captain Frank Monroe and a young woman with a leather satchel slung over her shoulder.

Mason rapped his knuckles on the edge of the briefing table, his gravelly voice piercing the silence. “Listen up. This is Rachel Donovan. Some of you might already know her name. For the rest, she’s Joe Donovan’s daughter. She’s grown up in and around this job more than most of you, and she’s got the instincts to prove it.”

Will stilled. The name hit him like a jolt. Joe Donovan, his first sergeant at Summit Falls Police Department, the man who had hauled him through rookie mistakes, taught him the rhythm of the street and shoved him toward every hard lesson he needed. His mentor. His friend. The man who used to call him “kid” even after almost a decade in. Will owed much of his career to Joe, and more than once, his life.

And now here was Joe’s daughter.

Rachel stood beside him, straight-backed but not stiff, her hands neatly clasped in front of her. She wore a pale blouse tucked into slim slacks, professional and deliberately modest—clothing chosen to blend in, not stand out. Still, her figure defied anonymity—long lines and pronounced curves that even careful tailoring couldn’t quite hide.

Her chestnut hair was pulled back, with a few loose strands softening her face, and a braid draped over one shoulder. Sea-green, almost mystical eyes scanned the room, wide and searching—curious but cautious; when she met someone's gaze too long, she quickly dipped her chin as if to avoid drawing attention. Pretty, undeniably, but understated, and intent on staying that way.

"She's sharp," Mason continued. "Already flagged things on the Serpents' socials that the rest of you missed. Don't mistake her quiet for timidity. She pays attention, and she's not afraid to speak when it counts. Treat her like part of the team."

Rachel offered a slight nod, her voice low but steady. "Thank you, Chief. I'll do my best."

Casey leaned back in her chair, a smirk playing at her mouth. "Adorable. Straight out of the Disney Princess academy." Her eyes flicked deliberately over Rachel before swinging back to Mason. "Only difference? This one's got better curves."

Mason's glare snapped her way. "Murphy."

Casey lifted her hands in mock surrender, grin unrepentant.

Rachel flushed, ducking her head slightly, her fingers tightening around the strap of her satchel.

Will didn't move, but he noticed the flicker—the way Rachel tugged her blouse closer as if she could erase Casey's words. She wasn't flaunting herself. Quite the opposite. And maybe that contrast, hiding what she couldn't quite conceal, was what drew the eyes all the same.

Monroe clapped Will on the shoulder. "Figured you'd appreciate this one, Anderson. Joe always said you had a knack for turning rookies into detectives."

Will's throat tightened. He managed a nod. "Joe taught me more than I can ever pay back." His gaze flicked to Rachel, softer now. "Guess that makes us family of a sort."

Rachel's lips curved into a tentative smile. "He talked about you," she said quietly, like she wasn't sure she should. "Said you were the stubborn one. Wouldn't take no for an answer once you had your teeth in something."

That earned her a faint chuckle from Will. "Sounds about right."

Casey tipped her chair back further, boots landing on her desk. "Great. Another overachiever. Just what we needed." She gave Rachel a long look, eyebrow cocked. "You ever been shot at, Rookie?"

Rachel blinked. "Uh... no?"

"Ever been chased across a swamp in the middle of the night by a meth head with a machete?"

"...no."

Casey grinned, sharp and wolfish. "Well, stick close. Around here, we collect weird stories, much like Jedi collect lightsabers. You'll get plenty of material."

Rachel laughed softly, tension loosening from her shoulders. But her eyes kept moving, cataloguing details: the scuffs on Casey's boots, the burn mark on her jacket sleeve, the half-finished doodle of an X-wing on her notepad. Reckless, quick-witted, but sharper than she let on. The kind of person who played trauma for laughs but never stopped watching.

And then there was Will. Tie slightly crooked, shirt sleeves rolled to his forearms, scars faint against his skin. His desk was organized but worn, pens aligned by habit, not vanity. He studied the room differently than Casey: steady, deliberate, weighing angles before acting. The protector. The anchor.

Will smirked faintly despite himself, but unease lingered low in his chest. Rachel Donovan wasn't just any intern. Her arrival felt like the start of something that was going to ripple far wider than any of them could see.

Rachel gave a polite nod, her gaze flicking across the room with quick, surgical precision before she tucked a strand of dark hair neatly behind her ear. "Thank you for having me," she said, her voice quiet but steady, carrying more control than nerves.

"She started nursing school at Ravenwood University," Mason continued, "but life had other plans. Taking some time off. In her downtime, she has been training hard again in mixed martial arts and Brazilian jiu-jitsu—already a blue belt, she began training at sixteen. Smart, disciplined. I figured this would be a good way for her to find her footing again."

Casey Murphy leaned back in her chair, copper hair catching the fluorescent glow, and let her eyes run Rachel up and down. A grin tugged at her lips. "Blue belt, huh? Guess you're already tougher than half the guys here. Not that it takes much—most of them couldn't fight their way out of a stormtrooper shooting gallery."

The bullpen chuckled, tension easing.

Rachel's cheeks flushed faintly, but her answer came quickly, like it had been waiting on her tongue. "Only if they don't see it coming."

Casey smirked wider. "Careful, rookie. That kind of line makes me think you're auditioning for the Sith, not the Jedi. But don't worry—every Jedi needs a Padawan. Looks like I just found mine."

A ripple of laughter rolled across the bullpen. Rachel's mouth curved in a small, careful smile, her eyes flicking toward Casey as though testing whether she was serious or joking.

Will Anderson rose from his desk, tall and steady, pen set aside. He extended a hand, measured and professional. "Let's make this official, Will Anderson. Homicide."

Rachel accepted. Her grip was firm, not overcompensating, the kind of handshake that said she'd practiced. But her eyes lingered on his longer than most rookies dared, sharp and unblinking, like she was reading something past the surface. Then she released his hand letting it slide against his as she pulled away, squared her shoulders slightly, bracing herself against the weight of the room.

"Detective Murphy," Casey added, tipping her chin. "Welcome to the circus, Padawan. First lesson: the coffee here tastes like engine oil, so learn to love bad bourbon instead. We have plenty of both."

Rachel gave a slight nod, her satchel sliding smoothly to the floor as she took the empty desk beside theirs. Everything she pulled out was tidy: a tabbed notebook, pens clipped in a perfect row, sticky notes already color-coded.

She smoothed the notebook open, pen poised, but her mind was already sketching patterns—how they moved, how they spoke, what they revealed without meaning to.

Chief Mason cleared his throat, gravel thick in his voice. "She'll be shadowing you two. Paperwork, ride-along, whatever you need. I want her to see the job from the inside. And I want her treated like one of us. Clear?"

Will and Casey exchanged a glance. They'd broken in rookies before, fresh grads, transfers, eager academy kids, but this was different. This was Joe Donovan's daughter.

"Clear," Will said at last.

"Good," Mason replied. He clapped a hand briefly on Rachel's shoulder. "Joe always said his girl was tougher than she looked. Prove him right."

When the chief left, Rachel settled into her chair, uncapped a pen, and immediately started writing. She didn't fidget, didn't glance around. Her focus locked in like she was determined to capture every detail, every word, before it slipped away.

Will noticed. The sharp eyes, the deliberate poise, the faint coil of tension in her frame, like someone bracing for impact. She was polite, deferential, and careful. But beneath it all, there was something else.

Not nerves.

Not eagerness.

Something hungrier.

He pushed the thought aside, reminding himself she was Joe Donovan's kid. That alone was reason enough to give her a chance.

Out for a Ride Along

The morning air outside the precinct was thick with the sticky cling of August. Patrol units came and went, the hum of radios carrying across the lot, a steady backdrop of clipped voices and static.

Casey adjusted her sunglasses, tugging them higher against the glare, and popped open the passenger door of the unmarked sedan. "Shotgun's yours, Rookie," she said, jerking her chin toward the seat.

Rachel hesitated just long enough to betray nerves, then slipped inside gracefully, placing her satchel on the floor like she was checking into a lecture hall instead of a cop car. Her hands were folded in her lap, but her eyes moved constantly, scanning the dash, the police radio mount, and the faint scuffs on the gearshift. Cataloguing. Measuring.

Will slid into the driver's seat, motions practiced and unhurried. He turned the key, the engine rumbling to life, and glanced sideways. "First rule of a ride-along," he said, voice even but carrying weight. "You don't talk to suspects. You don't interfere. You watch, you take notes, and you let us do the talking. Clear?"

"Yes, sir." Rachel's tone was respectful, almost eager, like a student answering the professor she most wanted to impress.

From the back, Casey snorted. "Don't 'sir' him too much, kid. His ego won't fit in the car."

That earned a faint smile from Rachel. "Noted."

"Second rule," Casey added, leaning forward with an elbow hooked over the seat, "you see something, you write it down. Don't blurt it out mid-interview. People clam up the second they realize you're dissecting them. People will talk themselves into handcuffs if you let them."

Rachel nodded quickly. "Understood."

'Casey gave a quick nod, then added, "Third rule—don't take anything said to you personally. People won't see you for you; they'll see the badge, the department, and the whole weight of what we stand for. Sometimes they'll spit at that. Sometimes they'll cry to it. Either way, it's not about you. Don't let it stick. There's more out there that loves us than the few loudmouths that don't."

They pulled away from the precinct, the city streets rolling by in streaks of sunlight and shadow. Rachel sat upright, posture attentive, eyes flicking out the window but always coming back to her notebook.

Their first stop was Ravenwood. Campus security had flagged a student witness who'd been near the quad when Brock Prescott's body was discovered.

Inside the student union, the smell of coffee and fryer grease clung to the air. Students hunched over laptops and textbooks, though more than a few stole glances at the detectives. Rachel trailed half a step behind, quiet, her gaze flicking between faces, shoes, postures, as if every detail mattered, as if she were taking attendance in a class only she understood.

The witness, a thin sophomore named Hannah Moore, wrung her hands as Casey guided her to a table in the back.

"It happened fast," Hannah said, voice trembling. "I was walking back from the library. I heard shouting and then..." She swallowed hard. "Then I saw the crowd forming. Brock was already on the ground."

Casey leaned in, her tone steady but soft enough to coax. “Did you see anyone with him? Even before you noticed the crowd?”

Hannah shook her head. “No. Just... people running. And someone pushed past me. Tall, I think. Dark Hoodie. That’s all I remember.”

Will’s eyes narrowed slightly. He leaned in, voice calm. “What color was the hoodie?”

“Gray. I think. It happened so fast. Everyone was yelling.”

“Did you catch anything else?” Casey asked, gentler. “Shoes, voice, smell, anything stick?”

Hannah frowned, staring at her hands. “Sneakers. Dark. And he... he smelled like some type of cologne. Strong. Cheap. I’m sorry, that’s all.”

“You did fine,” Casey reassured her, giving the girl’s hand a light squeeze.

Behind them, Rachel’s pen scratched steadily. Will glanced back and caught a glimpse over her shoulder. She wasn’t just writing Hannah’s words. She was sketching a rough outline of the quad, with arrows indicating the girl’s path, the crowd’s movement, and an X marking the body’s location.

He raised a brow. “That’s... pretty sharp for someone who just walked in cold.”

Rachel looked up, startled, then snapped the notebook closed like she’d just broken a rule. “Sorry. Habit. In nursing, we had to map symptoms and track patterns. It’s just... how I was trained.”

Casey gave a low whistle. "Not bad, Rookie. Might actually earn your keep."

Hannah blinked at them, lost, but Will forced a small smile as he stood, thanking her.

They left the union and stepped back into the sweltering air. As they crossed the lot, Casey shoved her hands in her pockets, her sunglasses slipping down her nose. She angled a look at Will. "Kid's sharp. Almost too sharp."

"Maybe she just pays attention," Will said.

"Uh-huh." Casey arched a brow. "That's what you're going with?"

Will didn't bite. He started the engine, his eyes flicking briefly to the intern in the passenger seat. Rachel sat calmly, pen capped, gaze fixed out the window. Relaxed posture. Distant eyes. As if she were still running the interview in her head, frame by frame.

"She's Joe's kid," Will said finally, voice even. "She'll do fine."

Casey leaned back, unconvinced. "Sure. But I've seen Padawans before, and that one's already practicing her lightsaber moves in the mirror."

Watcher's Journal

Fragments were all the witnesses ever kept.
A sleeve in gray. The shove of a shoulder. A trace of cheap fragrance clinging to the heat.
Loose pieces on the board.
Enough to feel useful.
Never enough to change the position.

Gentleness always came first—the rook's move.
The steady hand. The careful voice.
Questions were asked twice, then again, until repetition began to resemble the truth.
That line of play had been mapped days ago.

The real story lived in movement.
Where the pawns compressed.
Where the light failed to cover the square.
Where a body could be placed and still be unseen.
A capture made without spectacle.

Once written, the paths were easy to follow. Forced, even.

Engines turned. Attention drifted. The board thinned.
The square emptied.
The gap widened.

I listened.

I waited.

There was no effort in it at all.

The Rook's New Message

Casey Murphy dropped into her chair at the precinct, the vinyl groaning under her weight. She balanced a Styrofoam cup of station coffee on one knee, its thin lid already bent, already leaking heat. The bullpen hummed around her—the background music of a dozen lives unfolding at once. Phones rang. Printers ground through reports. Boots thudded down the hall in uneven rhythms. Overhead, the fluorescent lights buzzed, too bright, too clean, like they were trying to bleach the night out of her eyes.

She shoved her copper hair back from her face and jabbed the laptop awake. The screen blinked to life, her inbox already swollen with press inquiries about the Ravenwood murder. Subject lines crowded together, all urgency and speculation, none of them asking anything she could actually answer.

Casey lifted the cup and took a sip.

Regret hit immediately.

The coffee was bitter in the wrong way—burnt, thin, like it had been brewed yesterday and reheated out of spite. It coated her tongue and refused to leave, an oily aftertaste that distracted her just long enough to make her scowl. She rolled the cup slightly between her fingers, considering the trash can across the aisle. One good flick and it would be gone.

Jack'd Up was three blocks away. Real coffee. Strong enough to reset her brain, hot enough to burn the fog out of it. She could already picture the chalkboard menu, the hiss of the espresso machine, the smell of beans instead of disinfectant and toner. Five minutes, maybe seven if the light caught her wrong.

Not yet.

She set the cup back on her knee and stared at the inbox, letting the noise of the bullpen wash over her while her mind refused to settle. Ravenwood sat heavy behind her eyes—the lake, the crowd, the way the scene hadn't quite lined up no matter how many times she replayed it. Everyone else saw chaos. She kept seeing gaps. Pauses. Moments where something should have been there and wasn't.

The coffee sat between her and the keyboard, an irritant she couldn't ignore, like a wrong note in a song. Too early in the day for distractions. Too early to be this tired.

Casey exhaled through her nose, fingers hovering over the keys.

She'd earn Jack'd Up later.

First, she needed answers.

She skimmed the subject lines with a dry snort:

Statement request.

Comment on Sigma Epsilon Rho.

Do police suspect foul play?

"Breaking news," she muttered, blowing steam from her coffee before taking a scalding sip. "Frat boy dies, vultures circle. What a shocker."

Will Anderson set a stack of files on the corner of her desk, his movements neat, deliberate. His shirt sleeves were rolled past his forearms, and he carried the kind of exhaustion that didn't come from one late night but from years of them.

"Comes with the territory," he said simply. "Ignore the noise."

Casey smirked at him over the rim of her coffee. "Easy for you. You don't answer half your emails anyway."

Before he could fire back, her inbox pinged again. She clicked the newest message, which had no subject or sender. Just a timestamp glowing like a quiet alarm at the top of the screen.

Two lines stared back at her in stark black against white:

The rook shields the twins but cannot see the board.

Your pawns are Sigma Epsilon Rho.

Watch. Question. Follow.

Casey blinked, her brows shooting up. A cold knot curled low in her stomach, though she masked it quickly with sarcasm. "Well, that's not ominous at all." She spun the laptop toward Will with a flick of her wrist. "Take a look at this little gem."

Will leaned in, frown deepening as he scanned the text. His jaw worked once, muscle ticking. "Anonymous?"

"Anonymous." Casey leaned back, feigning casual, though her knuckles tightened around her coffee cup. "Also weirdly dramatic. Somebody's been binging *The Queen's Gambit* one too many times."

"Or too many true-crime podcasts," Will said flatly, unimpressed. He didn't like giving threats oxygen, that much she knew.

Casey tapped one painted nail against the screen, her grin sharp but uneasy at the edges. "'Pawns are Sigma Epsilon Rho.' That's Brock Prescott's frat. They didn't even bother spelling it out. Like they assumed I'd already know."

Will shook his head slowly. "Cranks send crap like this all the time. They skim the headlines, mash them into a metaphor, and hit send. Half of them just want to see their words show up on the evening news."

"Sure," Casey said, voice breezy, but the words gnawed at her. Somebody hadn't just called out the frat. Somebody had called *her* the rook. Not Will. Not Kristen. Her.

She tried for humor, letting her chair creak back under her weight. "So what's next? Knights, bishops, queens? Do I get a crown if I survive this case?"

Will didn't smile. His eyes stayed on the laptop, gaze sharp as glass. "Don't give them credit. Treat it as noise until it proves otherwise."

Casey snapped the laptop shut, the sound loud in the hum of the bullpen. She drummed her fingers against the Styrofoam cup, trying to shake it off. But her pulse still carried the echo of the words, steady and insistent:

The rook shields the twins but cannot see the board.

Your pawns are Sigma Epsilon Rho.

Watch. Question. Follow.

The email hadn't just landed in her inbox.

It had been aimed.

Whoever sent it wasn't guessing. They weren't shouting into the dark.

They were already watching the board from above.

Out of the blue, Chief Robert Mason appeared in the doorway, his presence pulling the bullpen to attention the way it always did. The man didn't need to bark orders; just standing there with his perpetual scowl and battered coffee mug was enough. He looked like he hadn't slept in a week, but then again, he always did.

"Morning," he grumbled. His eyes swept the room, landing on Casey and Will. "Anything useful come in?"

Casey hesitated, then flipped her laptop back open, the glow splashing against her face. She angled the screen toward him. "Depends on your definition of useful. This dropped into my inbox after midnight."

Mason leaned forward, squinting at the short lines. His lips moved as he read, then he gave a dry, humorless chuckle. "Some kid with a keyboard and a thesaurus. Don't let it get under your skin."

Casey crossed her arms, unimpressed. "It mentions Sigma Epsilon Rho. That's not public. Not officially."

"Campus rumor mill works faster than we do," Mason shot back, waving a dismissive hand. "Those frat boys don't keep their mouths shut. Trust me, it'll be on Twitter by lunch."

Casey bit the inside of her cheek, jaw working. "So you want me to ignore it?"

"I want you to file it, log it, and move on," Mason said firmly. He pointed at the evidence board, his tone sharp enough to cut. "We chase facts, not riddles. Stick to what we can prove."

With that, he disappeared back into his office, door closing with a solid, final click.

Casey exhaled, muttering under her breath, "Glad to know the chess club's got his blessing."

Will, still at his desk, glanced at her. His mouth quirked, but his eyes didn't match. "You heard him. File it and move on."

Casey stared at the screen instead, the words glowing like they'd been etched into the glass. *The rook guards the twins but cannot see the board.*

She closed the laptop, but the weight of the message stayed lodged under her skin.

Will noticed the way her hand lingered on the lid, the way her jaw was tight. He didn't say anything else. Not yet. But he'd caught it too—the difference between noise and something that cut a little too close.

Watcher's Journal

The cursor blinks.
Steady. Patient. Like a pulse.
Words matter. They aren't thrown. They're placed.
The rook shields the twins but cannot see the board.
Your pawns are Sigma Epsilon Rho.
Watch. Question. Follow.
Enough to sting.
Enough to see if she's paying attention.
She will pretend it's noise. She always does at first.

Casey Murphy hides behind humor and momentum. She moves fast, talks faster, laughs like nothing ever gets close enough to bruise. That works on witnesses. Sometimes with partners. It won't work on me.

She loves too hard. That's the flaw. Friends. Loyalty. The twins. She guards what she loves without ever checking the cost to her of standing there.

That's why she's the rook.

Straight lines. Predictable paths. Power without perspective.

I picture her at her desk—not because I imagine, but because I've watched. Hair pulled back just enough to function. Files are stacked out of order. Coffee, she pretends not to hate—sarcasm as armor.

Armor always has seams.

On campus, pawns mistake noise for importance, crowns borrowed and already cracked.
In the precinct, the rook laughs too loudly, too often.

The board is set.

I wait for the next move.

One square at a time.

Day Drinking

The Ravenwood fraternity house squatted at the edge of campus like a fortress that had seen one too many battles. Its redbrick façade was scarred with beer stains and graffiti, half-scrubbed away; porch railings were warped from years of bodies leaning too hard on them. Above the heavy oak door, the gleaming brass Greek letters—ΣΕΡ—glimmered like trophies, proud and untouchable. *House of the Serpents.*

Loud bass rattled the glass panes, a dull, repetitive thump that made the porch boards vibrate beneath their feet. The humid August air carried the stink of stale beer, sweat, and weed—sweet and acrid all at once, the scent of nights blurred and forgotten.

Casey adjusted her badge on her belt as she climbed the steps, her lip curling. "You'd think with one of their pledges lying in the morgue, they'd turn the music down for at least a day. But no—mourning isn't on the syllabus, apparently."

Will didn't answer, just rapped his fist against the door hard enough to rattle the frame.

It swung open a moment later, revealing a broad-shouldered student with a backward cap and a polo shirt stretched across his chest like it had been painted on. His grin was instant and smug, practiced for mirrors and girls at the bar.

"Detectives," he drawled, voice dripping with mock respect. "To what do we owe the pleasure? You here to bust us for underage drinking? Or maybe a noise complaint?"

"Ethan Voss?" Will asked, already knowing the answer from the campus records he'd reviewed earlier.

"That's me," Ethan said, leaning his bulk against the doorframe as if he owned not just the house but the street it sat on. "Social chair, Serpent's chapter. You want to come in, or are we doing this little performance out on the lawn?"

Casey didn't wait. She brushed past him with a muttered, "We'll take it inside."

The living room was a shrine to indulgence. The air was humid, with the sweat of too many bodies, and the floor was tacky with spilled beer. Couches sagged under the weight of two more brothers: Derek Langley, legs spread wide like he was holding court, and Ryan Cho, leaning back with his sneakers kicked up on the armrest, a lazy smirk on his lips. The table in front of them was cluttered with red cups, a half-empty bottle of vodka catching the light like a jewel among the wreckage. Empty pizza boxes slumped in a corner. Posters of half-naked models curled on the walls, glossy and cheap, corners darkened by fingerprints and smoke.

It didn't smell like grief. It didn't even smell like guilt. It smelled like arrogance—like the rules that applied everywhere else simply stopped at the Serpents' front door.

Casey's eyes flicked over the scene, sharp and disdainful. She muttered just loud enough for Will to hear, "Welcome to the snake pit."

"Wow," Casey muttered under her breath, eyes sweeping the wreckage of pizza boxes, empty cups, and stale smoke. "Classy."

Ryan Cho smirked from his sprawl on the couch, twirling an empty red cup in his fingers. "You heard about Brock? Shame. The kid couldn't handle his liquor. Guess he picked the wrong place to pass out."

Will's jaw flexed, the muscle ticking. His voice was calm, but there was steel in it. "He was murdered. You want to try that again with a straight face?"

Derek Langley, lounging like he was in a throne room instead of a beer-stained frat den, shrugged lazily. "Look, man, people hate us. Jealousy's a disease. Some activist nutjob probably saw Brock and decided to make a statement. Doesn't mean it's on us."

Casey stepped forward, boots scuffing against the sticky floor, planting herself between the brothers and the vodka bottle like she was cutting off their supply line. Her voice dropped sharp and dangerous. "Funny thing about statements. They usually come with evidence. And evidence has a way of pointing back to the people who thought they were untouchable."

Ryan laughed, tossing the red cup back onto the table. It bounced and rolled, dripping a faint trail of beer. He raised his hands in mock surrender, grin widening. "Untouchable? Lady, we've got lawyers on retainer before we even take pledges. Good luck pinning anything on us."

Casey's eyes narrowed to slits, shoulders tensing as if she was one smart-ass comment away from putting him through the table. But Will shifted closer, laying a steadying hand on her arm—cooling the temperature before it boiled over. His tone was clipped, professional.

"Membership list," he said, turning his gaze on Ethan Voss. "Full roster. Officers, pledges, anyone active last night."

Ethan smirked, leaning back against the doorframe with his arms crossed like he was in a beer commercial instead of a murder inquiry. "That's private."

Will didn't blink. "Not anymore. You can either hand it over now, or we will come back with a warrant and conduct a full house search; we cannot predict where a roster may be kept. Your choice."

For a moment, the only sound was the bass still faintly thumping through the walls, like a second, mocking heartbeat. The brothers exchanged a look, silent communication passing between them. Then Ethan sighed dramatically, as if this was all beneath him, and fished out his phone.

"Fine," he drawled, tapping at the screen with deliberate laziness. "I'll email you the list. Don't say the Serpents don't cooperate with law enforcement."

Casey's glare could have curdled milk. "Yeah, you're just pillars of civic duty."

Ryan smirked wider, but for the first time, a faint flicker of unease appeared in his eyes.

Back at the Office

The precinct bullpen buzzed with phones and early morning chatter—reporters calling, detectives arguing over leads, the constant rattle of keyboards. But Rachel's corner of the room felt like a quiet island, insulated from the storm. She'd tucked herself neatly into the desk beside Will's, her satchel perched precisely by her feet, laptop glowing faintly against her pale skin.

Casey stalked past, her boots clicking hard against the linoleum, muttering, "Serpents. God, I'd love five minutes in a locked room with those smug bastards." She yanked a stray pen from her pocket and jabbed it into her palm as if it were one of their throats.

Will raised an eyebrow but stayed silent, folding his arms as he leaned against the edge of Rachel's desk. His gaze drifted from Casey's restless pacing to Rachel's screen. She was scrolling with the precision of a surgeon, pausing only when something snagged her attention.

"They're arrogant," Casey pressed, pacing tight circles like a caged animal. "So damn smug it makes me want to—" She cut herself off, fingers slicing the air in a sharp gesture.

Rachel didn't look up, her voice calm in the storm. "Sometimes arrogance leaves fingerprints." She tapped the trackpad, zooming in on a blurred corner of a photo. "Here. Ryan Cho. Claimed he was at the house, but this check-in puts him at the union fifteen minutes after the body was found."

Will bent down slightly, scanning the screen. Rachel shifted just enough to make room, her posture straightening. Her blouse pulled taut across her shoulders as she angled the laptop toward him. A faint trace of vanilla—

subtle but impossible to miss—lifted from her, carried by the hum of the overhead vents.

"You've got an eye for detail," Will said, his tone measured but sincere.

Rachel tilted her face up to him, a smile flickering at the edges of her lips. "Or maybe I'm just good at reading people. Runs in the family, right?" Her voice carried a teasing note, but her gaze lingered on him a beat too long before falling back to the screen.

Casey appeared at Will's shoulder, peering down. "Well, aren't you two cozy." Her smirk was razor-edged.

Rachel flushed, ducking her head quickly, fingers flying over the keys. "Sorry. I didn't mean—"

"Relax, kid, I'm messing with you, comes with the territory," Casey cut in, twirling the pen like a knife between her fingers. "Just don't let his poker face fool you. He's not half as charming as he looks."

Will shot her a warning look, jaw flexing, but he said nothing. He straightened, putting a deliberate inch of space between himself and Rachel's chair, suddenly aware of the heat crawling under his collar.

Rachel's hair slipped forward as she bent closer to her work, the glow of the screen reflected in her eyes. She resumed typing with quiet efficiency, but her knees stayed angled—not toward Casey's desk—but just slightly toward Will's, a subtle alignment she never corrected.

And then he caught it—the faintest tug of her lower lip, teeth sinking in for just a heartbeat before she released it. It wasn't nerves. Not this time. The gesture was too fleeting, too unconscious, and it sent a ripple of heat straight through him. She didn't even notice she'd done it. But Will did. And it left him suddenly, uncomfortably aware of how close her chair sat to his.

The Next Morning

The bullpen was buzzing as usual, the constant ring of phones and shuffle of papers layered beneath the harsh drone of the fluorescent lights. Will stepped in with a folder tucked under his arm, scanning the room until his eyes landed on Rachel.

She was already at her desk, posture straight, tapping brisk notes into her laptop while cross-referencing the Serpents' member list. A paper cup of coffee balanced precariously close to the desk's edge, steam curling upward in lazy tendrils.

"Detective Anderson," she said brightly, glancing up. Her smile was quick, almost expectant. "I grabbed you one too. Two sugars, right?"

Will slowed, his brow arching in surprise. "That's right." He took the cup she slid toward him, the warmth bleeding into his palm. "Good memory."

Rachel brushed it off with a faint shrug, eyes darting back to the screen. "Just paying attention."

Casey strolled by, smirk already in place. "Careful, Rookie. Keep spoiling him like that, and you'll turn him into Jabba the Hutt, demanding tribute every morning."

Will shot her a flat look. "Really?"

"What?" Casey spread her hands innocently. "He's got the coffee; all he's missing is the palace and the slave dancers."

Rachel laughed, light and unguarded, but her forearm knocked against her cup. The coffee tipped, a dark arc spilling across her blouse. She gasped, jolting up from her chair as the thin cotton went instantly translucent, clinging to her skin.

"Oh my God," she muttered, taking in a gasp of air, fumbling for napkins, blotting furiously at the spreading stain. Her cheeks burned crimson as she hunched over, trying to hide the sheer outline of her bra beneath the damp fabric. "I can't believe I did that."

Will was already setting his cup down, shrugging out of his jacket with practiced ease. "Here."

"No, it's fine—"

"Rachel." His voice was firm, steady, and carried that weight that ended arguments before they began. He stepped in close, draping the jacket over her shoulders. The heavy fabric settled around her like armor, instantly swallowing her frame. "Don't sit in that all day. You'll stink like burnt beans."

Her hands clutched the lapels tight, pulling the jacket closed. The scent of him, cedar, faint aftershave, something clean and steady, filled her lungs. She looked up at him with wide, grateful eyes, her voice hushed. "Thank you. You always... step in at the right moment."

Will cleared his throat, suddenly conscious of how close they stood. He took a step back, straightening his sleeves. "That's what partners do. Even the temporary kind."

From across the room, Casey's voice cut in, smug and merciless. "Smooth move, Skywalker. One jacket loan and suddenly you're everybody's hero. Careful, next she'll be calling you Obi-Wan."

Rachel ducked her head, laughing softly, but the sound was wrapped in shyness. Her gaze, however, followed Will's retreating back as he returned to his desk, jaw set as though nothing had happened.

Casey slid against Rachel's cubicle wall, arms folded, grin sharp. "Nice touch, kid. But if you want the full cinematic effect next time, spill it in your lap. Damsel-in-distress points go through the roof. Works every time."

Rachel pressed her lips together, cheeks still pink, fingers smoothing the oversized jacket over her thighs. "It was an accident."

"Uh-huh." Casey gave her a mock salute. "And I'm Yoda. Wise beyond my years, destined to be ignored."

Rachel smiled faintly but didn't argue. She kept Will's jacket on for the rest of the day, the weight of it grounding her, the scent of him clinging long after the stain had dried.

Coffee Run

The Tahoe rumbled down Main, its engine a steady growl beneath the hum of tires. Late afternoon sun bled across the windshield, streaking the dash in amber and gold. Dust motes floated in the beams of light, catching on Casey's sunglasses as she sat reclined in the passenger seat, nursing her iced coffee. The straw clicked rhythmically against the plastic lid, a sound deliberately timed to get under Will's skin.

"You know," she said casually, her voice sing-song, "you're getting predictable."

Will's brow ticked, though his eyes never left the road. "How so?"

Casey slurped loudly through her straw, just to make the point.

"First, the rookie brings you coffee exactly how you like it, and you light up like a kid on Christmas.

Then she spills hers all over and boom, you're throwing your jacket around her shoulders like Han Solo. I'm telling you, Anderson, you've got a type."

Will shot her a sidelong look, jaw tight. "She's Joe's daughter. That's it. End of story."

Casey smirked, turning her cup in her hand, the ice clattering inside. "Uh-huh. Sure. Next thing you know, she'll be calling you 'Master Jedi' and following you around with a notebook like your Padawan learner."

"I don't watch Star Wars," Will said flatly, shifting in his seat.

Casey clutched her chest in mock horror. "And yet you're raising teenage twins. The Force weeps."

Will exhaled slowly, adjusting his grip on the wheel. "You going somewhere with this?"

"Just an observation." She leaned her head back against the headrest, a grin tugging her lips upward. "Rookie's got those big eyes and that whole 'oops, I'm clumsy' routine down pat. Classic undercover Disney Princess move. If I didn't know better, I'd say she's working an angle."

Then, "Just don't confuse protecting someone with knowing them."

Will's hands tightened subtly on the leather wheel. His tone stayed even, but the weight behind it was unmistakable. "You do know better."

"Do I?" Casey angled her head toward him, sunglasses sliding down just enough to reveal her eyes. "Look, I'm not saying she's bad news. But she's not just some shy little intern either. Kid's sharper than she lets on. You just... keep both eyes open, okay?"

Silence settled between them, broken only by the steady hum of the Tahoe. Finally, Will said, quieter than before, "Rachel deserves a chance. Don't read into it."

Casey lifted her cup in a mock toast, ice clinking. "Sure thing, Dad. Just remember, Obi-Wan thought Anakin deserved a chance too. Didn't exactly pan out."

Will shook his head, exhaling through his nose.

Casey's grin widened. "Don't worry, partner. If she starts humming the Imperial March, I'll let you know."

She thumbed her phone and put it on speaker. "Hey, Rookie. We're almost at your place if you want to hop in. Headed to campus security to check video."

Rachel's voice came through faintly, tinny with background noise. "Perfect. I'll meet you out front."

Will pulled the Tahoe into the curb outside her apartment complex, the sunlight cutting sharper now, dipping lower across the rooftops. Rachel hurried down the steps, her hair slightly damp, a clean blouse tucked neatly into dark jeans. She had Will's jacket folded over one arm, clearly laundered already, the faint smell of detergent trailing behind her as she slid into the back seat.

Casey's eyes flicked down, one brow lifting. "Well, look at you trading in the slacks. About time, rookie—if you've got it, rock it. Those jeans don't exactly keep secrets."

Rachel flushed, tugging at the hem of her blouse as though that might make the denim less noticeable. "It's laundry day," she muttered.

"Uh-huh," Casey drawled, smirking. "And I only drink coffee for the antioxidants."

"Sorry about earlier," she said quickly, cheeks still pink. She held out the jacket toward him. "I wanted to make sure it didn't stay ruined."

Will glanced at it in the rearview, his expression unreadable. "You didn't have to do that."

Rachel smiled softly. "I know. But I wanted to."

Casey twisted in her seat, eyebrow arched, smirk primed. "Look at you. Fresh shirt, jacket returned, ready for round two. Very proper."

Rachel's eyes flicked to Will before she answered. "I figured I should be ready. You never know when things might spill again."

Casey barked a laugh. "Oh, she's learning."

Will's knuckles flexed against the wheel. He kept his eyes forward, but the faintest twitch at the corner of his mouth betrayed him.

The Tahoe eased back into traffic, sunlight blazing against the hood as the three of them headed toward campus.

Ravenwood University Security

The Ravenwood University security office smelled faintly of burnt coffee and disinfectant, the hum of monitors filling the cramped space. Fluorescent lights buzzed overhead as Officer Nick Fox, a stocky man with thinning hair and a permanent squint, guided them toward a wall-mounted campus map.

"Here's the layout," Fox said, tapping the laminated surface with a stubby finger. Red dots marked each exterior camera. "Most of the quad and the fraternity row are covered, except..." He trailed off, circling one area near the east lawn.

"That's where Prescott was found," Casey said, arms crossed, eyes narrowing.

Fox nodded. "Correct. Thing is, those cameras? Weren't working that night." He moved to the console, punching up the feed. The monitors flickered, showing blank static and frozen timestamps. "Thunderstorm rolled through about six hours before. Fried a couple of the circuits. Power surge tripped the backup too. It was all hands on deck with the body, so we didn't catch it until morning. Maintenance checked them and found the fried circuits."

"Convenient," Will muttered, jaw tightening.

Rachel, perched at the edge of a rolling chair, was already jotting notes in her spiral notebook. Her handwriting was small, neat, and efficient. She began sketching the campus layout in the margin, boxes for buildings, arrows for walkways, the gap where the cameras should have been. Her brow furrowed in concentration as she shaded in the blind spot.

A pen slipped from her lap, clattering to the tile. "Shoot," she murmured, bending to retrieve it.

Her blouse, cut with short shirt tails, rode up as she leaned forward, tugging free of her already low waistband. The hem lifted just enough to reveal the low rise of blue cotton underwear, the curve of her hips, and the bare hint of skin above. For a brief moment, the top of her butt crack showed before she straightened again, tucking the blouse hastily back into place and giving her waistband a discreet adjustment.

Will, standing just behind her, had caught the glimpse. He exhaled slowly through his nose and shifted his stance, eyes snapping back to the monitors as though they'd never strayed.

Across the desk, Casey's gaze flicked from Rachel to Will. Her eyebrows shot up, and she pulled an exaggerated face, silently mouthing the words: *Twice in one day.*

Will ignored her, though his jaw ticked.

Rachel, oblivious, reclaimed her seat and kept sketching. "If we can't rely on the footage, at least this diagram can help track angles and sightlines. Someone might have seen something even if the cameras didn't."

Casey smirked, sipping her iced coffee like it was the most entertaining show she'd seen all week. "Look at you, Rookie. Disney Princess with a blueprint. Didn't see that in the training manual."

Rachel flushed faintly but didn't look up. Her pencil moved with quiet certainty, tracing the blind spot as if she were already planning how to close it.

Will cleared his throat, steadying his voice. "Good thinking. Bag the notes, we'll need them later."

Fox frowned at the static feed, shaking his head. "Shame the storm knocked it out. Cameras catch everything—except when you really need 'em."

Casey shot Will another sideways glance, her smirk still firmly in place. Will kept his focus squarely on the diagram, refusing to take the bait.

The Tahoe rolled down the quiet avenue back toward the precinct, sunlight slanting through the windshield and flashing in broken patterns across the dash. Will drove in silence, one hand loose on the wheel, his jaw set. Casey had her iced coffee balanced between her knees, straw bobbing as she swirled the ice. Rachel sat in the back, notebook propped on her lap, pen still poised as though the diagrams were fresh in her mind.

Casey twisted in her seat, leaning over the backrest to peer at the notebook. "So, Rookie, where'd you learn to sketch like that? You looked like an architect back there, mapping out blind spots."

Rachel glanced up, surprised by the attention. "My mom used to make me draw floor plans whenever she rearranged furniture. Said it helped visualize the space. I guess it stuck."

Casey hummed, tapping her straw against her lid. "And the color shading? I noticed you had your pencils out. Blue for the camera zones, right? I see you chose blue today. Was there a reason?"

Will's eyes flicked to her in the rearview, a side-eye sharp enough to cut.

Rachel tucked a strand of hair behind her ear, thoughtful. "Blue's neutral. Calming. I wanted the blind spots to stand out against it without looking chaotic. If the page gets messy, details get lost."

"Mm..hum," Casey smirked faintly, satisfied with the answer but already circling to her next jab. "So did you see any cracks in the security coverage?"

Rachel didn't hesitate. "Plenty. The gaps between camera sightlines are big enough for someone to walk a clean path from the frat houses to the east lawn without ever being caught on film. If you time it right, no one would notice."

Will's grip on the wheel tightened, color creeping up his collar as he glared at Casey again, silent but loaded with warning.

Casey, unfazed, let her grin sharpen. "Okay then, Rookie. Last one. If *you* were the suspect, how would you slip through without exposing yourself?"

Rachel froze for a beat, then lowered her eyes to the notebook. The pen hovered as she considered, her voice careful but steady. "I'd wait for noise to cover me, a storm, traffic, a party. Anything that makes people stop paying attention. Then I'd move through the blind spots like I belonged there. Not sneaking. Just... walking with purpose. Most people don't see what's right in front of them if it doesn't look out of place."

Casey whistled low, sitting back in her seat. "Damn. Somebody's been paying attention."

Will shot her a look sharp enough to kill the grin off her face, his jaw flexing. His flush hadn't faded.

Rachel glanced up, wide-eyed. "Was... that the right answer?"

Will cleared his throat, his voice rough. "It was a good answer."

Casey sipped her drink, smirking again. "Yeah. Real good."

The Tahoe rolled on, the silence thick with unspoken things.

Ryan Cho

Rachel leaned into the passenger seat of Will's SUV, a notebook balanced on her lap, braid slung forward like it was part of her uniform. "Ryan Cho," she said, tapping her pen against the page. "He claimed he was at the house, but this social media check-in puts him at the union fifteen minutes after the body was found. He lied."

Will kept his eyes on the road, jaw tight. "Which is why we're going to talk to him. But remember, you shadow. I ask the questions."

Rachel smiled faintly, tilting her head. "Of course. I'll be your shadow. And you know what they say about shadows."

He cut her a look. "What?"

"They stay with you. No matter how hard you try, you can't shake them." Her tone carried a lilt of playfulness, but the weight behind it lingered. Her eyes held his just a breath too long before she lowered them to her notes, the corners of her mouth still curved in that quiet, knowing smile.

Will shifted gears, letting the silence settle. She always knew how to toe the line between innocent and deliberate, and it put him on edge.

Rachel broke it again. "Speaking of hard times, I see Kristen's been having a rough go. The press won't let up. I bet you're not giving her a hard time about all of that, right?"

Will's tone was even. "Kristen doesn't need anyone piling on. Least of all me."

Rachel hummed, the sound low, almost approving. “Didn’t think so. You’re the kind of man who stands by people... even when it costs you.”

They found Ryan Cho lounging outside the fraternity house, phone in hand. Will’s voice carried no softness when he approached.

“Ryan. Need a word.”

Cho looked up, smirk ready. “Detective. And the intern. What’s this about?”

Will’s eyes narrowed as he looked at him. “You lied to us. Said you were at the house, but you checked in at the student union fifteen minutes after the body was found.”

Cho shifted, rolling his shoulders as if trying to make himself look bigger. “Alright, fine. I was at the quad. Didn’t want Derek or Ethan to know. I was... meeting up with Sheri. Langley’s sister. At her dorm. Having relations, you know? On my way back is when the crowd formed.”

Will’s brows knit. His voice was calm, clipped. “Meeting up how?”

A grin split across Cho’s face, the kind of grin that made Will’s skin crawl. He jabbed his thumb toward Rachel, eyes flashing with crude humor. “She knows. Relations. A good time.” Then, as if he were still twelve years old, he pumped his fists back and forth, hips jerking in a grotesque imitation of the act, skidding toward Rachel.

The air snapped taut.

Rachel’s pen stilled against her notebook. Her face went blank for a heartbeat, then sharpened, every syllable slicing through the room. “I’d rather drink poison than be seen in the same room with an ogre like you. Let alone whatever pathetic thing you're pantomiming."

Cho blinked, faltered, his smirk flickering.

Will stepped in, his shadow falling over the frat boy, his voice low and dangerous enough to hollow out the air between them. "Watch your mouth, Cho. Now."

The smirk vanished. Cho shifted his weight, his cocky facade thinning under Will's stare. For the first time, unease crept into his posture.

Cho muttered, "Whatever. It's the truth."

"Guess we will find out." Will retorted.

Back at the SUV, Rachel slid into her seat, shaking her head. "He's lying. We should see the sister."

Will shook his head, starting the engine. "Not yet. We need to get back to the PD and sync with Casey. We'll check Sheri later."

As Rachel climbed into the elevated passenger seat, something slipped from her lap and clattered onto the pavement.

"Damn it—my phone!" She leaned down to reach it, shifting her weight as she balanced halfway out of the SUV, one hand braced against the door frame.

"Careful—" Will started, then stopped. His eyes caught the movement and turned away at once, registering only the brief, unmistakable awareness that she hadn't been as covered as she thought. Nothing more. Enough to know.

She straightened quickly, phone secured, smoothing her skirt with a small, practiced motion before settling back into the seat.

Will kept his gaze forward, hands steady on the wheel, the moment already filed and dismissed.

Rachel's laugh floated up as she recovered, phone in hand. "Got it." She brushed herself off as if nothing had happened, then shut the door gently behind her.

The Ride Back to the PD

The SUV hummed quietly as they merged back onto the main road, its headlights cutting through the mid-afternoon haze. Rachel sat turned slightly toward him, her braid sliding over one shoulder, her notebook balanced casually on her thighs as though the encounter with Cho hadn't rattled her at all.

"Thanks again for standing up for me," she said, her voice low, deliberate. "I know you'll... stand up for me anytime I need you to."

Will kept his eyes locked on the road. "That's my job."

But her tone lingered in his ears, low and knowing, like she'd meant more than the words themselves.

Will clenched his jaw, replaying it.

Don't overthink it. She's young. She's grateful. That's all.

Except his mind wouldn't let go of what had happened outside the frat house. Not the movement—but the choice. The way she'd stayed balanced half out of the seat a moment longer than necessary. Long enough to be seen. Long enough to make him aware that she knew it.

He tightened his grip on the wheel. Damn it, Will. She's Joe's kid. Twenty-two. You should be protecting her—not letting her decide what you notice. Not letting her control the moment.

And that was the part he didn't like at all.

Rachel shifted in her seat, stretching her legs out as if she owned the space, then slid forward as she leaned the seat back a bit, allowing her skirt to climb up her thighs a little, exposing more skin. "Feels good to be useful," she added, tone feathered with something lighter, almost playful. "Better than just being the shadow. Though shadows... stick close, don't they?"

Will's gut twisted. Every phrase, every glance felt balanced on a knife's edge, innocent on the surface, dangerous if he let himself read into it. And that was the trap, wasn't it? Whether deliberate or not, she was walking too close to a line she didn't even know existed.

At least, he hoped she didn't.

He forced his voice steady, protective. "Rachel. You don't need to prove yourself to me or anyone else. You're here to learn. Nothing more."

She looked at him then, wide-eyed, lips parted like she might argue. But she only nodded softly, braid slipping forward again. "Yes, Detective, of course, and I hope to learn a lot from both of you."

The silence stretched, thick with the words unspoken.

Will tightened his hands on the wheel, gaze fixed hard on the road. *Protect her. That's all. Protect her.*

But the unease curled tighter in his chest. Because for the first time, he wasn't sure if Rachel was the one being tested.

Or if he was.

The SUV rolled into the precinct lot, the orange wash of early sunset and long shadows bleeding across the brick facade. Rachel hopped out first, smoothing her skirt with practiced ease, as though nothing unusual had happened. Will followed, slower, jaw tight, replaying every word, every glance from the ride.

Inside, the bullpen buzzed with the night shift settling in. Casey sat perched on the edge of her desk, coffee in hand, her boots crossed at the ankles. The moment she saw Will, her eyes narrowed.

"You look like you just saw a ghost," she said, hopping down. "Or like Chewie shaved his fur in your patrol car."

Will exhaled through his nose, trying for neutral. "Long interview. Cho folded."

"Uh-huh." Casey's gaze flicked to Rachel, who was already sliding into her chair, notebook open, pen poised like the model intern. Then back to Will. She didn't miss the storm behind his eyes. "What'd he say?"

Will cleared his throat. "Enough to tie him to the scene. Claimed he was with Langley's sister. We'll follow up."

"Good. Because you're giving me the whole Vader vibe right now, broody, menacing, like you want to Force-choke someone." She tilted her head. "What's going on?"

Will rubbed a hand over his jaw, the memory of Rachel's words—and the moment they'd followed—still nagging at him.

"Just... instincts. Plus, he made a run at Rachel, that smartass." He kept his voice low. "Something doesn't add up. And I don't like it."

Casey studied him for a long beat. Then she leaned closer, her tone gentler but edged with warning.

"Trust your instincts, Will. They're the only reason you're still breathing in this circus."

Will nodded, but his eyes drifted to Rachel across the room. She was bent over her notes, braid draped forward, every line of her posture picture-perfect.

Too perfect.

Casey followed his gaze, then back to him. One eyebrow arched. "Careful. You're starting to look like a man who's questioning the wrong things."

Will forced his eyes back to her, voice even. "No. Just a man making sure the shadows don't swallow us."

Casey didn't press, but she didn't buy it either. She sipped her coffee, smirking faintly. "Fine. But if you start quoting Anakin Skywalker about sand, I'm staging an intervention."

Will almost smiled, almost. But the unease in his chest hadn't loosened at all.

Will: SUV got awkward.

Casey: Define awkward.

Will: Her phone dropped. She leaned out the door. Skirt rode up.

Way up.

Casey: Sounds like a rookie strip tease.

Will: Felt deliberate. Red thong. Not exactly subtle.

Casey: Or not exactly graceful. Kid's all elbows. Wrong skirt, wrong move, wrong timing.

Will: You think it's just clumsy?

Casey: Yeah. If she wanted to play you, you wouldn't be guessing. Don't start reading games where there aren't any. Keep your head clear.

Will: ...Noted.

Across the room, Rachel scribbled in her notebook, oblivious, while Casey slid her phone face down on the desk. The smirk lingered, but so did the edge in her gaze when Will finally glanced up.

Watcher Observes

The coffee shop window framed the quad like a stage. Students drifted across the green, backpacks bouncing, voices bright with laughter. Normal. Ordinary.

At a corner table, a latte cooled beside an open nursing textbook, pages unturned. The gaze fixed outside, unblinking.

Ellie Anderson. An identical twin with raven hair braided with a faint streak of light blue, swinging earbuds in, a stack of art supplies balanced against one hip. She laughed at something her friend said, head tipped back, carefree. Pure. Untouched.

The Watcher stirred the coffee slowly, spoon clinking against ceramic. No one noticed the watching. Why would they? The figure blended easily, plain clothes, notebook open, posture relaxed. Nothing remarkable. Nothing to see.

Across the quad, Ellie bent to tie her shoe. A boy in a letterman jacket lingered too close, grin sharp, eyes sticking even after she turned away.

The Watcher's jaw tightened. He didn't belong near her.

Those eyes were hungry. Not the hunger of affection or curiosity, but of ownership. Boys like him looked for cracks, small vulnerabilities, the glimpse of skin at a collar, the arch of a back bent low, the slip of a hem when someone crouched. They saw openings as invitations, hesitation as weakness, silence as permission.

What he wanted was simple: to take. To test boundaries until they bent, to press until a "no" shrank into nothing. To stain what was unmarked, to leave fingerprints that never washed away.

Fingers brushed the chess piece in a pocket, the smooth weight of the pawn grounding the moment. Rolled between thumb and forefinger, its edges pressed faint grooves into skin. Pawns had to be protected. Directed and corrected, when necessary. Fragile by design, but fragility was a lie, pawns could become anything if guided.

Ellie didn't know that yet. None of them did. They wasted their moves, drifting across the board without seeing the traps waiting to swallow them. A smile at the wrong boy, a party invitation, a drink poured when no one was watching. That's how innocence bled away, not all at once, but piece by piece, until there was nothing left.

And the boy in the letterman jacket? Contamination. Not just close, circling. His type always believed pawns were theirs to claim, to consume, to discard.

The Watcher's jaw tightened again as the boy vanished into another crowd. Not today. Not while the board was being set.

The latte had gone cold by the time Ellie disappeared into the art building, her braid flashing in the sunlight one last time before the door shut. The Watcher lingered a moment longer, eyes on the empty space she had left behind.

Then the notebook closed, slid neatly into a bag. On the surface, nothing unusual, plain clothes, steady stride, another body lost in the stream of students crossing the quad. Invisible in plain sight.

But inside, the pulse thrummed steady. Deliberate. Every step a calculation. Every glance, surveillance.

Pawns were never safe on their own. Not unless someone stronger moved them, sheltered them, controlled their path.

And the Watcher was willing to do what no one else would.

Watcher's Journal

Pawns are the first pieces targeted. Their paths are narrow, their moves are predictable, and their defenses are weak.

Predators circle them not for challenge, but for convenience. A pawn bent is a pawn that has been claimed.

The board applauds this as a natural order.

But the board is wrong.

Pawns are not meant to be consumed. Pawns are meant to be shaped, moved with purpose, guided into power.

And any hand that seeks to spoil them must be cut away.

Kristen's Courtroom Failure

The courtroom was packed, warm with the press of bodies, the air thick with the smell of coffee and sweat. At the prosecution table, District Attorney Kristen Anderson sat with her files spread neatly before her, posture crisp and composed for the gallery's benefit. Up close, though, the strain showed in the way her fingers dug crescents into her pen. Her suit was dark, tailored with precision, the kind of armor meant to project control, but the shadows under her eyes betrayed the long nights she had spent behind it.

Across the aisle, Tyler Brentwood lounged with the cocky ease of someone certain the system bent in his favor. His suit was too sharp, his hair too perfect, and his lawyer leaned close, whispering smug reassurances that pulled a grin onto the boy's face.

From his seat in the gallery, Will watched his wife's jaw tighten as she forced her attention to the judge's bench. To everyone else, she was the DA—unyielding, unshaken. To him, she was Kristen, carrying the weight of the whole room on her shoulders and daring it to break her.

Kristen rose for closing arguments, forcing her voice steady.

"Ladies and gentlemen, this case is about accountability. About a girl who deserves to be believed."

She moved before the jury box, her heels clicking against the tile. "The victim, Nancy Hall, remembers the drink. She remembers the sudden blackout. She remembers waking up bruised, humiliated. That is not a coincidence. That is not bad luck. That is—"

"Objection." The defense attorney was already on his feet. "Inflammatory. The state has provided no medical evidence to prove intoxication or assault."

The judge nodded. "Sustained. Keep it to the facts, Ms. Anderson."

Kristen's stomach knotted. The facts. What did she have left to give them? Blurred security footage. A toxicology report run too late to be of any consequence. A victim whose voice shook under cross-examination until she contradicted herself.

She pressed forward anyway, words hollow even as they left her lips. "What happened to her happens far too often, and it ends the same way—silence, fear, shame. Today, you have the chance to break that cycle."

The defense attorney rose again, slicing her argument to pieces, hammering on "lack of evidence." By the time the jury filed out, Kristen already knew.

The verdict was delivered in less than an hour. **Not guilty.**

Tyler Brentwood smirked openly this time, his lawyer clapping him on the back as though they'd just won a game. He strutted from the courtroom, his fraternity brothers hooting in the hallway.

Kristen sank into her chair, pen rolling from her hand to the floor. She didn't move to pick it up. The victim sat three rows back, shoulders hunched, face pale. Kristen couldn't meet her eyes.

The next morning's paper screamed the failure in black ink:

"DA's Office Fails to Convict Fraternity Member."

Kristen's own photo stared back, weary eyes, tight smile, the perfect image of defeat.

She sat at her desk, the newspaper folded beside her laptop, a bottle of whiskey hidden in the bottom drawer, its amber contents already lower than they should be. Her hands trembled when she reached for her coffee, and she told herself it was from lack of sleep.

The email arrived at 9:04 a.m. No subject. No sender. Just one sentence:

A queen who betrays her pawns is no queen.

Her chest constricted. Betrays. The word echoed, slicing deeper than she wanted to admit.

A flash of memory jolted up, unbidden—

Steve's presence. The sweet chemical taste of something slipped into her drink. Darkness pressing in. The heavy weight of a body she hadn't invited. Hands tugging at her body. The camera light blinking red. The violations that occurred after the blackmail began

Kristen squeezed her eyes shut, the nausea rising. She'd buried that night for years, telling herself she was strong, telling herself it hadn't happened the way she feared. But the Watcher's words cracked that lie wide open.

The knock at her door made her jolt.

Will Anderson stepped inside, holding two files. His eyes softened when he saw her face. "Rough morning."

Kristen shut the laptop quickly, too quickly. "That obvious?"

Will glanced at the paper on her desk. "Front page doesn't help. Kris... you did what you could."

Her laugh was short and bitter. "Tell that to Nancy. The girl who sat in the courtroom and watched me lose. She's going home with nothing but scars and a jury that doubted her."

"Stop," Will said gently but firmly. "You didn't lose this. The system did. Lack of evidence isn't the same as lack of truth."

Her throat worked. She wanted to tell him about the memory of Steve, just like the recurring nightmares that she still had. About her own night in front of a camera lens, drugged and powerless. About the shame that had silenced her then, the shame that still shackled her now. But the words lodged like glass in her chest.

Instead, she forced a smile that didn't reach her eyes. "Thanks, honey. Really. But I'm fine."

He studied her, gaze lingering a beat too long, before finally nodding. "Call me if you need anything."

When he left, Kristen let the mask drop. She opened the laptop again, staring at the message until the words began to blur.

A queen who betrays her pawns is no queen.

Her hand trembled as she reached for the drawer. The whiskey burned down her throat, but it didn't wash away the taste of betrayal.

Second Pawn Off the Board

The frat house reeked of stale beer and sweat long before they crossed the threshold. But once inside, another smell pushed through, metallic, coppery, heavy in the back of the throat. Blood.

The living room looked like a storm had torn through it. Couch cushions gutted, bottles shattered, sticky trails of liquor smeared into the carpet. Red streaks led from the hall to the center of the room, where the body lay sprawled across the floorboards.

Derek Langley.

Casey recognized him instantly, smug grin, careless swagger, the same kid who'd laughed through their questions days earlier. That grin was gone now. His eyes stared blankly at the ceiling, wide and glassy. His throat was opened nearly ear to ear, a jagged slice that had bled him out across the hardwood. The dark pool beneath him still glistened, reflecting the strobe of police lights through the blinds.

He begged in the end.

The sound was thick with blood, gurgling through a ruined throat. Fists had landed blows, wild, desperate, but precision beat rage. Every counter was practiced, every strike measured.

Pawns fight as though they matter. But pawns are meant to fall.

Casey crouched, breath caught in her chest. His knuckles were raw, split open like he'd fought hard and lost badly. His ribs bore dark, ugly bruises, some boot-shaped. Whoever had done this hadn't been sloppy. They'd been angry. They'd wanted him to hurt.

But it was his left hand that froze her.

A pawn. White plastic, small and unremarkable, except it wasn't pristine this time. It was smeared red, sticky, tacky against his skin. Blood had seeped into the grooves, filling the tiny scratches until the piece looked as if it were half-dipped in crimson.

"Holy Sith," Casey muttered, pulling a bag from her kit. She pried the pawn loose carefully, the piece clinging before releasing with a wet pop. She held it up, grimacing. "Not just a calling card. This is a full-on transmission."

The piece fit perfectly in his hand.

The fingers were curled around it carefully, almost tenderly, blood slicking down the palm until it marked the pawn forever. A signature. A truth.

White against red. Purity marked by consequence.

Will crouched beside her, eyes hard as he scanned the scene. "More brutal than Prescott. Whoever did this... they're escalating."

A crime tech called from the corner, gloved hands holding up a small vial. "Detectives! Found under the couch.

Residue matches what we pulled from under the vic's nails. Preliminary test shows it's synthetic. Designer drug."

Casey straightened, glancing toward the body, then back at the tech. "The same stuff running through campus parties?"

"Looks that way. Lab will confirm."

The drug was still in his pocket.

Tiny glass vials, promises of destruction for whoever they chose next. He had laughed about them before the knife met skin, before the grin cracked into panic. He wasn't laughing now.

Poison disguised as pleasure. Serpents always carried venom.

Will's gaze lingered on Derek's face, then slid back to the bloody pawn in Casey's hand. "The killer isn't just targeting the Serpents. They're tying it to the drug."

Casey looked around the wreckage, the gutted couch, the sticky footprints tracked through blood. "Then it's not just revenge. It's a crusade."

Outside, the crowd pressed against the police tape. Students whispered and filmed, faces pale in the wash of red and blue lights. Every phone was a glowing eye, every whisper a rumor sprouting wings.

Casey shoved the bloody pawn into its evidence bag and sealed it tight. "You still want to call this a crank, Will?"

Will didn't answer right away. His jaw flexed, the weight of the scene pressing down like lead. Finally, he said it, voice low and certain:

"The game's already started."

Watcher's Journal

They crowned the Serpents, called them kings, and let them poison the board without consequence.

Kings believe they are untouchable. That pawns exist to serve them, to sacrifice for their amusement.

But kings fall the hardest. Kings bleed the deepest.

Tonight, another crown cracked. Another piece removed.

Still, the board demands balance.

Sheri Langley

The dorm room smelled faintly of nail polish remover and takeout cartons. Sheri Langley sat cross-legged on her bed, a pillow hugged tight to her chest, eyes darting between Will and Casey. Rachel stayed quiet by the desk, notebook open, pen poised.

Will leaned on the doorframe, voice steady. "Sheri, Ryan Cho claims he was with you the night Brock Prescott was killed. We need you to confirm that."

Sheri shifted, biting her lip. "We were... just hanging out."

Casey arched a brow. "Hanging out how? Watching TV? Talking? Anything your roommates might've noticed?"

"They were in their rooms," Sheri said quickly, almost too quickly. "I don't think they saw him."

"Did they hear you?" Casey pressed. "TV? Voices?"

Sheri squirmed, avoiding their eyes.

Before she could answer, the door swung open. One of the roommates stumbled in, a petite brunette with smeared lipstick and a tipsy grin.

"Kari Black," Sheri muttered under her breath.

Casey turned, seizing the opening. "Kari. Did you see Ryan Cho here the night Prescott died?"

Kari blinked, then laughed, the sound a little too loud. "Didn't see him. But I sure as hell heard him." She waggled her brows. “Grunting through the walls, Sheri calling his name like it was prom night.”

Sheri’s face went crimson. She buried her head in the pillow. “Okay. Fine. I’ve been seeing him. I didn’t want Derek to know. He’d never approve of me being with a Serpent.”

Casey exchanged a glance with Will. “Cho said you were having relations. Guess he wasn’t lying for once.”

Sheri’s voice cracked. “Please don’t tell my brother. I mean—” She stopped, realizing the words she’d just said.

Will’s tone softened but stayed firm. “Sheri... You know Derek is dead. He was found mutilated this morning. A pawn stuffed in his mouth. We need to know what you can tell us. Who hated him enough to do this?”

Her eyes flooded. “Enemies? God, Derek had plenty. He and Brock hated each other. There was this girl they both dated, neither of them still with her, but... there was bad blood.”

Casey cut in, her tone edged. “What about you? Ever have... relations with Brock Prescott?”

Sheri flinched, whispering, “No. Never.”

Before Will could press, Kari staggered closer, eyes glassy, grin loose. She leaned into Rachel, inhaling deep. “Mmm. You smell delicious.”

Then, without warning, her tongue dragged across Rachel’s cheek. Her hand slid brazenly under Rachel’s skirt, gripping her backside and the other one on her chest.

Rachel moved in a blur. The notebook slipped from her hand, pen clattering to the floor. She seized Kari’s wrist, pivoted hard on her hip, and in one smooth motion hurled her to the carpet.

With a thud, Kari landed flat on her back, groaning.

Rachel dropped into a crouch over her, fist cocked, eyes blazing. Her voice was a razor's edge. "I didn't ask you to touch me. And as a woman, you should damn well know better."

The room froze. Sheri stared, wide-eyed. Casey's jaw tightened. Will shifted forward, caught between breaking it up and letting Rachel finish what she'd started.

For a heartbeat, it wasn't the shy intern sitting at her desk. It was something sharper. Coiled. Trained.

Casey finally found her voice. "Holy hell, Rookie. You just went full Jedi on her."

Rachel blinked, breath ragged, as though just realizing what she'd done. She loosened her grip and stood slowly, brushing herself off, forcing her mask of composure back into place. "She... crossed a line."

Casey and Will exchanged a look, half impressed, half uneasy.

Because whatever mask Rachel wore as the eager, book-smart intern... a crack had just shown through.

Sheri looked at Will and then to Rachel and said, "I promise I don't know anything else!"

The SUV hummed low as it rolled out of the Ravenwood campus, headlights washing over the quiet streets. Inside, the silence was thick.

Rachel sat in the backseat, staring out the window, notebook clutched too tightly in her lap. Her braid had come loose during the scuffle, strands falling across her face. Her jaw worked like she was chewing on words she couldn't quite spit out.

Casey glanced in the rearview, then let out a long whistle. "Well, Rookie... that was one hell of a throw. I've seen black belts at the Y that couldn't stick a landing like that."

Rachel's cheeks flushed. "She touched me. I wasn't going to let her—"

"Hey, no judgment," Casey cut in, lifting a hand. "She deserved to be body-slammed into the next zip code. I'm just saying... I didn't expect my intern to go all Jedi Temple Guard on a drunk roommate." She smirked, voice pitched into mock drama. "'This is not the boob you're looking for.'"

Rachel gave a shaky laugh despite herself, but her grip on the notebook didn't ease. "Sorry if I made things awkward. I didn't mean to lose control."

Will's hands tightened on the wheel, eyes fixed forward. His tone was calm, but there was weight behind it. "You didn't lose control, Rachel. That was controlled. Precise. Too precise to be a first instinct."

Rachel met his gaze in the rearview, unblinking. "I told you—I've trained. Self-defense for the last six years, BJJ, and some Krav Maga. You spend enough time on campus, you learn not to freeze when someone crosses a line."

Casey twisted in her seat, studying her. "Training's one thing. Hip-tossing a drunk girl without spilling your notebook? That's muscle memory. What are you, undercover Black Widow?"

Rachel forced a small smile, tucking her hair back. "I just... don't like being touched without permission. Makes me... angry." Her voice dipped on the last word, almost fragile.

Casey softened, turning back around. "Fair enough. Anger, I get. Hell, you've seen my lightsaber temper. I'd have decked her too. Been known to drop kick a few sleazeballs, most recently Steve, that perv."

The SUV fell quiet again, the only sound the thrum of tires on asphalt.

Will's gaze flicked to the rearview once more. Rachel had calmed, face tilted back toward the window, but his gut didn't buy it.

She wasn't just reacting. She'd moved like someone who'd practiced that throw a hundred times. Like someone who'd been waiting for the excuse.

Casey broke the silence with a sigh. "Next time, Rookie, just... maybe a little less WWE Smackdown during witness interviews. We want cooperation, not concussions."

Rachel chuckled softly, but Will's thoughts didn't ease.

Because Rachel Donovan's mask had slipped.

And what he'd glimpsed beneath it wasn't just competence.

It was something dangerous.

Back at the PD

The fluorescent lights in the conference room hummed as Will, Casey, and Rachel filed inside. Casey dropped her files on the table, grabbed a chair, and pointed her pen at Rachel with mock sternness.

"Okay, Rookie—rule of thumb. No hip-tossing drunk girls unless you're in the octagon or I'm getting it on camera. HR tends to frown on suplexes."

Rachel gave a soft laugh, brushing a strand of hair back into her braid. "Understood, Detective. It won't happen again."

Casey smirked, leaning back. "I'll give you this though—you pulled it off smooth. Almost too smooth. Guess all that time on the mats pays off." She tipped her head, looking at Will. "She's been rolling since she was sixteen. That's six years of armbars and guard sweeps, partner. No accident she dropped Kari like that."

Will's jaw flexed, but he didn't comment. He pulled out a chair and sat, folding his arms across his chest. Rachel lowered herself neatly into the chair opposite him, notebook already open, pen poised like she was back in class.

"I only reacted," she said evenly. "I don't like being touched without permission."

There was a quiet in that statement that carried more weight than her tone allowed. Will caught the undercurrent but held it, testing for cracks. Rachel didn't look away.

Casey cleared her throat, breaking the silence. "You don't have to explain yourself, Rookie. Hell, given what you've lived through, I'm surprised you didn't break her arm."

Rachel blinked, but her expression didn't falter. She dipped her head in a polite nod, scribbling something across the page.

Casey glanced at Will, waited until Rachel's pen was moving, then leaned closer and dropped her voice so only he could hear. "She's twenty-two, Will. She is less than a year out from getting drugged and gang-raped by three guys who thought filming her was funny. You saw the video just like I did. Don't ride her too hard when she defends herself. She's earned the right to."

Will's chest tightened. He didn't answer, only stared at the notepad Rachel was filling with careful bullet points. Perfect penmanship. Perfect posture. Not a hair out of place.

But under the neat mask, he wondered how much was discipline—and how much was armor.

Casey sat back and yawned, stretching her arms overhead like she was shaking the tension out. "Alright, what's for dinner tonight, Anderson? I saw we call it a day and cool off in your backyard. Fresh saltwater pool dip sounds pretty good right now, would help relax this ol girl. What do you say? Can I swim in your bacta tank?"

Will says, "Well, it's usually taco Tuesday, Kristen's turn to pick up. I'll have Kristen grab extra from La Tia Traviesa. They primarily serve Mexican-American style, so speak up if there's something you may not like."

"I'm good with whatever." Casey said, "Same here." Rachel followed.

Casey looked at Rachel, "Got a suit or need to borrow one?

Rachel says, "I can run home and grab one."

"Ok then, go Padawan go," Casey joked, "And Rachel—try not to judo flip anyone else before to make it to the pool, okay?"

Rachel smiled faintly, closing her notebook. "I'll try, Detective."

She gathered her things with quiet efficiency, gave them both a slight nod, and slipped out the door.

The moment it closed, Casey let out a low whistle. "Kid's tougher than we give her credit for. But she's still a kid."

Will didn't answer right away. He was staring at the door, jaw tight, unease thrumming in his gut.

Update to Captain Monroe

The night air outside the dorm was cooler, sharp against Will's skin as he and Casey walked Rachel back toward the SUV. Rachel's shoulders were rigid, her notebook clutched too tight, as though she was still bracing for the next move.

"Take five," Casey said gently, opening the back door for her. "We'll handle this part."

Rachel slid inside without a word, jaw tight.

Will pulled out his phone, thumb hovering a second before he hit the speed-dial. Captain Frank Monroe answered on the second ring.

"Tell me you've got something," Monroe said, his voice gravel worn down by too many years and too much bourbon.

Will exhaled. "Depends on your definition of something. We pressed Sheri Langley. She admitted Cho was with her the night Prescott was found. Alibi looks like it might hold, though I'm not buying it clean. Her roommate Kari half-confirmed it—loudly, and drunk."

Casey leaned against the hood, arms crossed. “Confirmed it with way too much detail. And then tried to climb all over our intern. Rachel put her down hard. Fast reflexes.”

Monroe groaned. “Christ. I don’t need a lawsuit from a tipsy sorority brat claiming your intern broke her collarbone.”

“No one’s pressing charges, girl had it coming, she crossed a line,” Will said quickly. “But it tells us something. Rachel doesn’t spook easily. She’s sharper than she lets on.” His tone darkened. “Maybe too sharp.”

Casey shot him a look but stayed quiet.

Monroe let the silence stretch. “Alright. I’ll take your half-a-win. Cho’s still dirty in my book, but if he’s wrapped around Langley’s sister, that complicates things. Dig deeper. See who else Prescott pissed off. And Will—keep the intern out of the headlines. I don’t need reporters asking why Joe Donovan’s daughter is hip-tossing students on university property.”

Will nodded to himself. “Understood.”

Monroe’s sigh rasped through the line. “Good. Now go get some sleep before one of you ends up in the morgue alongside these frat boys.”

The call ended. Will slipped the phone back into his pocket and glanced toward the SUV, where Rachel sat watching the two of them through the tinted glass, face unreadable.

Casey muttered under her breath. “Cap’s right. This is getting messy.”

Will’s jaw tightened. “Messy’s not the half of it.”

Cool in the Pool

Will heard the splashes before he pushed through the sliding door. Laughter carried across the patio, Casey, Rachel, and the twins tangled in some inside joke that sent water flying. The late sun caught the ripples, turning the pool surface into shifting bands of gold and blue.

He stepped out, phone in hand, scanning an email as he lowered into a chair. The metal arms were hot under the August heat. He barely looked up until Casey passed him, water dripping from her crimson two-piece. The Gamecock logo stamped across her top was unmistakable, a piece of her alma mater pride she never let him forget.

"Fair skin burns, Anderson," she quipped, wringing water from her hair as she headed for the shade. "Gotta keep the tan lines away so I can still sport my Leia bikini."

Will shot her a side glance over the top of his phone, unimpressed. "You'd scare half the neighborhood with that thing."

Casey grinned, whipping her wet hair in his direction. Droplets spattered across his Carolina-blue shirt, turning it mottled navy. "See? Dark blue looks way better on you than that powder-puff Tar Heel shade."

Will lowered his phone, narrowing his eyes. "Watch it."

Casey plopped into her chair, smirking. "What? You're still clinging to Duke's little brother complex? Come on,

Will, deep down even you know USC would steamroll your precious UNC."

That got him to sit back. "We'll see how you're running your mouth when the Tar Heels sweep basketball season again."

"Basketball." Casey groaned theatrically. "Always basketball with you Chapel Hill types. Down in Columbia, we care about football. Real football. You know, the kind with grit and bone, not squeaky shoes and shorts."

Will crossed his arms. "We'll revisit this in March when you're crying into your garnet pom-poms."

From the pool, Rachel had been quiet, only her head and shoulders above the surface, hair slicked back, water glinting off her skin. She tilted her chin, eyes catching his across the patio. "Funny. For someone so sure of himself, you don't sound like you're winning this argument."

Casey whooped. "Ohhh, Rookie's got teeth!"

Rachel drifted closer to the edge, propping her arms on the ledge, her smile faint but sly. "Numbers don't lie, Detective. Three against one... and I haven't even shown you my best moves yet."

Emily squealed and splashed her sister. "Did you hear that? She's destroying him!"

Ellie grinned. "Dad's toast."

Casey raised her drink in triumph. "Tar Heel, you're outnumbered and outclassed. Admit defeat."

Will smirked faintly, but the heat creeping up his collar wasn't just from the sun. Rachel's words, playful enough to make the twins laugh, innocent enough for Casey to cheer, carried a sharper edge under the surface. *I haven't even shown you my best moves yet.*

She was still smiling at him when she sank back into the water, disappearing to her shoulders, as if she'd never said anything at all.

Will turned back to his phone, jaw tight, but the line looped in his head, stubborn and unshakable, long after the laughter faded.

The twins had been racing each other in the shallow end when Rachel climbed the pool ladder. Water streamed from her hair and down her shoulders, sunlight catching on her skin as she stepped onto the deck and reached for a towel.

Emily froze mid-stroke. Ellie nearly swallowed a mouthful of water.

Rachel wore a navy-blue string bikini—clearly borrowed, clearly last-minute. It fit, technically, but just barely, the kind of suit meant for someone bolder or better prepared. The twins stared openly, forgetting entirely that they were supposed to be swimming.

"Oh my God," Ellie breathed.

Emily elbowed her without looking away. "That's... not fair."

Rachel caught their expressions and paused, one hand on the towel, brow creasing in confusion. "What?"

Emily flushed. "Nothing. Just—wow."

Rachel laughed, a little embarrassed, a little amused, and wrapped the towel loosely around her shoulders before sitting on the edge of a lounge chair.

Will had been half-focused on his phone when the sudden silence tipped him off. He looked up, took in the scene, and immediately looked away again, clearing his throat as he set the phone down. He fixed his attention on the far end of the pool with exaggerated care.

Casey, stretched out beside him with sunglasses on, tilted her head just enough to peek over the rim. She took Rachel in with one long, slow look, then let out a low whistle.

"Well damn," she said cheerfully. "You rob a runway on the way over here, Rookie?"

Rachel's cheeks warmed. "It was borrowed. I didn't exactly pack for a pool."

"Oh, I can tell," Casey grinned. "That suit's hanging on for dear life. Respect."

Emily slid lower into the water, hiding her face. Ellie didn't even blink.

Casey leaned toward Will, voice stage-loud. "Relax. It's a swimsuit, not a crime scene. Though I will say—" she turned back to Rachel, pointing with her straw, "—next time you give me zero warning, I'm breaking out my Leia slave bikini just to keep things balanced."

Rachel snorted despite herself. "Pretty sure that'd cause more chaos, not less."

"Chaos is my brand," Casey said proudly. "And don't worry—Will here doesn't care what anyone wears. Man's seen enough crime scenes to be immune to human anatomy."

Will shot her a look. "That is not—"

"Oh hush," Casey waved him off. "If anything, this is good exposure therapy."

Rachel tilted her head, studying Casey with a thoughtful glint. Then she adjusted the towel more securely, leaned in just a fraction, and smiled.

"Well," she said lightly, "if that's the case, maybe I should thank you for the warm welcome. I was worried I'd underdressed."

Emily burst out laughing, splashing water as she tried to cover her face. Ellie finally looked away, shaking her head like she'd just witnessed a magic trick.

Casey laughed outright. "Oh, I like her. She bites back."

Rachel settled into her chair, towel in place, confidence fully intact. "I pay attention," she said. "You never know when it'll come in handy."

Will kept his eyes on the pool, but the corner of his mouth twitched despite himself.

Casey wagged her straw at her, still grinning. "Noted. You can stay."

Emily whispered to Ellie, loud enough for Will to hear, "Okay, she's officially cooler than Casey."

Ellie just shook her head, still staring at Rachel like she'd rewritten the rules of gravity.

Will just shook his head. "I'm definitely getting too old for this shit."

"Shut it, Sgt Murtaugh," Casey said, throwing her towel at Will, cover up your face and let us be free."

Kristen slid open the patio door, the warm aroma of seasoned meat drifting outside with her. "Food is ready!

We've got a full taco and quesadilla buffet bar tonight." Her eyes flicked toward the pool, settling on Casey and Rachel in their swimsuits. With a grin, she added, "You girls might want to tie your strings a little tighter, because if this food is as good as it usually is, and those strings pop, dessert's going to be on display early."

Emily and Ellie howled, laughter bubbling so hard they tumbled right off their floats and splashed into the pool.

Rachel's face flamed as she grabbed her towel, wrapping it hastily around herself before making a beeline for the door.

Will just shook his head, smiling faintly, caught somewhere between embarrassment and amusement. No safe words came to mind.

Casey, meanwhile, smirked and called back, "Don't tempt me, girlfriend. I'm not stretching this sacred suit. I'll let these pull out these strings and let it go in a skinny minute if it means more room for Naughty Auntie's food. Wouldn't be the first time around here."

That sent Emily and Ellie into another round of cackles as Kristen laughed and waved them all inside.

Anderson House – Dining Room

The buffet spread across the kitchen island looked like a feast: sizzling quesadillas still steaming on their platters, tacos piled high with shredded lettuce and spiced meat, bowls of guacamole and salsa glistening under the light. The sharp tang of cilantro and lime cut through the warm, rich smell of melted cheese and grilled tortillas.

Kristen, hostess to the bone, set down the final dish, a tray of roasted corn still hissing from the oven, and waved everyone in.

Emily and Ellie barreled inside from the pool, water dripping onto the tile, their hair plastered to their cheeks. The blast of air conditioning raised goosebumps on their arms, but they hardly noticed as they lunged toward the food, squealing at the sight of all the toppings. Casey swept in behind them, skin still damp, scooping tortillas onto her plate with the speed of a practiced thief. "Fuel for the force," she muttered, stacking them high.

Will moved quietly among them, pouring tall glasses of iced tea. The clink of ice against glass was a cool counterpoint to the sizzling quesadillas. Rachel lingered in the doorway, towel clutched around her shoulders, the chill air raising the scent of chlorine from her hair.

Kristen noticed. She pulled out a chair directly across from her. "Rachel, sit here. You've been drafted to the big kids' table."

Rachel hesitated, then slipped into the chair, towel falling away as condensation from her tea glass chilled her palm.

Kristen's gaze was warm but sharp, her DA's edge never fully tucked away. "So, Rachel. You've seen me at my worst, bun crooked, no makeup, barking orders into two phones while Will pretends he's not rolling his eyes. Now you get to see me in my natural habitat: food and family."

Rachel gave a small laugh. "Honestly, this is... nice. Very different from the bullpen."

"Different, but not easier," Kristen said, spooning guac onto her plate. The avocado was creamy, flecked with onion and lime. "In both places you've got to keep people in line and make sure nobody does anything stupid. At least here the worst mistake is over-salting the queso."

Casey, already chewing, raised her taco like a toast. "Preach."

The twins collapsed into giggles, chips crunching as they told exaggerated tales of "Naughty Casey" breaking every rule in sight.

The room buzzed with laughter and the rustling of tortillas. Still, Rachel felt Kristen's eyes flick to her every so often, weighing. Will caught it too. He slid a bowl of salsa across the table, the smell of roasted peppers rising with it. "Careful with that one. Extra heat."

Rachel dipped a cautious spoonful, the chili bite stinging her nose. "Thank you for having me," she said softly. "I... didn't expect this."

Kristen's mouth curved. "We keep it real here. No courtrooms, no crime scenes, no badges. Just tacos, teasing, and trying to mortify each other whenever possible." She leaned back, the snap of a chip punctuating her words. "You're initiated now."

Rachel's shoulders eased. The cold tea slid sweetly down her throat, a soothing contrast to the spice. For the first time all evening, she felt less like the intern rookie detective or Joe Donovan's daughter, and more like herself.

Casey launched into a dramatic retelling of the time she "rescued" a plate of nachos from a rookie. The twins clinked chips like glasses, salsa dripping down their fingers as they cackled. Rachel folded her towel neatly over the chair back, her damp hair cooling against her skin.

Then Kristen set down her fork, her gaze steady across the table. Her voice was light but edged with purpose. "So, Rachel. What's next? Are you planning to stay in law enforcement, follow your dad's footsteps? Or is this just a stopover before nursing calls you back?"

The chatter dipped, the crunch of chips filling the pause. Casey arched a brow, watching with interest.

Rachel glanced at Will, then back at Kristen. "I... don't know yet. Nursing was always the plan. But once I started working with the department—" she lifted a shoulder, steady despite the weight of eyes on her—"it felt like maybe I belonged here more than I expected."

Kristen studied her for a beat, then nodded. "Fair answer. Just remember, whether it's a hospital or a squad room, both places need people who don't scare easily."

Casey raised her taco in salute. "Amen."

The twins echoed with clinking chips, laughter spilling out again.

Will pushed the salsa bowl closer to Rachel, his tone calm but confident. "She doesn't scare easily."

Rachel ducked her head, the spice still tingling on her tongue, cheeks warming despite the chill of the AC. Her smile lingered.

Twins in Danger

The sun was warm on the bricks of Ravenwood's quad, September clinging to summer even as the trees whispered of autumn. Emily angled her phone against her knee, the glare catching the glass as she scrolled for filters.

"Come on, El, one picture," she said, tugging her twin closer. Her braid brushed Ellie's shoulder as they leaned in. A snap, a laugh, and it was done.

Ellie rolled her eyes but smiled anyway. "You're obsessed."

"It's called having a presence," Emily shot back, already captioning: *Campus sunshine with my built-in bestie.* She posted it before Ellie could protest, tucking the phone back into her bag.

By morning, Ellie's mood had soured.

She froze in the hallway outside the lecture wing.

Up ahead, a girl passed by in the same pale blue sweater Emily had worn yesterday. Same braid trailing down her back. Same silver hoop earrings flashing in the light. From behind, the resemblance was so exact it caught Ellie's breath in her throat.

"Em?" she called.

The girl didn't turn. She moved with the tide of students, her steps measured, posture unnervingly stiff. For an instant, Ellie swore it was Emily, the way the braid swung, the slope of her shoulders.

But then her real sister jogged up from behind, coffees in hand.

"What?" Emily asked, out of breath. "Why are you staring at me like that?"

Ellie's head snapped between her and the crowd. The girl was gone.

"You were just—" She stopped, pulse hammering. "No. Never mind. Thought I saw you up there."

Emily laughed it off, shoving a cup into her hand. "Clone me? Please. The world can barely handle one."

Ellie forced a smile, but her gaze lingered on the hallway. Something itched at her memory.

The braid.

It had been tied with a red elastic.

Emily never used red. Ever. Said it clashed with the streak in her hair. Always yellow elastic with that outfit. Always.

Her stomach turned cold. Whoever that girl was, she hadn't just copied Emily's sweater or earrings. She'd studied her closely enough to get almost everything right.

Almost.

Ellie gripped her coffee tighter, eyes sliding to the windows, the doors, the blur of faces around her. The unease stayed knotted in her chest all through class.

Because someone out there wanted to be Emily so badly they wore her skin.

And if Ellie hadn't noticed, no one else would have.

Ellie Confides in Casey

Ellie waited until she was sure Casey would be home before stopping by. The living room lights spilled softly and golden through the blinds, wrapping the space in warmth that never quite touched the pit of unease in her stomach. She folded herself cross-legged on the couch, tugging at the loose cuff of her sweatshirt like it could anchor her.

On the other end, Emily sprawled against the armrest, a bowl of popcorn balanced on her stomach, thumbs flying across her phone while the movie played ignored in the background.

Casey padded in from the kitchen, setting down a steaming mug of tea in front of Ellie. She crouched low, searching Ellie's face the way only an older sister could. "Alright. You said something freaked you out on campus. Talk."

Ellie's eyes darted sideways to Emily, who hadn't looked up once. She leaned closer, lowering her voice as though the walls themselves might be listening. "I saw... someone. Dressed exactly like Em. Same sweater, same braid, same earrings. I even called her name. But it wasn't her. She was behind me the whole time."

Casey's brows drew together, skeptical. "So... a girl in a sweater?"

Ellie's shoulders snapped tight. She shook her head hard. "No, you don't get it. It wasn't just similar. It was exact. Even the braid. The only thing wrong was the tie, red instead of yellow. Whoever it was, they were trying to be her. And it felt... off. Like they'd been studying."

Emily finally looked up, smirking. "People copy outfits all the time, El. It's called fashion. Relax." She popped another piece of popcorn into her mouth and went back to her phone.

Ellie bristled, heat rising in her cheeks. "No, this wasn't just clothes. It was the way she moved. It was as if she was trying to walk like you. It felt—" Her voice cracked, the word *wrong* sticking sharp in her throat. She swallowed it back, knuckles white as she clutched her sleeve.

Casey leaned against the coffee table, arms folded, studying her. Her cop brain measured the fear in Ellie's eyes against the logic of campus life. "Creepy, sure. But the campus is crawling with people. You sure you're not spooking yourself?"

Ellie's voice dropped, low and certain. "I know what I saw."

The quiet in the room stretched. Emily crunched popcorn, oblivious. Casey reached forward, laying a steady hand on Ellie's knee. "Okay. I'll make a note. If you see her again, you let me know right away. Got it?"

Ellie nodded, but her lips pressed into a tight line. The reassurance slid off like rain off glass. The image of that red elastic, bright, glaring, wrong, burned too deep.

The drive back to campus was quiet, the streets thinning as the city wound down for the night. Emily drove with one hand on the wheel, music low, tapping out the rhythm against the steering column. Ellie sat rigid in the passenger seat, staring out the window as the amber glow of streetlamps slid across her face in intervals.

She almost convinced herself to let it go. Almost.

Then, as they slowed for a light near the campus gates, Ellie's breath caught.

On the corner, under the lamplight, a figure stood facing away from them. Not the pale-blue sweater this time, something worse. A red Kansas City Chiefs pullover, the hood tugged low. Emily's pullover. The one she wore on game days and lazy Sundays, the one with a faint grease stain on the pocket that she swore she'd never wash out.

Even from across the road, Ellie saw it clear as day, the braid swinging out of the hood, tied with that same glaring red elastic.

Her stomach dropped.

Emily followed her sister's stare, eyes narrowing. "No way..." Her grip tightened on the wheel. "That's—"

The light flipped green. A horn blared behind them. Emily jumped, slamming the gas. The Tahoe lurched forward, headlights flooding the intersection.

Ellie twisted in her seat, heart hammering. The figure was gone. The sidewalk was empty, as if no one had been there at all.

Emily's voice was tense and lower now. "That was my hoodie. No one else has that exact one. Not here. Custom-ordered by Mom for my birthday. What the hell Ellie."

Ellie dragged her gaze back to the windshield, throat dry. "I told you."

The silence between them was heavier than the night pressing against the glass. For once, Emily didn't argue.

By the time they pulled into the dorm lot, the warmth of Casey's living room felt a world away.

Ellie kept seeing that flash of red under the lamplight, the braid swaying just so.

Whoever this was, they weren't just mimicking.

They were escalating.

Emily Believes

They pulled into the dorm lot, the engine ticking as Emily killed the headlights. Neither of them moved at first, the silence heavy in the small space.

Emily blew out a sharp breath, forcing a laugh that didn't quite land. "Okay... so maybe someone bought the same hoodie. It's a Chiefs thing. Popular team. Could've grabbed it at a thrift store."

But her hands stayed clenched around the wheel, knuckles pale.

Ellie turned slowly, her voice steady even as her pulse thudded in her ears. "No. Not with the braid. Not with the earrings. And not with *your* hoodie. There's a stain on the front pocket, Em. I saw it. Same spot."

Emily blinked, startled, then scoffed too quickly. "Coincidence. Just a coincidence."

But Ellie caught the flicker in her sister's eyes, the quick calculation, the doubt she didn't want to admit.

Ellie's stomach churned. She gripped the strap of her bag so tight her fingers ached. "Whoever that was... they've been watching you. Close enough to know your clothes, your habits. Close enough to copy *you.*"

Emily finally looked at her, phone dark in her lap now. The smirk she usually wore was gone. "El... you really think somebody's out there playing dress-up as me?"

Ellie didn't answer. She didn't need to. The chill sitting in her gut said it for her.

Because this wasn't just about a sweater or a braid anymore.

Someone out there knew them. Someone out there wanted to *be* Emily.

And if they were close enough to know about the hoodie...

They were close enough to know where Emily lived.

Close enough to be in her clothes.

Dorm Discovery

The twins didn't speak much as they climbed the stairs to their dorm, footsteps echoing hollow in the stairwell. Emily had her phone out again, screen glow washing her face, though her scrolling was slower now, distracted. Ellie stayed close behind, eyes darting at every landing, every open door.

When they reached their floor, the common lounge sat mostly empty, the big TV humming quietly with a late-night news rerun. A couple of backpacks were dropped near the couches, but no one was around.

Emily moved ahead, but Ellie stopped dead in the doorway.

There, draped over one of the chairs.

A red Kansas City Chiefs pullover.

Her stomach dropped clean out. It wasn't just a similar hoodie. It was *the* hoodie. She knew every fray at the cuffs, the faint grease stain near the pocket, the tiny snag in the fabric just above the hem—Emily's.

"Em..." Ellie's voice was barely a whisper, her throat dry.

Emily turned, a frown tugging at her mouth. When she saw it, her phone slipped lower in her hand. "That's—"

She cut herself off.

The hoodie was abandoned, limp over the chairback. But there was no bag beside it, no books, no drink cup. Nothing to say, no one had been there at all.

Emily moved forward fast, snatching it up. She turned it inside out, searching for something, a tag, initials, a mark that would prove it wasn't hers. But the moment she caught sight of the grease stain on the pocket, her hands trembled.

"It's mine," she whispered.

Ellie's breath came sharp. "Then how did it get here?"

The hallway behind them stretched long and quiet, shadows pooling under the exit sign. The silence pressed down hard, as though someone were still close enough to hear them.

Emily clutched the hoodie to her chest, forcing a shaky laugh that fooled no one. "Somebody... must've grabbed it from my laundry. That's all."

But Ellie's eyes stayed on the darkened corners of the lounge, every nerve bristling.

No one had walked past them on the stairs. No one had been in the hall when they arrived.

Yet the hoodie had beaten them here.

And whoever left it behind could still be watching.

Emily clutched the hoodie tighter, as if holding it might somehow explain it away. Her fingers brushed the pocket, and froze.

"Wait."

She reached in, frowning, and pulled out a folded scrap of paper. It was damp from fabric and faintly crinkled, but the ink bled sharp and deliberate.

Emily unfolded it slowly. Ellie leaned in, heart in her throat.

The handwriting was neat, almost elegant, each letter precise.

Pawns should be cautious where they walk.

The board is larger than they think.

Neither girl spoke. The hum of the lounge TV seemed impossibly loud, buzzing against the silence that wrapped around them.

Emily's hand trembled as she shoved the note at her sister. "This is... this is a joke. Has to be."

But Ellie's stomach turned to ice. "No, Em. This isn't a joke."

Her eyes kept flicking to the hallway, the doorways, the corners where shadow pooled thick. The hoodie, the red elastic, the note, none of it was a coincidence. Someone had been close enough to follow them, close enough to listen, close enough to *know*.

Ellie folded the note again with shaking hands, voice low. "Casey needs to see this."

Emily finally nodded, hugging the hoodie like armor. But her eyes betrayed her, wide and darting, as though she already knew the truth Ellie had felt all along.

They weren't just being watched.

They were already on the board.

Watcher's Journal

The twins represent what I lost.

I study them so I don't forget what innocence looks like.

Pure lines, unbroken. Pieces with potential.

They waste it—flirting, laughing, drifting too close to contamination.

They don't see the traps.

I see them. I will guide them. Even if they hate me for it.

Pawns can become queens. If they pass the board's test

Casey's Discovery

Casey froze in her doorway, single key still in her hand, she had just dug out of the packet of her favorite sonic pink Lululemon Speed Up running shorts, the faint jingle swallowed by the stillness.

At first glance, the apartment looked normal, the muted glow of daybreak bleeding through the blinds, the faint sour trace of old coffee in the air, the jacket she'd left draped across the back of a chair.

But the silence was wrong.

It wasn't the kind of quiet she knew, the lived-in hush of her place after a long day. This silence was hollow, emptied. A quiet that felt pressed into the walls, like someone had stepped inside, held their breath, and waited.

Her skin prickled, every nerve awake. "Spidey-senses tingling!" she muttered inaudibly.

Gun instinctively in hand before she even registered drawing it from, Casey moved forward, the weight of her Springfield Hellcat 9mm pistol steady against her palm, removed from under he tank top from its stretch belly-band holster, that hugged her like a second skin, it bounced with her when she ran, not heavy but present with every stride. She swept the living room in practiced arcs, her eyes cataloguing details, searching for the betrayals of familiarity.

There. A pillow angled slightly differently on the couch.

There. A coaster left in the middle of the coffee table when she knew she'd tucked it back neatly into the corner.

Someone had been here.

Her throat tightened, dry as sandpaper. Not again.

Her boots barely whispered on the hardwood as she advanced down the hall, every step careful, deliberate. The air felt heavier here, stale, with the faintest undercurrent of fabric softener that wasn't hers. She caught the faint, chemical tang of leather, too, gloves maybe.

"At least they are clean," her mind fired into her thoughts.

The bedroom door stood cracked open, darkness bleeding out into the hall like a stain. Her pulse hammered in her ears, drowning the silence as she nudged it wider with the barrel of her pistol.

Her breath stopped.

The top dresser drawer hung open, tilted slightly off its track.

Underwear spilled over the edge, not in neat folds but a chaotic jumble, fingers had been here. Touching. Choosing.

Her chest locked, a band of iron around her ribs. Memory slammed into her like a fist.

The last time.

The memory of coming to on her apartment floor, not that long ago, throat raw with the burn of chloroform, chemical sting clawing her sinuses. Her own front door blurred in her vision, her body heavy and wrong. The pressure of an attacker's weight on her back. Her fingers fumbling with her Sig from its holster. Then black.

And waking later. Shirt completely gone. Bra still on. Pants not undone. Blood dripping sticky and metallic beneath her nose.

The cold realization of what could have happened.

Of what almost happened.

And finding her drawer emptied moments before that. Every pair of underwear gone, trophies stolen like teeth ripped from a jaw.

A warning on the scorecard.

And it hadn't been a bluff.

Her hand trembled on the Sig now, not from fear but from rage. The weight of the gun was solid, familiar, the one thing in the room that hadn't been tainted.

Not again.

The words roared in her head as she forced air through her nose, steadying her stance. The shadows felt closer, pressing at the edges of her vision. Every breath tasted like metal, the memory of blood, the sting of chloroform, the ghost of violation.

She shoved the dresser drawer closed with a violent snap, the sound cracking like a gunshot in the silence. The folded lace and cotton inside shifted back into darkness, as if trying to hide the evidence of hands that had pawed through them.

That's when she saw it.

On the bed. Perfectly centered. Waiting.

Plain white paper, crisp and uncreased, as if it had been laid with careful hands. The words printed in heavy black block letters:

A rook protects pawns, but even rooks can be toppled.

Casey's vision tunneled, the world shrinking to that sheet of paper and the way it seemed to sneer at her from the quilt. The room itself blurred, edges vibrating with her pulse.

They hadn't just violated her space. They'd replayed the scene, *her* scene. Reminding her of the last time, of how close she'd come to being pinned, helpless, stripped of control. They wanted her to feel it again. To drown in it.

Her throat ached with the memory of gasping into the floor, her body dead weight under someone else's hand. That same ice tried to slide into her chest now, that cold helplessness. But it hit a wall.

Fury rose instead.

She crossed the room in three sharp steps and snatched the paper up. The texture rasped against her fingertips, smooth but cutting. She crushed it in her fist until the stiff edges bit into her palm, drawing faint red crescents.

Her chest heaved, every breath sawing hot and heavy under her ribs. The rage felt volcanic, molten heat pushing against fragile skin. Her jaw locked, teeth grinding against the swell of it.

But the fear wouldn't take her this time.

Not the way it had before.

Casey stood in the center of her bedroom, shoulders squared, gun still steady in her other hand, and glared into the shadows that pooled in the corners like waiting eyes.

"You're not toppling me," she whispered, the words sharp enough to cut glass. Her voice didn't waver.

"Not now. Not ever."

Catching her breath, her lips pressed into a line. "Wash it off. Leave it here."

Casey placed the Hellcat on the bathroom counter within arm's reach before stripping down, after undoing the belly band. Her skin was still sticky with sweat from the run, a sheen of salt mixing now with the clammy residue of adrenaline. The overhead light buzzed faintly, too sharp, too bright.

She stepped beneath the spray, twisting the handle until the water ran hot enough to sting. It hit her shoulders in a hard stream, steam billowing up around her, fogging the mirror. She braced her palms against the tile and bowed her head under the cascade.

The sound of the water filled her ears, drowning out the phantom silence of the apartment.

It should have been cleansing, and part of it was. The sweat slid away, rivulets tracing down her back, swirling down the drain. But no amount of soap could scrub out the crawling sense of violation, the image of that note perfectly centered on her bed, the replay of past events in this same apartment. *Time to move, maybe.*

Her throat tightened as she closed her eyes, forcing the rhythm of her breathing to match the drum of the water. Tactical, Controlled, Deliberate. In. Out. Slow. Steady. She refused to let her pulse stay erratic, refused to give whoever had broken into her space the satisfaction of lingering in her system.

By the time she shut off the tap, steam curled like smoke around her, and her skin glowed pink from the heat. She toweled off briskly, jaw set, eyes hard in the mirror's blurred reflection.

Whatever game the bastard thought they were playing, she wasn't going to stay a piece on their board.

Watcher's Journal Insert

The rook is stone. The rook stands tall.

Stone is heavy. Stone is unyielding. But stone does not see.

While the rook watches the pawns, the board shifts beneath it.

Even the strongest piece can be tilted. Even stone can crack.

Will's Reaction to the Break-In

Casey slammed the evidence bag on Will's desk. The note inside sat flat and innocent-looking, but the black letters still seemed to hum with menace.

A rook protects pawns, but even rooks can be toppled.

Will's jaw tightened as he read it. He looked up at her, his eyes darker than usual. "Where did you find this?"

"An hour ago. My place." Casey folded her arms, trying to make her voice steady. "My one drawer rifled. Same one as last time."

Will's head snapped up. "The underwear?"

"Yeah." She forced a grim smile. "I guess I should be flattered they're consistent, at least I don't have to buy new underwear in bulk again."

"Casey." His voice sharpened, more edge than reprimand. "That's not funny. You know what this means.

Whoever did this—they got inside your apartment again. They're escalating."

Her lips pressed tight. "I know what it means. Come and go without a trace, no forced entry, I need to get a Wookie."

Will leaned back, rubbing a hand over his face. Anger seeped through the cracks in his control. "They used chloroform on you before. Took your shirt while you were unconscious. You could've—" He stopped, the words catching in his throat. He lowered his hand, voice gravelly. "This isn't just a taunt. It's personal. They're not afraid to get close."

Casey dropped into the chair across from him, legs stretched out, arms crossed like armor. "That's the point. They want me rattled. Shaken. Guess what? It's not working this time."

He studied her for a long beat. "You're angry."

"Damn right I am. And anger's better than fear."

Will's gaze flicked back to the note, then to her. He exhaled slowly. "We're not taking chances. I'll have Mason assign a car outside your building. Deadbolts, alarms, locks—all of it. No arguments."

Casey arched a brow. "What's next? Bodyguard droids? Don't start treating me like a pawn just because that's what they want."

He almost smiled at the quip, but it didn't reach his eyes. "I'm treating you like my partner. And my partner doesn't get left exposed."

Something in his tone softened the air between them, though the heat of her defiance still simmered. She looked down at the note, then back up at him. "Alright, but remember this—if they're calling me the Rook, then I'm staying on the board. I'm not hiding in the box."

Will's hand closed into a fist over the desk. "Then we'll play it smart. But if they try again..." His voice dropped into something colder, heavier. "They won't get a second chance."

Intern Overhears

The bullpen had primarily gone quiet, the clatter of keyboards fading as the evening shift wound down. Casey and Will sat close at his desk, the evidence bag with the note between them. Their voices carried just enough to drift into the open space.

Rachel Donovan rounded the corner with a stack of files, pausing when she caught the murmur of tension.

"...drawer rifled. Same one as last time," Casey said, voice low but strained.

Rachel's brows knit together. She stepped closer, careful not to intrude too abruptly. "Sorry—I couldn't help overhearing. Did... did something happen?"

Casey looked up, stiff, then forced a calmer tone. "Nothing you need to worry about, Rookie. Just a little bad luck on my end."

Rachel hesitated, her eyes flicking between them. "It sounded serious. Someone broke in?"

Will leaned back in his chair, steady, controlled. "It's under control. We'll handle it."

Rachel's gaze shifted to the evidence bag, the paper inside catching the overhead light. "Is that... a note?"

Casey gave a wry half-smile, trying to disarm the tension. "Yeah. Fan mail. Sith-level creepy, but fan mail all the same."

That pulled a small laugh out of Rachel, but her eyes lingered on the note longer than most interns would dare.

"You said 'same one as last time,'" Rachel pressed, careful but curious. "What happened before?"

Will's voice softened, quiet but firm. "That's in the past. And it's not something we're dragging you into."

Casey leaned forward, her tone gentler now. "Look, Rookie, this job gets messy sometimes. That's why you're shadowing, to learn. Not to carry our baggage. Okay?"

Rachel nodded slowly, as if reassured, though her gaze flicked back to Casey before she turned away. "Okay. I understand. I just... wanted to make sure you're alright."

Will gave her a slight nod. "I appreciate that. Really. Now go finish those socials for me, catch us a lead."

Rachel returned to her desk, her pen scratching quickly across her notebook. From behind her, Casey muttered under her breath. "She's got good instincts."

Will's gaze lingered on the intern a beat longer, jaw flexing. "Good instincts," he echoed. "Let's hope that's all they are."

Rachel's Research

Rachel stood at the front of the bullpen with her laptop open, posture just nervous enough to be disarming. Her notes were arranged in meticulous order, though she smoothed the top page again as if she needed the excuse to steady her hands.

"So... I started with the public fraternity pages, but those were mostly noise," she said, clicking to the next slide. The screen behind her cast her in a pale glow. Photos tiled across it, smiling faces, red Solo cups, neon lighting.

"Theme parties, charity events, nothing useful. But when I scraped tagged photos, the patterns popped." She advanced the slide. A cluster of young men stared out at the room, grinning with arms slung around each other. "Same circle of guys. Here—" she pointed with her fingertip—"Ethan Price, Chad Wexler, Tyler Dean, Marcus Holt. You'll find them at the center of almost every Serpents event going back two years."

She clicked again. The screen filled with candid photos of women, blurred dance floors, sunlit campus lawns, pool parties. Rachel's tone cooled slightly, matter-of-fact but edged with something tighter. "And the same rotation of girls. Madison Greer, Talia Smith, Kelsey Summers, Kayleigh Caldwell. Different photos, different venues, but always orbiting the same four guys. It's not random."

Another click: two columns appeared, side by side, party dates against health center reports. "And whenever the Serpents throw an event—" she tapped the glowing correlation on the slide—"it lines up with missing time reports filed at the campus clinic. Dozens of them. Blackouts. Lost hours. Enough to be a pattern."

The bullpen hushed, a rare silence settling over the room. Even Casey tilted forward, her smirk giving way to genuine interest as she studied the faces on the screen.

Will's arms folded across his chest, but his eyes lingered on Rachel, sharpened with something more than professional respect. She wasn't guessing. She wasn't lucky. She'd pulled threads no one else had even touched.

"That's sharp work," he said finally, his voice steady but weighted. "You pulled threads our tech unit hasn't even touched. I say we start with the girls that are associated, they may know more than they realize. Then we move back to the fraternity circle."

Rachel ducked her head, a small smile threatening at the corner of her mouth.

From across the room, Casey broke the silence with a slow clap. "Well, damn, Rookie. First, you pull a Jedi meditation force vision, zeroing in on the frat boys, now you're serving up data like Elle Woods in pink tweed. Keep this up, and the rest of us are just extras in your movie."

Laughter rolled through the bullpen, the tension snapping clean. Rachel only smiled faintly, though her gaze lingered on Will before she bent back over her notes.

Her smile unfurled slowly, a flush rising in her cheeks as she ducked her head, tucking a strand of hair back. "Thank you. I wasn't sure it would be helpful, but... I figured it was worth losing a little sleep."

She closed the laptop and crossed the room. Each step was measured, not rushed. When she bent to set it on his desk, the brush of her shoulder against his was no accident. Her blouse shifted, neckline loose enough to hint, to tempt.

"Guess I'll have to make a habit of digging deeper," she murmured, lifting her eyes through her lashes.

The air between them tightened. Will cleared his throat, leaning back in his chair, but not before catching the faint scent of her shampoo—citrus and something warmer. He forced a barrier of space, though a pulse of heat had already betrayed him. "As long as you keep it professional," he said, the words clipped, his jaw tight.

Rachel bit her lip, a flicker of contrition playing across her face before she let it melt into something more careful. "Of course. Sorry. I didn't mean to—" She cut herself off, stepping back just enough to leave him wondering who had really drawn the line.

From her desk, Casey muttered, "Careful, Rookie. That's how Skywalker ended up kissing his own sister. Boundaries, remember?"

The bullpen chuckled, tension broken, but Rachel only smiled faintly and slid back to her seat. "Sorry, I did not mean for that," she said, straightening herself in her seat.

Still, her gaze lingered on Will a beat too long before she turned to her notes again.

The bullpen had thinned out after briefing, chatter dying as agents drifted back to their desks. Rachel stayed planted at hers, shuffling her notes into neat stacks. Casey leaned back in her chair across the aisle, arms folded, watching her like a cat sizing up a bird.

Finally, Casey tilted her head. "So... I gotta ask. Was that little shoulder graze and eyelash flutter back there and the cleavage peak, you trying to seduce Will, or am I just hallucinating from too much stale coffee?"

Rachel froze mid-page shuffle, eyes darting up. "What? No. God, no." She gave a breathy laugh that sounded more nervous than amused. "People have... told me sometimes I do things that *look* suggestive, but I swear, I don't even realize it. I'm just—being me. Clumsy, caught up in the work. Honestly, I didn't even register until I saw his face flush."

She winced, dropping her voice. "I was mortified. I never want to make anyone uncomfortable, least of all him."

Casey arched an eyebrow, unimpressed, her chair creaking as she leaned back with her arms folded. "Mmm-hmm. Thing is, Will's a 'Trust No One, the truth is out there' kind of guy. You know, like Fox Mulder on *The X-Files*."

Rachel blinked, caught off guard. "I... never saw that show."

Casey snapped upright, scandalized, as Rachel had just confessed to never hearing of oxygen. "Are you kidding me? Mulder's the believer, always chasing conspiracy theories, aliens, paranormal crap, you name it. And Scully's the skeptic, all science and logic. She's the sultry redhead who keeps him grounded, while he drags her into believing things she never thought possible. Classic partners. Classic tension. Basically, the blueprint for every cop show romance since the nineties."

Rachel smirked, finally loosening the death grip she had on her notes. "So what you're telling me is, it's kinda like you and Will. He's your Fox Mulder and you're his Dana Scully. Red hair and all."

Casey barked a laugh, rolling her eyes so hard it was theatrical. "Careful, Rookie. Scully had patience. I've got none. You keep batting those lashes at Mulder over there, don't be surprised if I start carrying holy water and garlic to keep you at bay." She mimed pulling a crucifix from an imaginary holster, grinning.

Rachel laughed too, but it faltered quickly, her gaze dropping to her hands twisting in her lap. "The truth is..." She hesitated, then let the words tumble out in a low rush. "I haven't really dated much. I've never even had a real boyfriend, not... not really. I get caught up in my work, and sometimes I say or do things without realizing they might come off as suggestive. Then I see someone's reaction and I just—" she shook her head, cheeks burning. "I hate that it looks intentional. It's not. I just... don't know what I'm doing half the time."

Casey studied her, some of the smirk softening into something wryer, almost protective. "Well, that explains why you're over here turning bright red every time Will breathes in your direction."

Rachel groaned, burying her face in her hands for a second. "Exactly. I didn't even realize what I was doing until I saw his face flush. I wanted to crawl under the desk."

Casey leaned forward, propping her chin on her hand. "Relax. Will's basically Mulder with a badge and a worse wardrobe. Trust issues stacked to the ceiling. You couldn't seduce him if you wrapped yourself in a UFO conspiracy and beamed down from Mars."

Rachel peeked at her, half-amused, half-embarrassed.

Casey went on, deadpan: "Mulder and Scully were all about the slow burn. Years of tension. Lots of meaningful looks. Sound familiar?"

Rachel cracked a small smile. "So what you're saying is, I'm living inside your favorite old TV show?"

Casey smirked back. "Pretty much. And yeah, Rookie, in this version? He's Mulder. And me?" She tapped her own red hair. "I'm Scully. Which means if you mess this up, you're officially the alien of the week."

Rachel laughed, the blush still on her cheeks, but lighter now, easier. She went back to her notes, grateful for the teasing deflection, even if her heart was still drumming against her ribs.

Sorority Sister Interviews

The sorority house parlor smelled faintly of vanilla candles and nail polish remover, a sharp contrast to the damp cold outside. Madison Greer lounged back on the couch, glossy hair draped over one shoulder, scrolling idly on her phone until Casey cleared her throat. Beside her, Talia Smith sat straighter, legs crossed neatly, hands folded over her knee, the picture of calm disinterest.

Will set his notebook on the coffee table, Rachel perched beside him with her notebook, while Casey leaned against the armrest, arms folded.

Will started it clean. "We're here to talk about Brock Prescott and Derek Langley. You both knew them?"

Madison's phone slipped into her lap. "Knew? I mean, yeah, everybody knew Brock. Golden boy, quarterback, frat star. I made out with him once at a keg party." She flicked her hair, smiling at the memory, before her face hardened. "But he ditched me the second some random girl showed up. Kayleigh's friend from high school, Tara DeLuca, from Jersey. Once Tara was in his sights? Please. They disappeared right after she started letting guys do body shots off her stomach. He missed out on me that night." Her smile sharpened into something brittle. “And I’m not second to anyone.”

Rachel’s brow tightened, but she kept her gaze on the laptop keys.

Talia shifted. “Brock wasn’t my type. Too much of a pretty boy. The guys called him ‘the golden boy,’ but I don’t go for that. Derek, I only knew because he’d hang around his sister Sheri’s place. Sometimes I’d go study biology with Kari Black and he’d be there.”

Her eyes flicked toward Rachel, narrowing with recognition. “I’ve seen you on campus before.”

Rachel looked up, caught off guard, then smiled politely. “I was a student until two semesters ago. Transferred out.”

Casey slid into the opening, her tone casual but edged. “We also noticed you both hang around with Ethan Price, Chad Wexler, Tyler Dean, and Marcus Holt. Same parties, same circles.”

Madison smirked. “They’re fun. We like them.”

Talia added, “I’m with Tyler, actually. And Kayleigh? She’s with Ethan. So, yeah, we’re around them a lot.”

Casey exchanged a glance with Will, then asked, “Have you ever heard about girls coming back from Serpent parties reporting memory loss? Gaps in time? Clothes put back on wrong, missing items...?”

Madison snorted, waving it off. “I’ve heard that crap. But look, most girls who show up at those parties? They’re pros at drinking. They know what they’re there for. They want to hook up, or they drink to get the nerve. Sometimes they drink too much, have too much fun, and the next day? Instant regret. Parents breathing down their necks, worried about getting knocked up, so they file a preemptive report. No evidence, no suspect. Just... cover your ass, because someone didn't cover the pecker. Happens all the time. Some girls don't like condoms, some don't care."

The silence that followed was sharp enough to cut.

Rachel stared at her like she'd grown two heads, disbelief written across her face. Will caught it. Casey caught it too, and when Madison's attention drifted back to her phone, Rachel mouthed across the space, *"Dumb ass."* Casey smothered a grin.

Will leaned forward, voice cool. "Have either of you ever had someone come directly to you about that? Someone who filed a report with the campus clinic but didn't go to the police? Or someone who was unconscious, couldn't consent, and was taken advantage of?"

Both girls shook their heads instantly. Talia leaned in, defensive. "No. Absolutely not. The guys aren't like that. They've never done anything like that."

Madison nodded vigorously. "They do the opposite, actually. If a girl gets too wasted, they've got a system. Two of the guys take her home. Make sure she's safe."

Casey's eyes narrowed. "The same two every time?"

Talia shook her head. "Not really. It could be any of them. Brock, Derek, Ethan, Chad, Tyler, Marcus. They've all done it. Whoever's around."

Out of the corner of his eye, Will saw Rachel jotting the names into her notes, her pen moving fast. He gave her a slight nod of approval, which she returned with the smallest flicker of pride.

Casey pivoted, casual again. "What about Kelsey Summers? Kayleigh Caldwell? We had questions for them too."

Talia shrugged. "They live here with us, but they're not home. Out running errands, making a liquor run for the mixer tomorrow night."

Casey gave a slow smile, tapping her pen against her notebook. "Of course they are."

Unexpected Visitors at the Station

The interview rooms in Oakhaven PD were cold by design, plain gray walls, metal tables, two chairs. The kind of space that stripped away comfort and left only words behind.

When Kelsey Summers and Kayleigh Caldwell walked in, still in their matching Omega Kappa Psi hoodies, Casey exchanged a quick look with Will. Opportunity had walked itself through the front door.

"Let's split them up," Casey murmured.

Will nodded. He gestured Kayleigh toward Room One. Casey guided Kelsey toward Room Two, Rachel slipping in beside her with her notepad.

Chief Mason passed through the bullpen at that moment, spotting Rachel. "Rachel Donovan," he said warmly, giving her shoulder a brief squeeze. "Good work so far. Trust your instincts."

Rachel flushed faintly, nodded, and ducked into the room behind Kelsey.

Interview Room One – Kayleigh Caldwell

The interview room's fluorescent light buzzed faintly overhead as Kayleigh Caldwell crossed one leg over the other, posture poised, arms resting neatly in her lap. She looked less like a nervous sorority girl and more like someone preparing for a deposition. Will clocked it immediately.

He settled into the chair across from her, notebook open, pen in hand. His voice was calm, steady. "Kayleigh, thanks for coming in. Let's start simple. You knew Brock Prescott and Derek Langley?"

Kayleigh's lips curved into a small, practiced smile. "Everyone knew them. Brock was the golden boy, always the center of attention. Derek was quieter, but always around. I didn't know either of them well, though. I found out what happened from social media, same as everyone else."

Will jotted something in his notebook, though the answer already rang familiar. "Any closer connection? Parties, classes, mutual friends?"

She shook her head smoothly. "Not really. I'm dating Ethan Price, so I'd see Brock or Derek at Serpent events, but that's it."

Will kept his expression neutral. "How long have you been with Ethan?"

"Since last semester. He's great," she said quickly, almost too quickly. "We're good together."

Will's tone stayed steady, almost gentle. "Kayleigh, what about your friend Tara DeLuca? She's from Jersey, right? Came down to visit you one weekend?"

Kayleigh nodded quickly. "Yeah. Tara came to a couple of parties. Why?"

Will glanced at his notes. "We heard she was with Brock Prescott that night. Apparently, cut in on your friend Madison with him. Some people say Tara and Brock disappeared from the party together. Did she ever mention anything unusual? Anything that worried her?"

Kayleigh's brows pinched, her voice low. "Tara told me he was... intense. Like, charming at first, then real pushy. She didn't say he hurt her, but she said she wasn't comfortable being alone with him. After that night, she didn't want to come back to the house anymore."

"Did you see anything yourself?" Will asked.

Kayleigh shook her head. "Not exactly. Just that Tara seemed off when she reappeared, she wouldn't drink the rest of the night, and she kept checking her phone like she couldn't wait to leave. Said she was tired. But Tara never really talks about stuff when she's freaked. She just... shuts down."

Following up, Will asked. "And Madison? She didn't like being cut out of the picture, did she?"

Kayleigh hesitated, twisting the tissue tighter. "Madison was mad, yeah. Embarrassed more than anything. But Brock... he always thought he could pick and choose. That's just how he was."

Will jotted it down, then looked up. "If Tara remembers anything else, anything at all, we need to hear it. Even small details can matter."

Kayleigh nodded, though her expression said she wasn't sure Tara would ever want to talk.

"Did you ever notice anything unusual at the Serpent parties? Girls losing time? Waking up not remembering how they got home? Clothes out of place?"

Kayleigh gave a soft laugh, dismissive. "No. Nothing like that. Everyone drinks, everyone hooks up, but it's always by choice. The stories you're hearing? Just guilt the next day. Some girls don't want to admit what they did, so they make excuses. But the guys? They take care of people. If someone's too drunk, they make sure she gets home."

Will tapped his pen against the table once, observing her. "The same guys every time?"

Her eyes didn't flicker. "No. It could be anyone: Ethan, Brock, Derek, Marcus, Chad, or Tyler. Whoever's around. They look out for people."

He leaned back slightly, studying her. "And you've never heard anyone complain about being taken advantage of?"

"No." Her smile didn't waver. "Never. The Serpents wouldn't do something like that."

The cadence of her words was almost identical to Madison's, the same phrases, the same dismissive laugh. If Will closed his eyes, he wasn't sure he could tell them apart.

He let the silence stretch, hoping the weight of it might crack her composure. But Kayleigh only straightened her shoulders, chin tilted just high enough to suggest she knew the game.

Finally, Will closed his notebook with a quiet snap. "Alright. That'll be all for now."

Kayleigh stood, smoothing her hoodie, smile still in place as if she'd just delivered the right answers on a test.

Will watched her leave, the echo of Madison's earlier words rolling in his mind. Too clean. Too neat. Too rehearsed.

Interview Room Two – Kelsey Summers

Kelsey sat slouched in the chair, arms crossed like armor, eyes darting between Casey and Rachel. Casey started smoothly, going through the same questions they'd asked Madison and Talia.

Kelsey rolled her eyes at first. "I don't know anything about Brock or Derek. Found out through social media like everybody else."

But when Casey steered toward the Serpent parties, Kelsey shifted. Her voice dipped lower, uncertain.

"I was going out with Carter Vance for a while," she admitted. "We'd party at the Serpent house. I'd go off with him sometimes, back to his place. But... there were nights I'd wake up and something was off. Like, I'd be in the same clothes I'd worn. Or in some of Carter's clothes. Sometimes nothing at all. No memory of getting there. No memory of making out, or anything in between."

Rachel leaned forward, concern softening her expression. "How many times?"

Kelsey glanced down at her lap. "Maybe six? Over the year. August to May. We broke up right before summer break. I went back home to Florida."

Rachel's brows knitted. "That boy was stupid. Seems like a lot of boys running around this campus and not a whole lot of men."

The words hung in the sterile room for half a beat before Casey snorted. Kelsey cracked a reluctant laugh, and Rachel's smile broke wider. The three of them laughed together, the tension fracturing for a moment.

Casey leaned back, but her tone sharpened again. "Kelsey, listen. If you think Carter did something to you when you were unconscious? Even if you said yes other times, it's not consent. It's not okay. There are rumors of undetectable drugs being used at those parties. We've seen videos of girls being assaulted by one or more guys in masks or with their faces blurred out. If you suspect it happened to you or *know* it happened to anyone, you need to tell someone. You need to tell us."

Kelsey immediately stiffened, her face twisting in offense. "That never happened to me. Carter didn't do that. I don't know anything about any of that. I'm not—" She pushed her chair back. "I'm not talking about this anymore."

She started to stand.

Rachel reached out quickly, her hand settling lightly on Kelsey's forearm. Her voice was soft, steady. "If it did happen... It's not your fault. Even if you can't say it, even if you never say it out loud. Casey has your back. So do I."

Kelsey froze at the touch. For a heartbeat, her eyes flicked to Rachel's, a sharp sideways glance that held something unspoken, recognition, maybe, or the crack of a wall she'd built around herself.

Then she pulled away. "I need to leave."

Rachel let her go.

Lobby — Oakhaven Police Department

Kayleigh was waiting, perched on one of the hard plastic chairs. She stood as soon as Kelsey emerged. Neither said a word. Their expressions were tight, guarded.

Will and Casey, watching from across the bullpen windows, noted the silence. The girls left together, hoodies pulled up, steps quick.

Casey muttered, "Two peas, same pod. But that one"—she tipped her head toward where Kelsey had gone—"knows more than she's ready to admit."

Rachel lingered at the glass, still thinking about the way Kelsey had looked at her. That sharp, searching glance. It wasn't nothing.

Oakhaven PD – Hallway outside Interview Rooms

Will and Casey stepped into the hall, Rachel trailing close behind, notepad hugged to her chest. The three of them watched as the two girls left together in silence, hoods up, pushing out through the glass doors.

Casey broke it first, low under her breath. "Well, that was about as much fun as a root canal."

Will looked at her, brow arched. "Kayleigh gave me the same script Madison did. Word for word. Almost rehearsed."

Rachel nodded, still frowning. "Kelsey was different. Nervous. She slipped up talking about Carter Vance. Said she'd wake up with no memory, in her clothes, in his clothes, sometimes nothing at all. Six times in a year."

Casey's smirk faded. "That's not a slip. That's a pattern."

Rachel hugged the laptop tighter. "She denied everything once I pushed. Offended, even. But... when she left, she gave me this look. Like she wanted to say something, but couldn't."

Will's jaw tightened. "So Kayleigh's clean on the surface, too clean. Kelsey shows cracks but shuts down when we push." He exhaled slowly. "One's protecting the party line, the other's protecting herself."

Casey shoved her hands into her jacket pockets. "Mulder and Scully say we dig deeper."

Rachel gave her a sideways glance. "Which one of you is Mulder again?"

Casey grinned faintly, but her eyes stayed serious. "Doesn't matter. Either way, Rookie, you just found the first thread worth pulling."

Will gave Rachel the briefest nod, subtle but weighted with approval. She met it with the faintest flicker of pride before looking down at her notes again.

Oakhaven PD – Hallway Outside Chief Mason's Office

Will headed down the corridor, scanning the frosted glass windows for Captain Frank Monroe's office. Empty. He turned the corner and caught the low rumble of voices from Chief Mason's office instead. Monroe was inside with the Chief.

Will hesitated, then rapped his knuckles lightly on the frame. The conversation cut off, and after a beat Mason's voice called, "Come in."

Inside, Monroe was sliding a folder across the desk, but Mason waved Will forward. "Give me something, Will."

Will set his notebook down. “We separated Kayleigh Caldwell and Kelsey Summers. Kayleigh? Clean. Too clean. She parroted Madison Greer’s answers almost word-for-word, Brock was the golden boy, Derek was quiet, the guys ‘look out’ for people at parties. Nothing new. Felt rehearsed.”

Mason grunted. “Sounds like she studied for the test.”

“Exactly.” Will flipped a page. “Kelsey was different. She admitted to blackouts while dating Carter Vance. Six times over the course of a year, waking up in his clothes, sometimes with nothing on, no memory of how she got there. She shut down when we pressed harder. Denied everything, got offended, wanted to leave. But she slipped, Chief. Enough to tell us there’s more she’s not saying.”

Mason’s expression hardened. “That’s the first real crack in the wall.”

Will nodded. “Rachel caught it. Kelsey gave her a look before she walked out, like it resonated, even if she couldn’t say it out loud.”

Mason drummed his fingers against the desk, thoughtful. “Good. That means we’ve got pressure points. Vance just moved higher on the board. Keep digging, quietly. If there are drugs in play, or worse, videos floating around like Casey suggested, I don’t want this buried under rumor and denial.”

“Yes, sir.”

Mason leaned forward. “And Will, keep an eye on Rachel. She’s sharp, but she’s new. Don’t let her get eaten alive by this case.”

Will's jaw flexed, but he gave a single nod. "Understood."

Hallway

Rachel slowed as she passed the office door, the faint murmur of Mason's voice carrying just far enough. She heard her name. Listened to the Chief say *"keep an eye on Rachel"* and *"don't let her get eaten alive."*

She paused for half a second, expression unreadable, then kept walking, laptop clutched tight to her chest.

Oakhaven PD – Detective Bullpen

Will stepped back into the bullpen, his notebook tucked under his arm. He barely had time to set it down before Rachel appeared at his desk, moving with uncharacteristic determination. Without waiting for an invitation, she dropped into the guest chair beside his desk, the one usually reserved for people with case updates.

Her eyes were sharp, locked on him. "I heard what Mason said."

Will looked up, caught off guard. "Rachel—"

"No, I want to know," she pressed, leaning forward, laptop still clutched against her chest. "Am I here to actually work this case? Or am I just Joe Donovan's daughter who needs babysitting? Because if that's the plan, I'll save you the trouble and step back right now."

The bullpen chatter hummed faintly around them, but for Will it felt like the whole room had gone still. He opened his mouth, and froze when Rachel, lost in her own intensity, pulled her legs up into the chair and wrapped her arms around them.

Her skirt hiked, and before Will could look away, bright yellow underwear flashed in his line of sight. His stomach clenched, eyes darting sideways.

Casey, sliding past behind him with a coffee in hand, caught it immediately. She arched her brow, a smirk tugging at her lips. With her free hand, she made a broad, silent "underwear" gesture in front of her own waistline, eyebrows raised.

Rachel's eyes widened as realization hit. She dropped her feet to the floor in a rush, cheeks flaming, and crossed her legs tightly.

Will, pretending calm, deliberately nudged a stapler off the edge of his desk. It clattered to the floor, giving him an excuse to bend and retrieve it, eyes on the carpet. "Accident," he muttered.

The moment passed, but Rachel's composure cracked. Her voice was quieter now, tinged with embarrassment. "Forget it. Just—forget it." She stood abruptly, nearly knocking her chair back, and strode quickly toward the hallway.

Casey leaned against Will's desk, sipping her coffee, watching Rachel's retreat. "Smooth talker, huh?"

Will didn't look at her, just set the stapler back on the desk with a sharp click. "Casey."

She lifted her hand in surrender, grin fading as she pushed off the desk. "Relax. I'll go check on her."

Women's Bathroom – Oakhaven PD

The door creaked open as Casey slipped inside. The sound of muffled sniffling echoed off the tile. Rachel stood at the sink, hands braced on the porcelain, her reflection streaked with tears she hadn't meant to shed.

Casey softened her voice. "Hey, Rookie. You okay?"

Rachel shook her head, laughing bitterly through the tears. "No. I just embarrassed myself in front of everyone. Again. I can't stop screwing this up."

Casey stepped closer, setting her coffee cup on the counter. "You didn't screw up. You went at Will like a pit bull, I respect that. The... wardrobe malfunction?" She shrugged lightly. "Happens. We've all had worse."

Rachel gave a watery laugh, swiping at her eyes. "Not in neon yellow."

Casey grinned. "Trust me, Mulder didn't notice a thing. He was too busy pretending that the stapler had a mind of its own."

That broke the dam, Rachel laughed, shoulders shaking, though tears still streaked her cheeks. Casey handed her a paper towel and leaned on the counter beside her.

"You're fine, Rookie. Embarrassment fades. But guts like that?" Casey nudged her with an elbow. "That sticks."

Rachel pressed the paper towel to her face, nodding, still red-eyed but steadier now.

Rachel dabbed at her eyes with the paper towel, the edges fraying in her hand. "I just... I can't stop making a fool of myself. Every time I think I'm doing something right, I end up—" She shook her head. "I don't even know if I belong here."

Casey leaned her hip against the sink, arms folded loosely, her expression softer than Rachel had ever seen it. "Listen, Rookie. You belong here. You're smart, sharper than half the guys out there, and you actually give a damn. That's more than most."

Rachel's laugh was brittle. "Yeah, but Will doesn't see that. To him I'm... just Joe Donovan's daughter who needs babysitting."

Casey tilted her head. "You're wrong. I've worked with Will for a long time. He's got two modes: *professional wall* and *internal panic attack, he'd rather die than admit to.* If he didn't respect your work, he wouldn't have let you anywhere near those interviews."

Rachel sniffed, frowning. "Then why do I feel like such an idiot around him?"

"Because you've got a crush," Casey said bluntly, like she was stating the color of the sky. "And because you care what he thinks. Doesn't mean you're an idiot. Just means you're human."

Rachel's cheeks flushed again. "God, I must look so obvious."

Casey smirked, patting her shoulder. "Relax. Mulder over there? He's so busy building walls around himself, he wouldn't notice if you danced naked through the bullpen—" She paused. "Okay, bad example, given recent events. But you get the point."

That dragged a laugh out of Rachel, shaky but real.

Casey leaned in, lowering her voice. "Here's the thing. Will's trust is like Fort Knox. Takes time to break through. But once you're in? He'll walk through fire for you. Think of him like Han Solo, grumpy, guarded, all walls and sarcasm. But underneath? The guy would put the Falcon into hyperspace for the people he trusts. So stop worrying about the blushes and the staplers. Focus on the work. The rest will take care of itself."

Rachel looked at her reflection in the mirror, eyes red but steadier, shoulders straighter. "You really think so?"

Casey grinned. "Kid, I know so. Now wash your face, pull it together, and let's go crack this thing before Mulder dies of repressed emotion. Or worse, before he starts quoting Obi-Wan on me."

Rachel gave a watery laugh, the corners of her mouth finally turning upward.

Oakhaven PD – Detective Bullpen

Will was jotting final notes when his phone buzzed. He answered briskly, but his tone softened when he recognized the voice on the other end.

"Kristen. Yeah... I'll stop by before we head out." His eyes flicked to Rachel, then back to his desk. "Alright. Thanks."

He ended the call, slipping the phone into his pocket.

Casey glanced up from her desk. "That the boss lady?"

Will gave her a dry look. "District Attorney Anderson, yes. She wants me to stop by her office before we head out after Carter Vance." He turned to Rachel. "You should come. You've only met Kristen at the house, never in an official capacity. Good for you to see how she runs things."

Rachel blinked, surprised but nodding quickly. "Of course. That... makes sense."

Casey stretched, grabbing her jacket. "You two lovebirds go play politics. I'll run next door to Jack'd Up and grab coffee. Meet you at the Tahoe."

Will shot her a look, but Casey was already slinging her bag over her shoulder, grinning as she strolled out.

Rachel stood, gathering her laptop and bag. "I'm just going to hit the bathroom real quick before we go. Never know how long we'll be gone."

"Alright," Will said, stacking his files. "I'll see you in Kristen's office."

Rachel gave a quick nod and slipped out, pulse quickening at the thought. Kristen Anderson, no cozy kitchen table this time, no polite dinner smile. This would be official, professional, and very likely intimidating.

Will watched her go, jaw tight, then exhaled slowly before heading toward the DA's office himself.

Frustration of Office

The DA's office smelled faintly of burnt coffee and paper. Kristen sat behind her desk, but her posture didn't carry the usual sharp authority. Shoulders sagged, a half-empty glass of bourbon sat near her files, and her blazer was tossed over the chair like it didn't matter.

Will closed the door partially behind him, giving her privacy. "Heard you wanted to see me."

Kristen exhaled through her nose, rubbing her temple. "Wanted, maybe. Needed—yeah." Her voice was tight, ragged at the edges. She tapped a folded sheet of paper on the desk. "This came today."

Will stepped closer. The note's words were simple, handwritten in dark ink:

A queen who betrays her pawns is no queen.

His jaw clenched. "Where was it left?"

"In my office inbox." Her laugh was bitter, brittle. "Could've been anyone who walked through this building. No prints, no cameras. Just waiting for me when I came back from court. First was an email, and today the note"

Will studied her face. There was fear, yes, but also something more profound: shame.

Kristen leaned back, staring past him, eyes unfocused. "You know what it feels like to drag a girl through hell just to stand in court and hear the words *lack of evidence*? I've done it too many times, Will. And then today... another one walks free. Another Serpent. And I get a note calling me a betrayer."

"You're not betraying anyone," Will said firmly.

Her gaze snapped to him, angry and wounded at once.

"Aren't I? Steve drugged my wine, Will. He didn't just take my power that night; he recorded it, wore a damn camera like it was his art. I woke up humiliated in my own bed, violated, pieces of it flashing back still, whether I want them to or not." Her voice broke, rough and uneven.

"And Emily..." She swallowed hard, eyes glossing. "She heard voices and came to ask me a question. She walked in on him, Will. She saw it. He dragged her around in the hall, struck her, and she couldn't breathe. He pulled at her—" Kristen's voice faltered, trembling. "He was going to rape her, too. My baby, or have you forgotten?"

Her fists clenched, nails digging into her palms. "The only reason she got away was because I stumbled to the doorway, barely conscious, and distracted him long enough for her to run. I'm still haunted by the things I didn't even see."

Her eyes burned into Will's. "So yeah, I caught my monster. He's behind bars and will eventually do Federal time. But every time another one walks free, it feels like I failed. Like I'm betraying all the girls who didn't escape."

The room went heavy, silence pressing around them. Will stepped closer, lowering his voice. "Steve's behind bars. You faced him. You survived. That doesn't make the others your failure."

Kristen shook her head, eyes glassy. "Tell that to the girls who sat on the stand and still lost. Tell that to the parents who look at me as if I've failed them. Every acquittal feels like I'm picking the Serpents over the victims. Maybe the note's right."

Will's voice hardened. "No. That's what they want you to think. That's what predators thrive on, doubt. They make you feel powerless, so you stop fighting. But you're still standing. That matters."

For a moment, she just looked at him, searching his face, then glanced down at the note again. Her fingers trembled slightly as she folded it back into her desk drawer.

"Rachel," Will said suddenly, realizing she had made it to the office, quietly stacking files from the conference table. "Why don't you wait outside?"

Rachel blinked, startled, but gave a polite nod. "Of course, Detective." She slipped out silently, but her eyes lingered on Kristen, drinking in every detail of the DA's unraveling.

When the door clicked shut, Kristen dropped her head into her hands. "I don't know how much longer I can do this, Will. My monster's gone. But everyone else's monster is still walking campus. And every time they walk scott free, I feel like I'm the one letting them out the door."

Will crouched in front of her chair, grounding her with steady eyes. "You're not the betrayer here, Kristen. You're in the fight with us. We'll carry this weight together. But don't let a note, or the voice behind it, convince you you're on the wrong side of the board."

Kristen let out a long, shaky breath. "Board. Pawns. Queens." Her lip curled faintly. "Feels like somebody out there thinks this is a game."

Will's chest tightened as she spoke, every word pressing heavier on his ribs. His jaw locked, teeth grinding, and for a long moment, he couldn't trust himself to speak.

Finally, he crouched beside her chair, voice low but hard as steel. "Kristen... none of that is on you. Steve did that. Steve chose it. And he's rotting in a cell because you had the strength to fight back, even when you were broken down, drugged, humiliated. That isn't betrayal. That's survival."

Will's gaze darkened. "It's not a game. And when we find out who's playing it, the board's going to flip."

Her eyes shimmered, but the shame stayed etched into her features.

Will's tone roughened, anger bleeding through. "The thought of him laying a hand on Emily—" He cut himself off, his hands flexing like he wanted to wrap them around Steve's throat. "If I'd been there that night, I swear to God he wouldn't have walked out breathing. And I'd have lived with that choice."

Kristen blinked at him, startled by the fury in his voice.

He steadied, forcing his tone back down. "But what you need to hear right now is this: you didn't fail Emily. You didn't fail those other girls either. The failure lies in the system, the gaps, and the shadows these bastards crawl into. You're not betraying pawns, Kristen. You're standing on the front line with us. Every day you show up, even when it kills you to do it."

For a long moment, she just looked at him, breathing unevenly, as though waiting for the shame to lift.

Will reached out, covering her trembling hands with his steady ones. "Don't let a damn note convince you otherwise. You're not the betrayer."

"You're the reason the rest of us still believe the fight matters."

Watcher Interlude

Pawns. So easy to overlook. They move one square at a time, hesitant, uncertain. Yet I see their worth.

The twins are pawns. Pure. Fragile. They think innocence is their armor, but innocence is just glass. One crack, and it shatters. So I watch. I correct. I steer them away from contamination, even when they don't understand why.

They believe I am their shadow. They don't realize I am their guardian. Pawns left alone are prey. Pawns guided can become queens.

And then there is the Queen already on the board. Strong. Dominant. A force to command. But she betrayed the pawns once. She chose law over justice—procedure over truth.

A queen who betrays her pawns is no queen at all.

The rook guards. The king plots. But the queen, the queen decides who lives and dies. And when she fails, pawns are lost.

I will not let pawns be lost again. Not while I move the pieces.

Watcher Journal – Corrections to be Made

Skin. Just skin. To them, it means freedom, confidence, and a sense of playfulness. To the boys who watch, it means something else entirely.

Tonight, one of the pawns laughed too loudly, leaned too close, her sweater slipping just enough to reveal what should not have been shown. She doesn't understand what eyes do when they see. She doesn't know what invitations are written without words.

I do.

The boys see openings, weaknesses, not innocence. They are predators dressed as suitors. They wait for signals, and pawns don't realize when they've already given them. A tilt of the head. A bare shoulder. A smile held a second too long.

These are traps, and the pawns walk into them without seeing the board.

I see. I have always seen.

If they cannot guard themselves, then I must guard them. If they cannot close the door, I will slam it shut for them.

Pawns must be corrected before they become casualties.

The Warning Text

Emily flopped onto her dorm bed, still in the cropped top she'd worn to the mixer. The fabric clung a little tighter than she realized, her skin warm from the crowded room. She was mid-laugh at something Ellie had said when her phone buzzed against the comforter.

She grabbed it, expecting a text from the guy she'd been talking to earlier.

Her smile faltered.

Unknown Number: *Cover yourself. You don't know what they see when you lean in like that.*

Her throat tightened. She stared at the words, the edges of her vision blurring. Suddenly, another image intruded, Steve's face. That grin. The one from her nightmares. The sound of his laugh behind her, low and mocking, just before he shoved her into the wall, not long ago. She could almost feel the weight of his breath against her neck.

Emily jerked, dropping the phone as if it had bitten her.

Ellie looked up from her sketchbook, startled. "Em? What—"

Emily swallowed hard, forced herself to laugh, though her voice cracked. "It's nothing. Just... some freak."

Ellie picked up the phone, eyes scanning the text. Her face drained of color. "This isn't 'nothing.' Who the hell would send this?"

"I don't know," Emily said, hugging her arms across her chest, suddenly too aware of how bare her skin felt. "I was leaning in, just talking. Like—what, am I supposed to live wrapped in a blanket?"

The phone buzzed again.

Unknown Number: *Pawns attract predators without realizing it. Don't invite what you can't survive.*

Emily's stomach dropped. She pressed her palms to her temples, and the flashback came again—Steve's weight pinning her, his voice a cruel whisper, the tug and heat of his hands on her bare hip before Kristen's voice had broken through the haze. She blinked it back, but her body was already trembling.

Ellie touched her arm. "This isn't a prank. They're watching you. Right now."

Emily bit down on her lip so hard she tasted blood.

Then the phone buzzed once more.

Unknown Number: *Stay pure. Stay safe. I'll be watching.*

Silence filled the dorm, oppressive and suffocating. Emily shoved the phone away as if it were toxic. "I can't—" she choked out. "I can't breathe in here."

Casey's Apartment

Later that night, the twins sat on Casey's couch, knees tucked up, as if they were little girls again. Emily's eyes were still red, makeup smudged, while Ellie sat stiffly beside her, jaw tight with anger more than fear.

Casey handed Emily a mug of hot chocolate and set another in front of Ellie. "Alright. Show me."

Ellie slid the phone across. Casey read the texts, her expression tightening just slightly, but she masked it with a snort. "Well, that's comforting. Looks like Creeper McWierdo found your number."

Emily wrapped her hands around the mug, staring into the steam. "Casey, it's not just the texts. When I read them, I—I remembered Steve. His face. His laugh. It was like he was right behind me again."

Casey's jaw clenched, but she kept her tone light. "Steve's locked away. He's not texting you from federal custody. This? It's someone else trying to play Jedi mind tricks."

Ellie shot her a look. "It's not funny."

"No, it's not," Casey admitted, her voice softening. She leaned forward, elbows on her knees. "But here's the thing: you don't let them win by spiraling. Creeps thrive on fear. They want you frozen. You hear me?"

Emily nodded, though tears still welled at the corners of her eyes.

Casey reached over, tugging Emily into a side hug. "You're not pawns. You're not weak. And if anyone thinks otherwise? They've got to go through me first." She smirked faintly. "And trust me, I don't miss."

That earned the tiniest laugh from Emily, muffled against her shoulder.

Casey squeezed her gently. Behind her light banter, though, her gaze was sharp, fixed on the texts still glowing on the phone screen. Her hand brushed her thigh where her service weapon usually rested, and for just a second, the mask slipped, her smile fading into the hard edge of someone who knew the threat wasn't a joke at all.

She drew in a breath, straightened, and clapped her hands lightly against her knees. "Alright, decision made. You two are crashing here tonight."

Ellie blinked. "Casey, we can't—"

"Yeah, you can," Casey cut in, tone brooking no argument. "Dorms don't come with armed babysitters, and last I checked, your RA isn't qualified to handle Mr. McStalkerface if he graduates from text messages to showing up in person."

Emily sniffed, her voice small. "You really don't mind?"

Casey leaned back with a scoff. "Mind? Please. I've got enough frozen pizza and bad movies to keep us alive till morning. You're safer here. End of story."

Ellie's jaw flexed, like she wanted to push back, but Emily curled closer against Casey's side, already comforted by the weight of the decision made for them.

Casey slung an arm around Emily's shoulders and shot Ellie a look that dared her to argue. "Trust me, kid. Tonight, this couch is a fortress. If they step through that door, I'll be Vader, and they'll be the ones choking.

Dark Webs

Will leaned against the table in the briefing room, sleeves rolled up, waiting. Rivers dropped a thick folder onto the desk, the DHS seal stamped in the corner. His face was carved with exhaustion.

"Intel guys picked up chatter on the dark web," Rivers said without preamble. "Fraternity chatter. Some of your Ravenwood boys are tangled up in Steve's underground video ring."

Will's jaw flexed. "I thought we buried Steve's operation."

"Parts of it. But it's still breathing. The drugs are evolving—synthetics that leave a less detectable trace and a less pronounced effect. Girls look almost normal, but they're compliant as puppets. Memory wiped clean after. Like robots that can't remember they were ever programmed."

Will's eyes narrowed. "Guinea pigs."

"Yeah." Rivers exhaled hard. "Facial recognition tagged several Ravenwood girls who've reported time gaps. Same names. Same gaps. Suspects? Always masked. Or digitally blurred." He paused, voice tightening. "But one older video slipped through. No mask. Guess who?"

Will didn't need to guess. "Julien Cain."

Rivers gave a grim nod. "Toying with a half-alert girl like she was one of his installations, vic has since graduated and moved away, still trying to track her down. You've seen his other work firsthand. The painted bodies. The staged corpses. This... It's the same sickness. Just recorded."

Will's hands curled into fists on the table.

"We think this has cartel fingerprints all over it," Rivers pressed. "We're still tracking Steve's network. Looks like the initiation into something called the Ouroboros Club involves exactly this—drugging, recording, assault. And it didn't start with just Steve. Or Julien. They lit the match, but now it's spreading. More members than just frat boys out for kicks. This is organized. Legacy-level."

Will's voice dropped into a low growl. "And the money trail?"

"Every time we pull a thread, it leads south. Cartels. Laundering through shell accounts, fake art sales, crypto wallets. Small-town Oakhaven's looking like a cartel hub—sex, drugs, money, girls turned into experiments."

Will stared at the folder, then lifted his gaze. "You want this stopped? I've got someone I can call. State Department black ops. Codename: *Oblivion.*"

Rivers arched a brow. "Oblivion?"

"He hasn't failed me yet," Will said evenly. "And he doesn't answer to red tape."

Rivers studied him for a long moment, then gave a short nod. "At this point, I'll take all the help I can get. Bring in your ghost."

Oblivion

Will shut his office door, pulling the blinds halfway. The bullpen noise dulled, leaving only the low hum of the air vent. He scrolled through his phone until he found the encrypted app, thumb hovering.

One word typed. **Oblivion.**

Send.

The reply came in less than a minute.

Location?

Will hesitated, then typed: **Oakhaven PD. Private line.**

His phone buzzed. The number was untraceable, the connection secure. He pressed it to his ear.

A voice, low and steady, came through. "Anderson. Been a long time."

"Too long," Will said, leaning back in his chair. "I wouldn't call if it wasn't important."

"Nothing you ever call me for is small." A pause, the faint scrape of a lighter. "So. What's burning?"

Will took a breath. "We've got a fraternity network tied into Steve's old operation. Synthetic drugs, dark web videos. The girls don't remember, but the scars don't fade. Cartels are laundering through it. We even found Cain's face in an old clip."

On the other end, silence stretched, heavy. Then Mercer's voice dropped, colder. "Cain. Figures."

Will continued. "DHS believes this Ouroboros Club is bigger than frat kids. Legacy-level. Organized. They're building a system that turns girls into experiments. I need it stopped before more bodies hit the ground."

"Sounds like you're asking me to wipe the board clean."

"I'm asking you to do what I can't. Official channels are bogged down in red tape. You're not."

Another pause, then a chuckle. "And you remembered my number after all this time. Thought you'd erased me."

Will's voice softened, just slightly. "Hard to erase the man whose daughter I pulled out of a nightmare. Summit Falls PD, remember? Your kid. Wrong boyfriend, worse dealer. She's still breathing because I bent the rules for her. You know I'd do it again. You came through the last time and I didn't think I'd have to call you again, but here I am."

The silence cracked with a faint exhale. Mercer's voice shifted, warmer for just a moment. "She's alive because of you. College degree now. Married. Clean. I don't forget debts, Anderson."

Will leaned forward, elbows on the desk. "Then help me cash this one in."

On the other end, the flint-hard tone returned. "Fine. You've got me. But when Oblivion steps onto the board... pieces disappear. Are you ready for that?"

Will's jaw tightened. "If it stops this, I'm ready."

"Then Oakhaven just became my next shadow."

The line went dead.

Casey's Reaction

Casey strolled into Will's office, holding an oversized styrofoam soda cup filled with Cheerwine, like it was a weapon. She set it on his desk and dropped into the chair. "You've been brooding in here like Vader in his meditation pod. What gives?"

Will closed the folder he'd been reading. "I made a call. To Mercer."

Her eyebrows shot up. "Orin Mercer? Oblivion Mercer?"

Will nodded.

Casey let out a low whistle. "Didn't think we'd ever dust him off again. Last time he saved our asses with those untraceable trackers, remember? We planted them on Kristen so we could follow her to Steve's lair. Completely stripped her bare, and they still didn't find 'em."

Will's mouth twitched. "Yeah. Too bad she walked into a Faraday cage before we could storm in. Steve almost got away because of it."

Casey leaned back, shaking her head. "I still remember that damn steel door slamming on it, those two idiots looking at my face, their sexist remarks. You know what I yelled when the two thugs popped it open?"

Will allowed himself a thin smile. "You were in your lime green underwear screaming 'It's a trap!' like Admiral Ackbar."

Casey smirked, unashamed. "Damn right I did. One of my finer moments of tactical genius."

Will chuckled under his breath, but the weight pressed back in quickly. "Mercer's tech nearly turned the tide then. I need him again now. Cartels, Cain, Ouroboros, it's bigger than us."

Casey eyed him, soda straw between her teeth. "So we're calling in Oblivion. Just make sure he doesn't drag us into another Faraday cage mess. I'm running out of Star Wars quotes for the end credits."

Will leaned forward, his tone flat. "This time, we don't miss."

Casey raised her soda in a mock toast. "May the Force be with us, then. Because it sounds like we're gonna need it."

Watcher's Journal

They laugh about traps.

They forget a rook can only charge in straight lines. Predictable. Bold. Brave. But boldness is also blindness. A steel door slams, and the board changes before the rook even sees the snare.

They believe they're the only ones playing. That only their moves matter.

But every board has more than one hand arranging the pieces.

And the pawns? They're always the ones caught first.

I won't let that happen again. Not while I'm moving the pieces.

But now... another hand has entered the game. A shadow that doesn't belong. They whisper his name like a curse—Oblivion.

He is not mine. He is not theirs. Yet he steps onto the board all the same.

No piece moves without cost. If Oblivion plays, then blood will follow.

Carter Vance

The interview room was a stark space, with angles and fluorescent lighting, deliberately plain, featuring only a metal table, four chairs, and the faint hum of the vent overhead. Carter Vance leaned back in his chair, as if he were at a frat mixer, not a police department. His white polo was crisp, the sleeves pushed up to show off his tanned biceps, a Rolex gleaming under the dim light.

On his left sat Sal Harris, his family's high-dollar attorney. The man's suit probably cost more than Will's car, his cufflinks flashing each time he adjusted his Montblanc pen on the table.

Casey and Will came in together. Casey tossed a folder onto the table and dropped into her chair, posture loose but eyes sharp. Will took the quieter route, sliding into the seat opposite Vance, legal pad ready, voice calm but steady.

"Carter," Will began. "Appreciate you agreeing to talk to us."

Vance grinned as if it were all a game. "Hey, I've got nothing to hide. Let's clear the air."

Casey flipped open her folder. "Let's start with Kelsey Summers."

A flicker passed across Vance's face, then he shrugged. "Kelsey? She was a partier. Liked to drink. So did I. We had fun. Whole school year, on and off. She was always a willing participant. If anything, she was the one initiating stuff; that girl was hornier than I ever have been, like all the time wanting it, if you can believe that. The girl even kept clothes at my place for when she stayed over."

Will's pen scratched across the page. "You ended it before summer?"

"Yeah. I saw her kissing some other guy, from a different frat. Homie doesn't play that." He smirked. "So, to the curb with her. That's it."

Casey leaned forward, voice flat. "You expect us to believe you've got no idea what happened to Brock Prescott or Derek Langley?"

Vance's smirk twitched, but he kept his tone light. "Only what I've seen online, same as you. People love to talk."

Casey didn't let it go. "Fine. Let's narrow it down. Who would want to hurt Brock? You run with him long enough, you had to know if he made enemies."

Vance shifted, crossing his arms over his chest. "Brock was loud. Always mouthing off, always trying to prove something. If somebody had it out for him, it could've been anybody he rubbed the wrong way. But me? I wasn't keeping score."

Her gaze sharpened. "Where were you the night he was killed?"

That cocky smile returned, a shade too quick. "At the house. Whole night. Ask anybody. The place was packed. You think I slipped out with a hundred witnesses around? C'mon."

Casey let the silence stretch before she spoke again. "And Derek Langley? Same questions. Enemies? Where were you before he turned up dead?"

Vance tapped a knuckle on the table, as if bored. "Derek was chill. No beef I knew about. We partied, we drank, that's it. The last time I saw him was a few days before... everything. He was fine then. After that?" He lifted a shoulder. "Don't know, don't care."

The lawyer's pen tapped once against his pad, sharp and deliberate. "Detective, unless you have actual evidence to confront my client with, this line of questioning is speculative at best."

Casey ignored him, eyes still on Vance. "You sure you're not leaving anything out? Funny thing about parties, people remember more than they realize."

Vance leaned back, spreading his hands like the whole thing was beneath him. "You've got my answers. If you don't like them, that's not my problem."

Casey didn't blink. "We've had multiple reports from girls who think they might have been drugged at Serpent House parties. You want to explain that?"

Vance sat up straighter, bravado sharpening. "That's not possible. We don't need to drug anyone. Girls show up because they want to be there. They throw themselves at us. Just because we throw better parties than anybody else doesn't make us criminals."

Casey let the words hang for a beat, then dropped her voice, razor-flat. "You think that may have something to do with their murders? Brock Prescott. Derek Langley. Girls saying they blacked out, woke up sick, not remembering what happened, you expect us to believe that's just a coincidence?"

For the first time, Vance's easy grin faltered. His jaw clenched, a flash of irritation in his eyes. "I don't know what happened to them. And I sure as hell didn't have anything to do with it. You can't pin that on me."

Casey leaned in. "Not yet."

The lawyer's chair creaked as he leaned forward, voice clipped. "Detective, that's enough. This interview is over. My client has cooperated more than required. We're done here."

Sal Harris rose smoothly, tugging his jacket cuffs into place. Vance shoved back his chair, the metal legs screeching across the tile, trying to cover his unease with a smirk.

Casey stayed seated, arms folded, voice low and sharp enough to cut through the lawyer's polish.

"Walk out if you want, Carter. Just remember, people who swear they 'don't know anything' usually end up knowing more than they realize... right before we catch them in a lie."

Vance's grin twitched, teeth clenched. For half a second, his mask slipped.

"Detective," Harris snapped, ushering his client toward the door.

Casey didn't move, just watched him go. "See you soon," she called after him.

The door clicked shut, the hum of the vent filling the silence.

Will set his pen down, calm as ever. "He's rattled. That's something."

Casey leaned back, exhaling slowly. "Yeah. And the more he talks, the more rope he gives us."

Squad room later that evening:

Rachel was waiting when Casey and Will returned. She was perched at her desk, half-finished report in front of her, chewing absently on the end of a pen.

Casey dropped the file onto the corner of Rachel's desk with a thud. "You missed one hell of a show."

Rachel looked up quickly. "I wanted to be there. Why'd Kristen say no?"

Will slid into the chair across from her, loosening his tie. "Because Harris was in the room. High-priced attorneys eat rookies alive, Rachel. Kristen, as the DA, didn't want him taking one look at you and deciding to use you as the weak spot."

Rachel bristled, but she swallowed it down. "So what happened?"

Casey leaned against the edge of the desk, her grin sharp. "Golden Boy Vance swore up and down he's innocent. Said Kelsey Summers was a party girl, that she threw herself at him, that he broke it off when she kissed another frat guy. Classic dirtbag excuses."

Will added, his tone steady, "He claimed no knowledge of what happened to Brock Prescott or Derek Langley. No enemies, no alibi beyond 'the house was packed.'"

Rachel frowned. "And the drugging reports?"

Casey's smile thinned. "Denied it, of course. The girls practically begged for attention. Real charmer."

Will met Rachel's eyes. "But Casey rattled him. Hard. He walked out hiding it, but he's nervous. Which means we've got a crack."

Rachel straightened, a spark of resolve pushing past her frustration. "Then we keep pressing. He won't hold up forever."

Casey tapped the file with one finger. "That's the spirit, rookie. But next time? You'll have your shot. Kristen can't keep you in the bullpen forever."

Enter Agent Rivers

The bullpen was quiet for once, the hum of computers and the rattle of the AC filling the space. Will's phone buzzed across his desk. He glanced at the caller ID, then picked up.

"Agent Rivers," he said, voice even.

On the other end, Evan Rivers's tone was brisk but warm. "Anderson, good to hear your voice again. Listen, we're standing up a task force. The cartel's funneling of product to the Ouroborus Club looks like it's fueling those dark web assault videos we've been tracking. DHS wants boots on the ground here. I know you and Casey have worked the underground sex ring cases before, and that mess with Julien Cain and Steve Creegan, so I want you both on it. We could use your local insight."

Will straightened in his chair, eyes flicking toward Casey across the room. "Appreciate that, Agent. We're in. I should also tell you, I've got an intern working with us. She's a student at the same campus where some of the victims were targeted."

Rivers perked up immediately. "Perfect. A younger perspective could be exactly what we need. Someone who actually lived in that environment knows the culture."

Will hesitated just a beat, then said her name. "Rachel Donovan."

There was a low whistle on the other end. "Joe Donovan's girl? Hell, I remember her. Last time I saw her, she was running around your old precinct of Summit Falls—first or second grade, maybe. Stopped in Joe's office, and there she was with crayons. Time flies."

Will allowed himself the faintest smile. "She's grown. Smart. She's been a real asset."

"Good to hear," Rivers said. "I'll call Chief Mason and make it official. We'll set up a task force room at your PD, I hear you've got space on the back side of the building, good for the tech gear."

"Sounds like a plan." Will ended the call and set the phone down.

Casey swiveled in her chair, raising a brow. "Well? Who was that?"

"Evan Rivers," Will said. "DHS. They're putting together a task force on Ouroborus, cartel connection, and dark web videos. Wants us on it."

Casey gave a low whistle. "The big leagues. Guess they finally noticed we've been cleaning up their messes for years." She grinned, leaning over her desk toward Rachel. "Gear up, rookie. The Feds are coming."

Rachel blinked, caught between excitement and nerves. "Wait—you mean I'm in on this too?"

Will's expression was calm but firm. "You're in. And Rivers is already making it official."

Rachel exhaled, the tension slipping off her shoulders. For the first time, she realized: this wasn't just an internship anymore. She was about to step into something much bigger.

Task Force Up and Running

Two days later, the back side of the precinct was buzzing. IT techs wheeled in racks of servers and monitors, the sharp smell of cardboard and plastic mingling with the usual coffee and old carpet. Detectives craned their necks as a cluster of men in DHS windbreakers threaded through the bullpen.

At their center, Agent Evan Rivers looked much the same as the last time they'd seen him, tall, broad-shouldered, a streak of silver at his temples. His stride was purposeful, but when he spotted Will and Casey standing by the task force room, a grin cracked his face.

"Anderson. Murphy." He clasped Will's hand in a firm shake before pulling Casey into a quick half-hug. "Feels like I was just here."

Casey smirked. "Last time was the golf course. You remember, we lost two good men that night, while Kristen told us all how much trouble we were in for letting her get kidnapped."

Rivers laughed, the sound booming through the hall. "Yeah. Hard to forget Eldon Price. Damn glad we got her out of that one." His expression sobered briefly, but then he looked past them, eyes landing on Rachel.

"You must be Rachel Donovan."

Rachel straightened unconsciously. "Yes, sir."

Rivers studied her for a moment, recognition dawning. "Hell, I remember when you were knee-high, sitting in Joe's office coloring while your dad tried to talk me into joining one of his softball games. And now here you are." He shook his head, smiling. "Time flies."

Rachel's cheeks warmed, but she met his gaze. "I'm here to help however I can."

"That's exactly what I want to hear." Rivers clapped Will on the shoulder. "She's got the Donovan backbone, that's for sure."

Casey raised a brow. "Careful, Rivers. If you start getting all nostalgic, the kid's gonna think we're ancient."

Rachel grinned despite herself.

Rivers gestured toward the newly cleared task force room, where cables snaked across the floor and monitors flickered to life. "Alright. Ouroborus is expanding its reach faster than we expected. The cartel supply chain is feeding their video operation, and we're going to cut the legs out from under it. I want this room to be our base. Full integration. We share everything."

Will nodded. "We're ready."

Rivers scanned the three of them, Will steady, Casey sharp, Rachel eager but resolute. "Good. Because if Ouroborus is back on campus territory, it's going to get ugly fast. We'll need every one of you."

The DA Arrives

The task force room was still in chaos, monitors glowing, techs stringing cable, the faint hum of servers already filling the air.

Kristen stepped in, heels clicking against the floor. She'd just wrapped court, her blazer sharp against the backdrop of wires and screens. Her gaze swept the room before landing on Rivers.

"Agent Rivers." Her tone softened, genuine. "I didn't get a chance earlier, thank you. For being here. And for what you did that night at the golf course."

Rivers straightened, dipping his head in acknowledgment. "We all had skin in that fight."

Kristen's mouth tightened, but her voice stayed even. "Still. You were there with Will and Casey when it mattered most. You helped get Ellie and me out alive." She paused, the memory flickering across her face. "And I am sorry. Truly sorry. Two of your tac guys paid the price for Price's trap in those tunnels. They went in hunting victims so Casey could pull Ellie out. That doesn't leave me."

For a moment, the room hushed around them, the shuffle of techs seeming to fade under the weight of her words.

Rivers's jaw worked, but his eyes were steady. "They knew the risks. They didn't hesitate, and I wouldn't expect them to. Casey did her job, Ellie walked out, and that's what mattered. My men... they'd tell you the same thing if they could."

Kristen let out a slow breath, nodding. "Doesn't make it easier."

"No," Rivers agreed. "But it means it wasn't for nothing." His tone shifted, lighter. "Besides, you've got good people here. Anderson. Murphy. And now Donovan." He glanced toward Rachel, who was bent over a monitor with a tech. "Price didn't break your team. Looks to me like it's stronger."

Kristen followed his gaze, her expression softening just a touch. “Stronger, yes. And stubborn as hell. Which might be the only reason we’re all still here.”

Rivers chuckled low, but his eyes stayed sharp. “Then it’s the right team for Ouroborus.”

The Pawn Dared, The Pawn Captured

The campus bell tower loomed against the night sky, its clock face pale in the glow of floodlights. The chimes had gone silent long ago, but the quad below pulsed with life—clusters of students pressed against the tape hastily strung by campus security, phones raised, their hushed voices spilling into the warm night air.

Tyler Brentwood lay draped across the low concrete wall that circled the tower, head tilted back, eyes glassy in the artificial light. His face was swollen, lips split, nose broken, the bruises blooming purple against his skin. Jagged cuts striped his arms and thighs, strategic, disabling, the kind meant to take the fight from a man before life.

Balanced on his forehead was a single white pawn. Its base was smeared red, sticky with his blood, the piece clinging like a broken crown. A hush had fallen over the nearest cluster of onlookers, all staring at the little chess piece as if it made sense of the violence.

Casey muttered low, arms folded as she scanned the crowd. “Well. Somebody wanted to make damn sure this golden boy didn’t get another second chance.”

Will crouched beside the body, gloved hands steady as he checked the pockets. A glass vial of crystalline powder caught the floodlight, followed by a cheap aluminum keychain canister. Inside, the faint chemical tang of dissolvable pills confirmed it, synthetic, the same cocktail that had been trickling through the city for months.

He set them carefully on a clean evidence sheet. "Not just using. Moving. Or trying to."

A student broke through the crowd with a choked sob, yanked back by campus security. Whispers rippled out: *DA's case. Dismissed. Brentwood. The tower.*

Casey's eyes flicked from the pawn to the body, then back to Will. "The message is loud and clear. Brentwood wasn't a player. He was a piece. Expendable."

Will's jaw tightened. He pulled his phone and stepped a few paces away from the gawking crowd, thumbing Rivers' number.

The line clicked. "Rivers."

"It's Anderson. Body at the Ravenwood bell tower. Tyler Brentwood."

A pause, then a low whistle. "The DA's poster boy?"

"Not anymore. He's posed. Pawn dipped in his blood, balanced on his forehead. Multiple disabling cuts before the kill. Synthetic vial and pill canister on him."

"I'll bring the team," Rivers said, voice flat. "Keep the scene locked down. Nobody touches a damn thing."

Will ended the call, sliding the phone back into his pocket. The noise of the crowd pressed in again—students whispering, the scrape of radios, the flashing campus cruiser lights bathing everything in red and blue.

Casey exhaled slowly, watching the pawn gleam under the harsh light. "Ravenwood's playing chess with bodies. And the students? They're already taking notes."

Will rose, eyes locked on Brentwood's broken face. His voice was low, meant only for her. "Then we'd better get ahead of the next move."

Call to Kristen

Will stepped away from the crowd, the press of voices and strobing cruiser lights fading as he slipped behind the shadow of a campus oak. He pulled out his phone, thumbed through it, and pressed Kristen's number.

She answered on the second ring, brisk as ever. "Hi, honey."

"It's me." His voice was low. "Kristen... Nancy Hall can finally have her vindication."

A pause, sharp, her breath catching. "Will... what happened?"

"Tyler Brentwood, just found at the Ravenwood bell tower. He's dead. Someone beat the hell out of him, cut him up so he couldn't fight back. Then they left him posed with a white pawn on his forehead—dipped in his own blood. And in his pocket—cartel synthetic. Vial and pill form, both."

Her silence stretched so long he thought the call had dropped. Then her voice came, softer, breaking. "I told them. I told them he was dirty. I stood in that courtroom and I fought, and they laughed me out of it."

Will closed his eyes, jaw tight. "This isn't on you."

Her breath hitched again, a raw edge slipping through. "I let Nancy Hall down. I let *all* of them down. And now the whole damn campus is watching a blood-soaked pawn to remind me of it."

"You didn't put him here," Will said firmly, forcing calm into his tone. "The cartel did. Whomever's moving pieces want it loud, want it seen. That's not your failure, Kristen. That's their message."

From the quad, Casey's voice carried, snapping at campus security to push the students back. The whispers rippled louder, phones raised, the body on the wall still a grotesque spectacle.

"Kristen," he said gently, "I called because you deserved to hear it first. Not from the press. Not from the gossip mill. From me."

There was a tremor in her reply, quiet but cutting. "Thank you... Will. Just—just bring me something I can use. Something that puts this to rest."

"I will," he said. And this time, he meant it like a vow.

Rachels Report

Will ended the call with Kristen and slipped the phone back into his pocket, exhaling hard. Casey's eyes were already on him, sharp and knowing.

"She didn't take it well, huh?"

Will shook his head once. "She thinks this proves she failed. That she let Nancy Hall down. And now the whole damn campus is watching it unfold like a circus."

Before Casey could answer, his phone buzzed again. Rachel's name lit the screen. He picked up. "Anderson."

"Detective, you need to know—it's everywhere already," Rachel said, her voice quick but controlled. "Photos from the bell tower, the pawn, Brentwood's body. Students are reposting it with their own commentary. And some of the threads are pushing a narrative: that Nancy Hall finally got her revenge."

Will's jaw tightened. "Already?"

"Yes. It's spreading fast. Hashtags with her name, memes about Kristen's case dismissal. It's less about Brentwood and more about painting Nancy as some vigilante symbol. If it keeps going, she'll be branded as complicit in all of this, whether she likes it or not."

"Understood. Keep monitoring, but don't repeat that to anyone else." He cut the call short, staring at the sea of students beyond the tape, their glowing phones like fireflies buzzing with poison.

Casey folded her arms. "Social media doesn't waste time. Kids with cameras, blood on campus—no surprise. But Nancy's name in the mix? That's gasoline."

"She doesn't deserve it," Will muttered. "She fought like hell to be heard. Now they'll twist her into some vigilante ghost story."

"And Kristen?" Casey tilted her head. "She doesn't deserve to be dragged either, but she will. You can't carry both of them on your shoulders, partner. The internet sure as hell won't wait for the truth before it picks a villain and a martyr."

He rubbed a hand over his jaw, the weight settling heavily. "They're both paying for Brentwood's sins, even after death."

Casey stepped closer, voice lowering, more steel than comfort. "No. They're paying for whoever's moving those pawns. Don't let the chatter write the case for us. Our job is to find the player—not get lost in the crowd noise."

Will met her eyes, steadying himself in her bluntness. “Yeah. You’re right.”

Casey’s smirk was faint, but her voice was firm. “I usually am. Now let’s get ahead of the next move before it’s checkmate.”

Dark Web Discovery

The task force room was dim except for the glow of laptops. Casey hunched over her screen, one hand gripping a mug of coffee gone cold hours ago. Will leaned against the table beside her, arms folded, eyes sharp.

A tech from DHS slid a flash drive across the table. "Rivers pulled this from a cartel server we flagged last week. Looks like Steve's work, old stuff that never got fully purged. Some are encrypted, while others are simply dumped in their raw form. Could be useful."

Casey shoved it into her laptop. The files populated, endless strings of numbers and aliases. Video after video, thumbnails in neat rows.

Casey exhaled through her nose. "God. How many lives are in here?"

Will's jaw flexed. "Too many."

They opened the first file. Grainy footage, handheld, sickeningly familiar: a girl barely conscious on a couch, laughter from men off-camera. Her drink had been tampered with. She shifted, sluggish, murmuring, unaware.

Casey's hand clenched the mouse until her knuckles blanched. "This is the same cocktail we've seen in toxicology. Their 'compliance drug.'"

"Pause it," Will said sharply. She clicked, freezing the frame. His voice dropped. "Look."

The girl's head lolled to the side. Half her face caught the camera light. Just enough to glimpse a profile. Young. Vulnerable.

Casey whispered, almost choking on the words: "She was at Ravenwood."

They scrolled forward. A second clip. The same girl, different night. This time, the angle was tighter, featuring chest-cam footage from a frat room with its wall coverings. Male voices jeering. She resisted, weak, slurred, arms pushed back down again and again.

Casey shoved away from the desk, pacing, both hands gripping her hair. "Son of a Bantha... she was one of them. She was the evidence, and the whole damn system just went full Alderaan on her, boom, gone, like it never existed."

Will didn't move, but his eyes narrowed, burning. "Back it up. Go slow."

Casey scrolled frame by frame until one of the men leaned into the shot, his face catching the overhead light.

She froze. Her breath caught. "No... no way."

Will leaned in, his voice low and certain. "That's Derek Langley."

The name dropped like lead between them.

Casey's voice rose, ragged. "He was on these tapes? He was one of them?"

"Clear as day," Will said grimly. "This isn't a rumor, it's not gossip. That's him, laughing, holding her down."

Casey pressed both hands to her mouth, staring at the frozen frame, fury and nausea battling in her chest. "So he gets the easy out. No trial, no reckoning. Just gone, like Alderaan, big bada boom, crashed and burned."

Will's jaw worked. "Not a coincidence. Whoever's cleaning this board knows exactly who the pieces are."

The silence after that was suffocating.

Finally, Casey swallowed hard, forcing herself back toward the screen. "What happens when this gets out? Ravenwood's golden boy, found murdered, and now we've got proof he was part of this?"

Will didn't answer at first. He just stared at Langley's frozen smirk on the screen. "It'll crack the whole façade. Students will panic, parents will demand answers, and donors will scramble to cover it up. And Rachel..."

Casey turned sharply, reading the weight in his voice.

"She's still Ravenwood," Will said quietly. "Still tied to that campus, those kids, that world. When she finds out, it won't just be a case file to her. It'll be personal."

Casey dragged a hand through her hair, exhaling hard. "We tell her, it crushes her. We keep it quiet, she finds out another way, and it looks like we lied. Either way, we risk blowing up her trust."

"She deserves to know," Will said, his tone steady but heavy. "But not yet. Not until we've got more than just a face on a frame. She needs truth, not fragments."

From across the room, Rivers spoke up, his voice even but carrying weight. "Just remember, she's task force now. You can't keep her in the dark forever without it circling back. And the last thing we need is cracks on the inside while we're chasing this."

Casey shot him a look, then turned back to Will.

"She deserves to know," Will repeated quietly. "But when the time's right."

Casey looked back at Langley's image on the screen, young, cocky, untouchable, and shook her head. "Truth like this... it'll cut her to the bone."

Will's eyes stayed on the monitor, his voice low. "Better a cut than a lie."

Watcher's Journal

They call it chemistry. Progress. Evolution.

I call it slavery.

Synthetic dusts poured into red cups, clear drops slipped into bottles. Masks on their faces, distortion filters over their crimes, but underneath it is always the same. A boy with a grin too wide. A girl who doesn't remember saying no.

They think the game erases itself if memory is stolen. That pawns forget when the board is reset.

But I remember.

The Serpents wear masks now, but every mask hides the same rot. Cartels feed them, money shields them, and still they pretend they are untouchable.

They are not untouchable.

Pawns will not be their guinea pigs. Not while I move the pieces.

Cartel Movement

Will's phone buzzed against the tabletop. He glanced down, half expecting another update from Rivers. Instead, the name on the screen made his shoulders stiffen.

Orin Mercer

The message was short, clipped, Mercer's style.

Cartel chatter is increasing; there's been a rise in the last 24 hours. Something's changing. Stay alert.

Will exhaled slowly, the weight of it settling in his gut. If Mercer was reaching out unprompted, it wasn't noise, it was a signal.

Casey noticed his change in expression. "That Obi-Wan, or someone else?"

Will slid the phone face down on the table, voice steady but grimmer than before. "Mercer. Says the cartel just went into overdrive."

Casey's smirk faded. "Well, that's comforting. Guess we're not just playing chess anymore. Sounds more like dejarik, holograms and monsters you can't always see."

Will's jaw tightened. "Yeah. And in that game, you don't always get all your pieces back."

Will was still staring at Mercer's text when his phone lit up again, **Kristen** this time. He answered on the first ring.

"Will?" Her voice was tight, rushed.

"What's wrong?"

"I just saw it," she said. "The same SUV. The black Escalade. The one that used to sit outside the house before—before those two cartel guys ended up dead."

Will straightened in his chair. "Where?"

"First, near the office. I thought it was a coincidence, but then... it was on our street when I pulled into the driveway. Same tinted windows. Same dent on the back bumper." She sucked in a sharp breath. "Will, I swear it's them."

Casey glanced over, eyebrows raised at his expression.

"Kristen, listen to me." Will's tone was steady, but his pulse was thudding in his ears. "Are you inside now?"

"Yes. Doors locked. Emily's here, Ellie's still at class. I keep looking out the window, but it's gone now."

"Stay put. Don't open that door for anyone. I'll get a unit to swing by."

There was a pause on the line, softer, more vulnerable. "Will... I don't like this. It feels like they're circling again."

He closed his eyes for a beat, jaw tight. "I know. I'll handle it. Just keep the girls close."

Kristen whispered back, "Promise me."

"You have my word." He ended the call, slid the phone down, and met Casey's eyes across the table.

She smirked faintly, but there was no humor in it. "So much for peace and quiet. Looks like the cartel just parked on our doorstep."

Will's expression hardened. "Then we make sure they regret it."

Watcher Interlude

The board shifts. New pieces slide into play.

Tonight the Escalade circled again, black, heavy, glass so dark it swallows faces. They think their masks protect them, that tinted windows make them invisible. But predators always reveal themselves. They move in packs, wait, and then circle.

To the rook and the king, it is a cartel. To me, it is proof: the predators are restless. The pawns are in greater danger than they know.

Every movement on the board leaves an echo. Tires on pavement. Engines idling. Shadows that linger too long outside a window. I see what they cannot, and I remember what they prefer to forget.

The predators believe they are hunters. But they are wrong.

They are pieces. Disposable. Replaceable.

And they will fall, one by one, until only pawns remain, the way the game was always meant to be played.

Will Updates Captain Monroe

Will stepped into the stairwell, the door clicking shut behind him, muting the bullpen noise. He pulled out his phone, thumbed to Monroe's number, and pressed it to his ear.

"Monroe."

"It's Anderson," Will said. "Wanted to give you an update before it gets lost in the shuffle."

"Go ahead."

Will leaned against the railing. "Our intern's been digging into the Serpents' socials. She pulled a thread the tech team missed, tagged photos, and cross-referenced with clinic reports. There's a correlation between their events and the missing-time cases. It's solid enough to put the fraternity deeper on our board."

A pause. Monroe's voice carried a low note of approval. "That's sharp work. She's fitting in?"

"She's competent," Will said, keeping it clipped. "Focused. I'll keep her pointed where we need her."

"Good. What else?"

"I had a sit-down with DHS Agent Rivers. Their intel guys scraped chatter off the dark web, fraternity chatter. Steve's old operation isn't dead. The synthetic drugs have evolved, harder to detect, stronger in effect. Girls look awake, compliant, but memories wiped clean. Cartel fingerprints all over it. And they've confirmed some of the Ravenwood girls are in the footage."

Monroe's voice tightened. "Any suspects?"

"Most are masked or distorted. But a couple of older clips slipped through. Julien Cain is on one. And Derek Langley shows up on another, face clear enough there's no mistaking him."

A hiss of breath crackled over the line. "Langley. And Cain. Jesus."

"Yeah," Will said. "Rivers believes this Ouroboros Club is tied to it. Not just frat kids for fun, organized initiation, legacy-level players. Cartels are funding it. We're still tracking the money, but every trail runs south."

Monroe's tone went grave. "So we're up against an operation, not just predators."

"Exactly. For now, we're still chasing leads. Rachel's mapping socials, Rivers' team is pulling dark web chatter, and Casey and I are running interviews. It's moving, but not fast enough."

Silence stretched a moment, then Monroe said, "Keep on it. And Will—don't let the politics slow you down. If this reaches campus parents, all hell breaks loose."

"Understood," Will said.

He hung up the phone, heavy in his hand. For a second, the stairwell's hum pressed in, the weight of too many pieces moving, none falling where they needed to yet.

Second Summer

Late morning. Campus coffee kiosk. morning sun, heat already rising off the sidewalk. Students drift around with iced lattes and headphones. Rachel waits in line, phone in hand, thumb tapping idle patterns on the screen. A familiar voice behind her catches her attention.

"Rachel?"

She turns. It's Kelsey Summers. Hair up in a loose braid, oversized sunglasses, gym clothes. Not the high-gloss version of herself she'd been in the interview. She looks smaller, thinner, tired.

Rachel offers a warm but cautious smile. "Kelsey. Hey."

Kelsey hesitates. "Didn't expect to see you here."

"I basically live off of coffee." Rachel steps aside so Kelsey can join her in line. "You heading to class?"

"Spin. Then maybe class. Depends on how dead my legs are." Kelsey forces a light laugh. Rachel doesn't return it.

There's a beat of silence. The barista shouts a name. Ice clinks. Students mill past.

Rachel speaks, quiet. "I've been thinking about what you said. About Carter."

Kelsey flinches just slightly. "I don't want to—"

Rachel cuts in gently. "I'm not asking you to say anything you don't want to. But... you said something about things feeling off. Waking up not remembering."

Kelsey adjusts her sunglasses. "I said I had bad nights. That's it."

"Bad nights shouldn't feel like missing time," Rachel says, voice even. "They shouldn't feel like someone else's memories."

Kelsey exhales, her shoulders dropping a little. "It's just... he was cold. He could be so charming in public, but then... private, it was like I didn't matter. Like I was something he *had*. Not someone he cared about."

Rachel nods slowly. "You ever feel like you were more alone with him than when you were actually alone?"

Kelsey finally looks at her directly. "Yeah," she whispers. "Exactly like that."

A pause. The wind shifts.

Then Rachel says it, softly: "I knew Carter. Before he started seeing you."

Kelsey blinks. "At Ravenwood?"

Rachel nods. "Briefly. Before I transferred out. Before I knew better."

Kelsey pulls off her sunglasses. Her eyes are bloodshot, rimmed red like she hasn't been sleeping. "You think he did something, don't you?"

Rachel doesn't answer right away. Then: "I think he's not who people think he is."

Kelsey swallows. Her voice is almost inaudible. "When Casey mentioned the girls being drugged... something came back. A memory. I thought it was a nightmare. A man on top of me. Arms holding me down. Light everywhere. Like floodlights. Like it wasn't private." She pauses. "I thought it was a dream from the rumors. You hear enough stories, you start to imagine yourself into them. Right?"

Rachel doesn't look away. "Or maybe you don't imagine them. Maybe you were *in* one."

The line moves. The barista calls out again. No one claims the drink.

"I don't remember saying yes," Kelsey says, more to herself than to Rachel. "But I don't remember saying no either. And I can't—I don't want to—" She falters. "What if I just don't know?"

Rachel's voice is firm now, though still low. "Then you don't know. That's okay. But if you ever *do* know—"

Kelsey nods quickly, eyes shining. "You'll believe me."

"I already do."

A silence stretches between them again, heavier this time.

Then Kelsey says, almost like it hurts to admit it: "Sometimes I think he wanted me unconscious. Like he liked it better that way."

Rachel closes her eyes for a moment. Breathes in. Breathes out.

"You're not crazy," she says. "And you're not alone."

Kelsey nods once, then backs away. "I've gotta go."

Rachel lets her. Watches her retreat down the path toward the gym, shrinking into the crowd.

When she's gone, Rachel finally orders her drink. Iced Americano. Black.

She steps to the side, staring off into nothing, her mind reeling.

She remembers Carter's voice in her ear.

She sips the coffee.
Scalding.
She doesn't even flinch.

Breadcrumbs

The bullpen door swung open and in came Patrol Officer Savanna Jo Coltrane. Kevlar vest strapped snug across her frame, duty belt heavy at her hips—on paper she looked like any other street cop. But the uniform couldn't quite disguise the rest. Tall, slender, long-legged, there was a grace to the way she moved that drew eyes without her trying. Every step was easy, balanced, unhurried, like someone who knew her own strength and didn't need to prove it.

Her braid swung neatly down her back, the same no-nonsense style she'd worn since her academy days. Sun-browned skin and those striking ice-blue eyes gave her a presence that filled the room even before she spoke. Not sharp and cutting like Casey's, but magnetic, pulling attention toward her in a way that made rookies forget whatever excuse they were about to mumble.

She set a report folder on the sergeant's desk. "Traffic stop on Fairview. Pulled a vial of synthetic from the console, two ounces of powder coke from the trunk. Suspect's in holding, car's in impound, paperwork's clean." Her tone was calm, clipped, but carried a natural lilt of Southern charm that made even bad news sound like smooth conversation.

Casey leaned back in her chair, copper hair catching the light, smirk spreading slow. "Well, hell. Barbie with a badge and brains. Thought I was the last one they let slip through the door."

Savanna's grin came easy, softening her eyes but not her words. "Sweetheart, I was hauling hay before you figured out eyeliner. Don't think I'm here for decoration."

The bullpen cracked up, the tension of the night breaking in a ripple of laughter. Casey arched a brow, but her grin only widened—recognition in her look.

Will, watching from his desk, saw it too. Farm-tough, model-pretty, and completely unaware of it, Savanna Jo Coltrane didn't need to posture. She carried herself like the street was hers already, and the room followed her without realizing they'd given her the floor.

Savanna's gaze slid past Casey then, zeroing in on Rachel at her desk. Rachel was bent over her notebook, pen tapping thoughtfully against the margin, her copper braid loose from the night before falling against her shoulder. Savanna's smile turned slow, wicked.

"Well, now. And who's the little hot tamale y'all got parked in the corner?" Her drawl was lazy, but her eyes glittered sharp. "Wrapped up like a Sunday-school picnic, but anybody with sense can see there's more heat under that blouse than she knows what to do with. Back home, we'd call that hiding fireworks in a feed sack."

Rachel's pen stilled. She looked up, cheeks coloring but eyes steady. "Excuse me?"

Casey barked a laugh, slapping the arm of her chair. "Oh, Coltrane, I like you already. Took me months to work up material that good."

Savanna tipped her chin at Rachel, grin widening. "Don't get me wrong, sugar. It's a compliment. You got that farm-strong kind of pretty. Doesn't matter how neat you tie the ribbon, everyone knows what's underneath. Hot tamale, through and through."

Rachel blinked once, then leaned back in her chair, folding her arms loosely across her notebook. Her lips curved into a slow, knowing smile. "Trust me, Officer Coltrane—I'm perfectly aware of the goods. I just don't feel the need to hand out free samples."

The bullpen erupted again, half whistles, half laughter.

Casey nearly doubled over, pointing at Rachel. "Oh, she *burned* you, Coltrane. Rookie's got fire after all."

Savanna chuckled low, her ice-blue eyes narrowing with amused respect. "Fair enough," she drawled. Then, with a wry tilt of her head: "But careful, sugar. Where I come from, it doesn't matter if you hand out samples or not—word gets around anyway. Folks notice. Best you can do is be ready when they do."

Casey slapped her knee, eyes glittering. "Preach it, Coltrane! And for the record, if the rookie ever shows up in a sting bikini, I'm buying front-row tickets."

The bullpen roared. Rachel buried her face in her notebook with a groan, her cheeks blazing.

Will pinched the bridge of his nose, muttering low. *Three of them in the same room. God help me.*

Coltrane's Brief

Casey was still grinning from their back-and-forth when Savanna hooked a thumb over her shoulder toward holding. "Speaking of decoration, I've got a present for you two. Name's Cole Stanton. Thirty-two, local. Not a frat kid—older, rougher around the edges. Picked him up on a traffic stop—

synthetic in the console, two ounces powder coke in the trunk."

Will's brows lifted. "That was your possession bust?"

Savanna nodded, leaning against Casey's desk, arms folded across her Kevlar. "Yeah. But here's the kicker. Stanton was begging me not to book him. Said he'd tell me anything if I let him walk. One of those types—struts like he's God's gift to women until he's cuffed, then bawls like a toddler caught with his hand in the cookie jar. He was crying so hard he fogged the cruiser windows."

Casey smirked. "My favorite. So what's he selling?"

"Not just selling. He's spooked." Savanna's ice-blue gaze shifted to Will. "Said he knows who's feeding cartel product onto campus. Didn't give me names—just enough to show he's terrified. The way he was shaking, I'd say he's got something to lose... or someone pulling his strings hard enough to choke him."

Will's jaw tightened. "He's in holding now?"

Savanna pushed off the desk with a faint grin. "Safe and sound. Still whimpering like a puppy in the rain. If he really knows something, you'll want to hit him before he sobers up and decides silence is safer."

Casey exchanged a glance with Will, her smirk fading into something sharper. "Well, looks like your traffic stop just dropped us a breadcrumb, Coltrane. Question is—does Stanton lead us to the player, or just another pawn?

Cole Stanton

The holding room stank faintly of sweat and metal, the overhead light buzzing like it was tired of shining. Cole

Stanton sat slouched in the chair, cuffs loose against the table ring. Thirty-two, rough around the edges, but tonight he looked more like a cornered animal than a dealer—dark circles under his eyes, dried sweat at his hairline.

Casey dropped into the chair opposite him, boot heels kicking up on the table. "Cole Stanton. Not exactly kingpin material. More like the guy who keeps the kingpin's ashtray full."

His jaw twitched, the bravado kicking in. "You don't know me."

Will slid the folder onto the table, flipping it open with calm precision. "Two ounces of powder coke. Synthetic in your console. That's not personal use, Cole. That's distribution. We don't need to know you—we've got enough to bury you."

Cole's eyes darted between them, quick and nervous. His mouth opened, shut, then he leaned forward, voice dropping. "Look... I was gonna tell Officer Coltrane. She said no deal, but I—I know things. I can help you."

Casey arched a brow. "Here we go. What's the pitch, Stanton? You want us to clap and say, 'good boy,' and let you waltz out the door?"

His shoulders hunched. "No. I just—I can't go down for this. You don't understand, they'll kill me."

Will's voice stayed steady. "Who?"

Cole hesitated, chewing his lip. Then it all spilled out in a rush, words tumbling over themselves. "There's a guy. Local. He's not cartel, but he's plugged in. Runs product through kids on campus—frats, sororities, parties, the whole machine. I just run errands, okay? I don't touch the big stuff, I don't make calls. I just keep my head down."

Casey leaned forward, boots thudding off the table. "You're telling me you're a pawn. That about right?"

Cole swallowed, nodding quick. "Yeah. Pawn. Disposable. But I can name the one moving pieces if you cut me a deal."

Will's eyes locked on him, unblinking. "Name."

Cole licked his lips, voice shaking. "You won't believe me. You'll say I'm lying. But I swear—it's someone with roots here. Someone with pull. They're in deeper than anyone realizes."

Casey glanced sideways at Will, her smirk gone, her tone flat. "Well. Looks like Farmer Coltrane's traffic stop just bought us a front-row ticket to the next move."

Cole's cuffed hands twisted, his knee bouncing under the table. "Alright. Alright." His voice dropped, hoarse. "I can't give you a real name. But on the street, they call him **Ghost**."

Will's eyes narrowed. "Ghost."

Cole nodded fast, nervous sweat shining under the light. "That's all I got. He's local, but not campus. Not frat-boy trash. He moves through the parties, through the bars, never sticks long enough for anyone to pin him down. Always a step ahead. You cross him, you don't just lose your stash—you disappear. People say he's more myth than man, but I've seen him. He's real."

Casey tilted her head, smirking faintly. "Ghost. Sounds like somebody watched *Top Gun* too many times."

Cole snapped, desperate. "Laugh all you want, but he runs half the synthetics in this town, the new pills, powder, all of it. I'm just the errand boy. You want the one pulling strings? He's your guy."

Will leaned forward, voice calm but hard. "Then you'd better pray Ghost doesn't find out you said his name in this room. Because if he's half as real as you claim... you've just made yourself the next pawn."

Cole paled, shrinking back into his chair. The word lingered in the room like a curse.

Ghost.

Another Pawn

The sirens had already gone silent when Will and Casey arrived. Campus police had cordoned off the alley behind the student center, their yellow tape fluttering in the damp night air. The August heat carried a sour edge, mixing sweat, trash, and the metallic tang of blood.

Deputy Coroner Lila Rowan straightened as they ducked under the tape. Her gloves were crimson to the wrists.

"Male, early twenties," she reported crisply. "Cause of death looks like blood loss, but..." She stepped aside so they could see.

The victim's body was slumped against a dumpster, head tilted back, eyes glassy and staring. His throat was a ruin, but it wasn't ragged chaos. It was precise. The kind of line made by someone who understood anatomy. Clear punctures in his arm trailed IV tubing still looped around him, cinched like a grotesque tourniquet.

Casey exhaled sharply, jaw tight. "Jesus."

Dr. Rowan nodded grimly. "And that's not all. There's... mutilation. Postmortem castration."

Will's expression hardened. He crouched, studying the body. In the dead man's mouth, crammed between his teeth, was a white pawn smeared with blood.

Casey muttered, "Son of a Bantha... that's escalation. This isn't just a message. It's personal."

Will said nothing for a moment, eyes on the tubing, the placement, the clean precision of the cuts. Whoever had done this hadn't been frenzied. They'd been methodical.

Rowan glanced at them. "You'll want to know, ID came back. Zach Whitmore. Ravenwood senior. His family's name is all over the donor lists."

Casey frowned. "Donor lists?"

"Cain Family Scholarship Fund," Rowan clarified, stripping her gloves. "His father sits on the board. Big money, old ties. Julien Cain was practically raised at the Whitmore house."

"As in Charles Whitmore," will interjected, "one of the golf course murders"

Casey swore under her breath. "So this kid's not just another frat boy. He's Cain-adjacent."

Will straightened slowly, the weight of it pressing down. "Then this isn't a kill for the campus. This is a strike at the legacy."

Casey kicked at the damp pavement, restless energy rolling off her. "Which means we're not chasing a message anymore. We're chasing a vendetta."

Will's gaze lingered on the tubing, the way it was tied, clean and exact. A nurse's knot. Medical knowledge, applied with precision. He didn't say it out loud, but the thought lodged hard in his chest: *this wasn't improvised. This was practiced.*

Watcher Journal

Some deaths serve the board, and some deaths serve the soul. Tonight was both.

The tubing slid easy, the vein swelled obediently, the body yielded as if it had been waiting. Anatomy doesn't lie, arteries split, pressure falls, silence follows. Veins remember the touch that first broke them. So do I.

He laughed once, years ago. Laughed when I couldn't move, when the drug kept me pliant, when my voice broke trying to say stop. His laughter was the scalpel that carved me out of myself. I carried that sound until tonight.

Tonight I carved back.

A pawn was placed in his mouth, pressed so deeply that it cracked enamel. Let him choke on what he once dismissed. Pawns rise, even when kings and queens betray them.

The others were messages. This one was correction. Punishment. Balance restored.

And yet, the silence after was not relief. It was hunger. The board is not finished. The predators remain. The legacy festers.

They think the pawns are weak. They forget pawns advance. They forget pawns can reach the end of the board and change everything.

Task Force Briefing – Same Night

The task force room hummed—monitors alive, maps pinned with colored flags, printouts fanned across the table. Will slid the evidence photos forward: the IV tubing, the throat wound, the blood-smeared white pawn.

Agent Rivers leaned in, jaw set. "Walk me through it."

Will kept his tone even. "Victim is Zach Whitmore. Senior at Ravenwood. Family's old money—major donors to the Cain Family Scholarship Fund. Charles Whitmore—the father—was one of the golf course victims. Julien Cain basically grew up in their house."

Casey tapped the photo of the pawn with a knuckle. "Killer stuffed this in his mouth. Not random. It's a signature. And the cut to the throat? Surgical. Not rage—technique."

Will added, "Tubing's tied with a nurse's knot. Arm prepped like a line placement. Whoever did this has medical training or real practice. This wasn't improvised."

Rivers' gaze flicked between them, then to the whiteboard where OUROBORUS sat in block letters beside a web of names. "You think this is a gang statement or a family vendetta?"

"Feels like both," Casey said. "The pawn reads as humiliation—making Whitmore 'the first move.' But choosing this target? That's a strike at the Cain-Whitmore legacy. Someone's sending a message to the old guard."

"And we've got chatter the cartel's supplying product to Ouroborus," Will added. "If their dark-web pipeline is intersecting with campus nightlife, that may be the delivery vector—for the drugging reports and for the killer's hunting ground."

Rivers exhaled through his nose. "Alright. We treat it like a hybrid: cartel supply on one axis, legacy ties on the other." He pointed at the tubing photo. "Get me a silent consult from Medical Examiner on the knot and angle of incision—anything that narrows us to a clinician versus a field medic. And lock down any leaks; donors mean politics."

Casey nodded. "We'll also need Whitmore family schedules, board contacts, and Cain's known associates. If this is a score-settle, there'll be pressure points."

Rivers glanced toward the bullpen window, where Rachel and a tech were cross-referencing campus camera grids. "Have Donovan pull campus infirmary rosters and student orgs with clinical access—nursing, EMT, pre-med, even vet science. Anyone with hands-on practice who parties at Serpent House."

Will's pen paused. "She can parse the knot language faster than we can. She's seen how nurses actually work lines."

Rivers gave a short nod. "Good. Move fast, keep quiet. If the killer's playing chess, we're already at move two."

Casey gathered the photos, mouth a hard line. "Then let's flip the board."

Atlanta

Fox Brothers BBQ was packed, the air thick with hickory smoke, tangy sauce, and the kind of noise that only came from families and students piling in before a game weekend. Will spotted Billy in line, UNC cap backwards, lacrosse hoodie loose over his shoulders, bigger and broader than the last time Will had seen him.

"Dad!" Billy grinned, clapping him into a quick hug before they ordered pulled pork sandwiches and a tray of ribs. They found a corner table beneath a wall crowded with old team photos and barbecue trophies.

Billy unwrapped his sandwich, took a bite, and shook his head with a laugh. "Man... this is good, but it's not the same. Eastern North Carolina barbecue? Totally different, vinegar, chopped fine. That's what I'm living on at school. But this?" He pointed at the smoky, sauced meat. "Not what I grew up with in South Carolina. Still... I can't lie. We head out to Lexington every now and then. That red sauce? Think I may be in love."

Will chuckled. "So you're cheating on Carolina barbecue with Lexington?"

Billy grinned, mouth full. "I'm an equal-opportunity eater."

They ate, the small talk coming easy, Kristen's cases at the DA's office, Emily's latest sketches, Ellie's swim times.

Billy's face softened at the mention of his sisters, pride laced with a touch of worry.

"They're good kids," Will said. "They're finding their footing."

Billy leaned back, wiping sauce off his hands. "And Casey? You two still chasing down every bad guy in the galaxy?"

Will's mouth tugged in the faintest grin. "Yeah. She's still Casey, loud, sharp, impossible to miss. Work's moving fast. We've got a new intern. Rachel Donovan. Joe's kid."

Billy froze mid-bite, eyes narrowing. "Rachel? She's actually working with you?"

Will nodded. "She's sharp. Digging into social media threads, pulling stuff even our tech team overlooked."

Billy frowned. "Dad... people are talking. Even in Chapel Hill. About a... club. Dark stuff. Girls are getting dosed at parties, and videos are floating around. Everyone swears it's out of South Carolina, but some say it started way out west. Nobody knows for sure. Just... rumors."

Will's jaw tightened. "Rumors usually have roots."

Billy leaned in, serious now. "You think Emily and Ellie are safe? Freshmen, campus parties everywhere..."

Will's gaze locked on him, steady. "They're my pawns. Nobody touches them. Not while I'm breathing."

Billy nodded, though the unease lingered in his face. "I'll keep my ears open, Dad. If any of this crosses to Chapel Hill, I'll hear it. And when I'm home, I'll keep an eye on the girls. Especially Emily and Ellie."

"Good." Will's voice softened. "That's all I ask."

Billy glanced at his watch and winced. “Curfew. Coach’ll kill me if I’m late.” He stood, tossing his cap back on. “Game’s at Roe Stamps tomorrow. You’ll be in the stands?”

“Wouldn’t miss it.”

They hugged, briefly and firmly. Then Billy slipped out into the Atlanta night, leaving Will with the hickory smoke, the tang of barbecue on his tongue, and the weight of shadows closing in around his family.

Scrimmage Time

Roe Stamps Field buzzed with pre-season energy. The turf gleamed under the early afternoon sun, bleachers dotted with UNC parents in Carolina blue and Tech supporters in gold. Will took a seat halfway up, the wooden bench warm beneath him, the familiar weight of a program folded in his hands.

Below, Billy jogged across the field in his UNC jersey, stick balanced easy in his hands. Bigger, faster, more confident than the boy who used to sling balls against the garage door back home. Will felt the usual mix of pride and worry tighten in his chest.

The whistle blew. The scrimmage snapped to life.

From the start, UNC pressed hard. Billy moved like he had something to prove, quick cuts, shoulder down, driving toward the crease. His stick clattered against an opponent’s, ball scooped and gone. The stands erupted in cheers, but Will’s eyes didn’t just follow the play. His gaze kept drifting, scanning the crowd, cataloguing faces. Habit. Or maybe instinct. He told himself it was just a game, just college kids. But after everything he’d seen, “just” didn’t exist anymore.

Midway through the second quarter, Billy laid a heavy cross-check into a Georgia Tech middie. The sound carried up into the stands, carbon fiber and padding colliding hard. The ref's whistle shrieked.

"Flag down!"

The yellow cloth arced high into the air and landed on the turf. Billy threw up his hands, protesting, but the penalty was already set. One minute for unnecessary roughness.

Will exhaled through his nose, jaw tight. Old instinct flared, the same temper he'd tried to curb in himself years ago. The kid was his in more ways than looks.

Billy jogged to the sideline, helmet tipped back, face flushed with frustration. Even from the stands, Will could read the fight still simmering under his skin.

The game rolled on. UNC adjusted, killed the penalty, and Billy was back out before long, carving through the defense with a stubborn energy that made Will's chest ache with pride and unease in equal measure.

He clapped with the other parents, but his eyes never stopped roaming the bleachers, the sidelines, the open gates beyond. He had promised Billy last night he'd be there. He was. But being there meant more than just watching. It meant guarding. Always.

When the final whistle blew, Will sat for a long moment before standing, the field below alive with stick slaps and helmet taps. His son was grinning, sweat-slick and red-faced, laughing with teammates, alive in a way that looked untouchable.

Billy spotted him in the stands. Helmet tucked under his arm, mouthguard hanging loose, he lifted his stick and pointed it up at his father with a wide grin. *Did you see that?*

Will raised a hand, the ghost of a smile tugging at his mouth. For just a heartbeat, it was simple again, a dad in the stands, proud of his boy.

But as the team jogged off the field and the crowd began to thin, his gaze swept the bleachers one last time, cataloguing faces, searching shadows. Pride and unease warred in his chest.

Billy was strong, growing into a man of his own. But Will knew better than most that nobody was untouchable. Not anymore.

Post-Game

Traffic hummed low as Will pulled out of the Roe Stamps parking lot, the taste of barbecue and stadium dust still clinging to the air. His phone buzzed against the console, Billy.

"Yeah," Will answered, voice softening.

"Dad!" Billy's breath came quick, still high from the game. "You see that?"

"I saw." Will's mouth quirked. "I also saw you take a flag for that cross-check."

Billy groaned. "Yeah, coach already chewed me out. Said I've got more brawn than brains when I get riled. Guess I get that from you."

Will let the silence hang just long enough to make his point, then said, "Keep your edge, but control it. You're no good to your team in the box."

"I know." Billy sighed, but there was a smile under it. "Still, it felt good. Needed to let some steam out."

Will nodded, eyes fixed on the road. "You played hard. You're making a name for yourself. I'm proud of you, Billy."

That quieted his son for a moment. Then: "Thanks, Dad. And... thanks for coming. I know things are crazy with your cases, but it meant a lot."

"Wouldn't have missed it," Will said.

"Alright. Curfew again. Bus leaves at six sharp tomorrow. Love you, Dad."

"Love you too, son."

The line clicked off.

Will drove on in silence, Atlanta's lights smearing across the windshield. For one night he'd been just a father in the stands, clapping for his boy. Pride swelled, Billy, charging across that field, strong and sure.

But with it came the sharper ache: Emily and Ellie. Freshmen on a campus already tainted by drugs, by predators, by tapes of girls who never got justice. They weren't on a lacrosse field with whistles and refs to call the penalties. Their game was played in shadows, where rules didn't exist and mistakes carried costs that couldn't be undone.

Three games ran through his mind at once: Billy's fight on the turf, Emily and Ellie navigating Ravenwood, and the one he and Casey waged every night on the board against a predator who thought life was nothing but pieces to be moved.

Will tightened his grip on the wheel. He'd cheer for his son, protect his daughters, and keep pushing the case forward.

Because in every game, he couldn't afford to lose.

Home Cooked Meal

The front door banged open just as Kristen was setting the casserole on the table. Casey swept in, hair windblown, jacket half-off, looking both flustered and hungry.

"Smells like heaven in here," she said, dropping into the first empty chair she found. "Tell me that's food and not just some fancy candle."

Kristen smirked. "Chicken casserole. Aunt Anne's recipe. Secret ingredient I'll never tell."

Casey dished herself a heaping scoop, took one bite, and froze mid-chew. Her eyes went wide. "Holy Bantha fodder. Kristen, this is better than anything I've ever put in my mouth. And I mean *anything.* You'd better invite me into the kitchen next time, wink wink."

Kristen shook her head, amused. "You can watch all you want, Murphy, but the recipe's staying in the family."

Will chuckled, rolling his eyes. "Billy asked about everyone over dinner last night in Atlanta. He's worried about the girls, about Kristen, even about me. But not you, Casey."

Casey arched a brow, mouth full.

Will grinned faintly. "He said you'd probably take out some creep with a force choke and then throw him out the airlock by his nuts."

Casey pointed her fork at him. "Damn right I would."

Laughter rippled around the table, warm and easy for the first time in weeks.

A little later, Emily padded down the stairs barefoot, her damp hair hanging loose, wearing an oversized T-shirt and boy shorts. She plopped into the empty chair without ceremony, reaching for a roll.

Will raised a brow. "Laundry outfit, or campus commute outfit? Because that doesn't look like travel wear."

Emily grinned sheepishly. "Laundry. I came home to do it, and I'm crashing here tonight. Easier to head back in the morning after dinner and dessert tonight."

Casey leaned back, eyes flicking over Emily's getup. "Wait a second. Nobody told me the official dinner attire around here was underwear." She tapped her fork against her plate with mock gravity. "If I'd known, I'd have worn something nicer. Maybe the black lace. Or hell, maybe nothing at all, make it a real dinner party."

"Casey!" Kristen groaned, smacking her napkin against the table.

Emily nearly snorted her drink through her nose, laughing so hard she doubled over.

Will just shook his head, though his lips tugged at the corners. "And people wonder why I worry less about you than anyone else."

Casey raised her glass. "Because I keep morale up, Anderson. It's a public service."

Kristen sighed but couldn't quite hide her smile. She pushed back from the table, heading toward the kitchen counter. "Well, morale's about to get better. My sister,

Brittany Jo Hensley, dropped off one of her famous peach cobblers this afternoon. Still warm."

Casey's eyes lit up. "Oh, hell yes. First the casserole, now cobbler? Kristen, if you don't lock me in as family after this, I'm filing a complaint."

Emily giggled, reaching for a plate. "You already act like family."

Two chairs sat empty, though. Will glanced at them as he reached for the basket of rolls. "Ellie's running late from swim practice. And Rachel texted, saying she couldn't make it. Meeting a friend for coffee, helping her study anatomy."

Emily snorted from her place at the far end. "Didn't Rachel ace anatomy back in nursing school? Sounds like somebody's trying to show off."

Kristen shot her a look, but Casey only smirked. "Extra credit never hurt anybody."

Kristen set the cobbler down in the center of the table, steam curling up into the air. "Then you know the rule: family doesn't get to know the recipe, either."

Casey groaned theatrically. "Fine, but I'm not above blackmail. This cobbler and that casserole? You two might actually kill me with kindness."

The laughter bubbled again, and for a while the only sounds were spoons scraping plates, warm chatter, and the kind of comfort food that made the world's ugliness feel far away.

After Dinner

Plates clattered softly into the sink, the warm hum of the dishwasher filling the kitchen. The twins' laughter still carried faintly from the living room where Casey and Emily argued about which *Star Wars* movie counted as the best, their voices sharp and playful over the TV chatter.

Kristen handed Will a dish towel, brushing her hair back with her wrist. "Billy's worried. You could hear it in the way you told the story at the table."

Will dried a plate, eyes lingering on the smear of peach cobbler left on the edge before stacking it neatly. "He is. Said the rumors about this... club, whatever Ouroboros is calling itself, are floating all the way to Chapel Hill. That's how wide it's spread."

Kristen leaned against the counter, arms folded, her wine glass cradled in one hand. "And he's not wrong to worry about his sisters. Freshman year, girls walking alone across campus, parties every weekend..." She trailed off, then fixed him with a steady look. "I worry too."

Will didn't deny it. He set down the towel, leaning on the counter beside her. "I promised him I'd keep them safe. All of them. He'll do what he can from a hundred miles away, but here? That's on me."

Kristen studied his profile, her voice softening. "You've been carrying it all, Will. Billy. Emily. Ellie. Even Rachel. And now she's missing a family dinner, suddenly she's out studying anatomy with a 'friend.'"

Will's jaw flexed. "She's Joe's kid. Smart. Capable. But I can't shake the feeling she's... playing at something. Too polished. Too deliberate. And if she is..." He trailed off.

Kristen touched his arm lightly. "Then you'll see it before anyone else. You always do."

He nodded once, but the hard set of his mouth didn't ease.

Kristen let the silence stretch, then added gently, "Just... don't let whatever you feel about Rachel bleed onto Emily and Ellie. They trust her. They still see her as someone safe. If you start treating her like a suspect in front of them, it'll rattle their sense of security too."

Will's eyes flicked toward the living room where Emily's laugh rang out. He swallowed, voice low. "I know. I won't let that happen."

For a moment, they just stood there, shoulder to shoulder, the smell of casserole and cobbler still hanging warm in the air.

From the other room came the sound of bare feet slapping across the hardwood. Ellie had finally made it home from swim practice, fresh from the shower, hair damp, tank top clinging to her, darting past in nothing but underwear. She squealed as Casey lunged for her, snagging her around the waist and pulling her onto the couch. Emily dissolved into giggles beside them, the three of them a tangle of limbs and laughter.

Will muttered, half to himself, "Is it just me, or has the Anderson family dinner dress code officially become underwear?"

Kristen shot him a look over her shoulder, smothering a smile. "Don't start."

Casey's voice rang out, shameless and loud. "Admit it, Emily! *Empire* beats *Return of the Jedi* any day!"

Emily shrieked back, "You're insane!" while Ellie groaned dramatically, "Can we *please* not do this again?"

Will and Kristen shared a quieter look, the corner of her mouth quirking despite the heaviness of their talk.

"Normal," Kristen said softly. "At least for tonight."

Will nodded, drying the last glass. "Yeah. For tonight."

But when his eyes drifted to the empty chair still pushed under the dining room table, the shadow of unease lingered.

Back on the Patio

The crickets and cicadas hummed outside while the last clatter of dishes faded from the kitchen. Will and Casey settled into chairs on the patio, the glow of a citronella candle flickering between them.

Casey stretched her legs out with a sigh. "You know, Anderson, I never thought in a million years I'd go from rookie cop on patrol to sitting here as Detective Will Anderson's homicide partner. Feels like I tripped and fell into somebody else's life."

Will lit a match, the flame catching on the end of the cigar Casey had pulled from the humidor in Kristen's kitchen. He took a drag and handed it to her. "You earned it, Murphy. Every step. Don't think I don't know it."

She puffed once, smirk curling. "Yeah? Funny, because half the time you look at me like you're still wondering what planet I landed from."

"That's only when you start speaking in Star Wars," Will deadpanned. "I had to watch the whole saga just to understand half your jokes."

Casey barked a laugh, smoke curling out with it. "And here I thought you were doing it for the culture."

They passed the cigar back and forth, quiet settling between them for a moment. Then Casey leaned her head back against the chair, a grin spreading wide. "Since you asked... I'm wearing a pair of cheeky Chewbacca underwear. You know, up front they look furry, so I don't have to worry."

Will exhaled through his nose, unimpressed. "I didn't ask."

"No," Casey shot back, eyes twinkling, "but I saw you looking under the table to see if I'd shed my pants at dinner. Thought I shouldn't leave you in the dark."

Will shook his head. "You're the sister I never wanted."

Casey punched him in the shoulder, not gently. "And you're the brother I got stuck with." She stood, brushing off her hands. "Alright, Skywalker. I'm heading out before I start confessing what's on the rest of my underwear."

Will leaned back, puffing on the cigar. "I've got something for you to take the edge off once you get home."

Casey's brows arched. "Oh?"

"You'll see." His tone was even, but his eyes glinted.

She narrowed her gaze, amused but curious. "Fine. But if it's another homework assignment, I'm calling HR."

Will just smiled, the kind that meant she'd have to wait as he slid out of his chair.

Casey's Call to Will

The night hummed with cicadas as Casey eased her car out of Will's driveway. Habit more than thought had her steering toward the PD instead of her place, headlights cutting through the quiet street.

That's when she saw it.

A black SUV sat parked up the road, dark windows reflecting just enough of her beams to prickle the back of her neck. She pressed the gas a little harder, keeping it in her mirror.

A few blocks later, she cursed herself and swung around, wrong direction. She needed to head toward her house. She made a sharp turn and rechecked her mirror. The SUV was gone.

Her phone was already at her ear by the time Will answered.

"Anderson."

"It's me," Casey said, voice clipped. "Listen, when I pulled out of your drive, I went toward the PD instead of home. Caught a black SUV sitting up the road, lights off. When I turned back the right way, toward my place, I'm pretty damn sure they flipped around after me."

Will's tone went hard and calm. "You get a plate?"

"Partial. Georgia tag, six-two, maybe a D. Couldn't catch the rest. The lights flashed too quickly. Could've been a second car too, but this one felt—" She broke off, jaw tight. "Cartel. Or damn close."

Kristen's voice cut in from the kitchen, sharp with alarm. "Cartel?" She grabbed her own phone, already dialing. "I'll give Rivers a heads up."

"Do it," Will said. Into the receiver, his voice steadied Casey like a hand on her shoulder. "I'll have dispatch send one unit toward your place, another past me. We'll box them in if they try to shadow. Stay on the line." Will grabbed his radio off its charger.

Casey drew a slow breath through her teeth, eyes flicking across her mirrors. "Copy that."

Kristen's call connected, loud enough that Will could hear Rivers on the other end. "You did the right thing calling me," the DHS agent said firmly. "I'll spin up surveillance feeds near Anderson's block. If cartel vehicles are creeping through neighborhoods, I want eyes on every camera within a mile. Text me that partial tag."

Kristen rattled it off, her voice low but clipped, and Rivers promised, "We'll cross-check it in minutes. I'll keep your people looped."

A woman's voice crackled through the radio Will was holding, low and even with a drawl that carried calm authority. Officer Savanna Jo Coltrane. "Copy that. Husband was polite, wife was chatty, and the retriever in the backseat looked like he'd rather lick me to death than bite. Vehicle's clear."

Back on Casey's line, Will's voice returned. "Unit just flagged down a black SUV with your partial. Pulled it over for a rolling stop. Not cartel, just a couple heading home from the country club restaurant. Golf clothes, dog in the backseat. Clean."

Casey exhaled hard, a half-laugh cracking. "Son of a Bantha. Spooked myself."

"Not spooked," Will corrected. "Cautious. Next time it's not golf clubbers, I want you alive to call it in."

Kristen cupped her phone, murmuring to Will, "Rivers says he'll keep teams on the feeds tonight. If something circles back, we'll know."

And then Rivers himself came clearer through the speaker, his voice low, edged with steel: "If cartel eyes are on Murphy, they're on all of you. Treat it like a warning shot. They're testing the fence."

The line went quiet.

Casey rolled her shoulders, tension finally bleeding out. "Alright. I'll take the escort the rest of the way... and maybe two fingers of that Buffalo Trace when I hit the couch."

Will's voice softened just a notch. "Take three. You earned it."

Targeting the Tower

Dinner at the Andersons had been loud, warm, messy, a comfort she didn't realize she needed. Out on the patio afterward, the night cicadas humming, Will had pressed a brown-papered bottle into her hands.

"Buffalo Trace," he said. "For when you finally sit down instead of running marathons around this case."

Casey grinned, hefting it. "And here I was out of adult beverages. Guess you *are* good for something besides paperwork, partner."

He gave her that patient, steady look. "Don't drink it all in one night."

She smirked. "No promises."

Her apartment was dark when she stepped inside, the hinges creaking like they always did. She shut the door with her hip and kicked off her boots, letting them clatter in a heap by the mat.

"Laundry, Murphy," she muttered, eyeing the basket already heaped with a week's worth of uniforms. "One of these days..."

In the bedroom, she peeled herself down layer by layer. Belt, holster, sidearm secured in the lockbox. Embroidered polo tossed into the basket. Finally, the last stubborn clasp gave way and she exhaled, rolling her shoulders loose. Tactical pants puddled at her feet, replaced by a soft, thinning T-shirt that had survived years longer than it should have.

The mirror caught her eye: hair coming loose, faint bruise on her forearm, dark crescents under her eyes. She smirked anyway. "Leia, eat your heart out."

Padding barefoot to the kitchen, she tugged open the fridge door, and groaned. It was practically empty. Just one lonely bottle of lemon-lime soda sat in the back like a forgotten prize.

"Figures," she muttered, grabbing it. "Should've known the twins would drink me dry." Emily and Ellie had raided her fridge last week after a late-night movie marathon, leaving behind nothing but crumbs and one soda.

She set a glass on the counter and uncapped the Buffalo Trace Will had given her. The bourbon splashed amber, sharp and sweet. She tipped in the soda, fizz rising like a hiss. She remembered that exchange student's advice, *kalimotxo*, mix it with cola or soda, it hits faster.

Casey grinned. "Why not? Tonight's all about shortcuts and stress relievers."

She took a long sip, wincing at the sugary edge, then carried it to the couch. *The Lincoln Lawyer* flickered to life on Prime, voices low and steady. She curled into the cushions, glass in hand, letting the day finally, finally bleed away.

By the second sip, her limbs felt heavier than they should.

By the third, a minute later, the room blurred.

Casey frowned at the glass, at the fizzing soda. "What the—"

It slipped from her hand, shattering on the floorboards.

And from the corner of her eye, a shadow moved toward her.

When consciousness crawled back, it wasn't air that greeted her.

It was water. And fabric.

Casey jerked awake into the darkness that clung to her face. Her arms were wrenched behind her, shoulders screaming from the angle. Zip ties bit into her wrists, each panicked tug only making them dig deeper, hot ridges burning against her skin. Her ankles were cinched the same way, tight plastic biting bone. She tried to kick, but realized with horror that her wrists and ankles were tethered together. Hogtied.

Wet. Naked. Cold. Trapped.

Her chest heaved, but every gasp dragged water and cloth against her mouth and nose. A soaked bag was tied down over her head, plastering against her skin with every inhale, suffocating. A strap or cord cinched it tight at her throat, sealing it in place.

She tried to scream but only gagged, choking around something shoved deep in her mouth, something coarse, familiar. Lace. Her lace.

Her own underwear stuffed between her teeth, sealed with tape. The humiliation burned even hotter than the fear.

Casey's mind fractured into shards. *What the hell is happening? What has happened?*

The hiss of freezing cold water answered her. The shower rained down relentlessly, pounding the cloth against her skin, filling the tub beneath her. It was already climbing past her thighs, her hips, licking at her ribs.

Her lungs screamed for air.

No. Not like this. Not drowned in my own damn tub.

She twisted, bucked, thrashed, the plastic bit deeper, her shoulders flaring white-hot with pain. Water sloshed higher, the bag tightening against her face as every splash soaked it through.

A sound cut through the roar, soft, low. A chuckle. Muffled. Mocking, noise of someone moving nearby, the digital click of a camera phone.

Casey froze. Was it real? Or was her oxygen-starved brain already betraying her? What are they going to do to me? What have they done to me?

Her pulse thundered so loudly that it drowned out the water. Panic clawed at her chest, sharp and merciless.

Breathe. Fight. Don't give them the satisfaction. Don't let them win.

But the water kept rising. Higher. Higher.

Her body spasmed, lungs convulsing. Her mind ricocheted between rage and terror, trying to hold on to thought, to strategy, but the bag stole her vision, the gag stole her scream, and the rising water stole everything else.

This is it. This is how they want me gone.

And then she thrashed again, because if she were going to die in her own damn tub, she'd make them work for it.

The pounding in Casey's ears shifted, water, heartbeat, and then... a voice.

"Casey?"

Faint at first, muffled through the bag. Then louder. "Casey? You home?"

The front door creaked open.

It was Emily.

Casey tried to yell, but the gag and water swallowed the sound. Mind racing, they thought they were going to get Emily now. No God, No! They were *still here.*

Emily's footsteps carried through the apartment, quick, uneven, her voice climbing with panic. "Casey?! Hey, Casey, I'm here! I need some womanly advice!" "Hey, Casey! You in –"

She followed the sound of the running shower, pushed the bathroom door open, and froze.

"Holy shit–"

Emily's bag slipped from her shoulder, thudding to the floor. For a beat, she couldn't move. Her best friend, her second mom, bound and naked in the tub, a soaked hood clinging to her head, water rising around her. It looked like something out of a nightmare.

Emily lunged forward, fumbling with the knots at Casey's neck, yanking the gag free. The wet lace tore loose, tape scraping skin as it came away. Casey coughed violently, choking up water, sucking in ragged gulps of air.

Emily twisted the shower knobs off with shaking hands, the cascade silencing. The only sounds left were Casey's rasping breaths and the frantic pounding of Emily's heart.

"Em–" Casey's voice was raw, shredded. "Next time, kid... knock first. Not exactly how I planned the slumber party reveal."

"Shut up! Shut up!" Emily snapped, tears in her voice. "Don't—don't joke about this!"

She spun, eyes scanning wildly until she spotted the knife on Casey's nightstand in the bedroom. She sprinted, grabbed it, and came back, her hands trembling so hard the blade shook.

Casey sagged against the side of the tub wall, blinking through water and humiliation as Emily sawed at the zip ties. Water still draining. Plastic snapped one by one until Casey's limbs came free, mottled with angry ridges.

Emily's cheeks burned crimson, tears streaking down. "I—I wasn't prepared to find you naked and bagged like a freaking hostage first thing in the morning! What the hell, Casey? Why does shit like this always happen?"

Casey gave a wet, shaky laugh, half delirious. "Welcome to detective life. All the secrets out of the way with you... just like my first week with your dad." She reached blindly for the bathroom counter, fingers brushing a razor. She gripped it tight, grounding herself, raising the razor as a conversation piece in front of Emily. "Your dad saw how I do business, Leia-in-the-bikini style."

Emily stared at her, shaking, torn between horror and relief. She steadied Casey as best she could, wrapping an arm around her slick shoulders. "You about died, and you want to talk to me about shaving your bikini line, god, you're so grounded." She wrapped her arms around Casey and buried her head against her wet shoulder.

Casey leaned into her, hair dripping on Emily's back, forcing a smirk. *Survive. Smile. Pretend it doesn't break you.*

But inside, she was trembling, not from cold, but from rage. From fear. From the memory of almost drowning, bagged and hogtied, gagged with lace that was hers. Humiliated in her own shower.

And from the sickening realization that the underwear shoved between her teeth hadn't gone missing last night at all. It had been gone since the previous break-in, when her entire drawer was completely emptied out, except for a creepy note. A violation she'd tried to laugh off, bury, pretend she could forget.

They hadn't just taken it.

They'd kept it.

Waited.

Used it.

This wasn't just about control anymore. It was a message, written in the most intimate theft imaginable.

Her own damn shower.

Her own damn lace.

Twisted into a weapon against her.

Casey's chest tightened, a fresh wave of rage clawing up her throat. She wanted to scream, to shatter something, to tear the whole apartment down until there wasn't a shadow left to hide in.

Instead, she forced a jagged laugh, rasping around the rawness in her throat. "Well... guess that makes me the galaxy's least glamorous Leia. Wrong chains, wrong setting. Ten out of ten, do not recommend."

Emily stared at her like she'd lost her mind. "Casey, that's not funny."

Casey squeezed her hand, her eyes sharp despite the exhaustion. “Kid... It’s either laugh like Solo with a blaster to his head, or let them see me broken. And I don’t break.”

Inside, though, she was shaking so hard she could feel it in her teeth. The memory of what had just happened, and the memory that she had none since last night.

Emily went and sat on Casey's bed, dazed and emotional. Casey, needing a drink of water to soothe her raspy throat, walked into the kitchen.

On the counter, propped against the empty Buffalo Trace bottle, sat a chess note scrawled in precise ink:

Rooks fall when queens betray pawns.

Casey hadn’t made it far. She sat on the kitchen floor, bare skin goose-pimpled against the cold tile, her arms wound tight around her knees, her head resting forward. Naked, soaked, her hair dripping onto her shoulders in dark rivulets. The folded note leaned against the half-empty bottle of Buffalo Trace on the counter above her, taunting in its quiet presence.

Emily paced the length of the kitchen, phone clutched tight in her hand. Her voice wavered as she spoke into it. “Dad—it’s Emily. You need to come. Now. It’s Casey—she was... she was in the shower, tied up, drowning—” She broke off, voice cracking. “I got her loose, but... she’s not okay. Please, hurry.”

She turned back toward Casey, frantic. “What do I do? I don’t know what to do.”

Casey didn't lift her head. Her breath came ragged, her shoulders trembling, but she managed a rasp of words. "You... already did it, kid. You got me out."

Emily bit her lip, pacing harder, glancing at the front door. It was still ajar, the night air bleeding into the room. "I thought—I swear—I thought I heard someone leave when I was cutting you free. What if they're still out there?"

She slammed the door shut, the frame rattling with the impact. The motion jolted the counter, and the folded slip of paper toppled to the floor, landing inches from Casey's bare feet.

Casey blinked, her eyes dragging to it. The black scrawl blurred at first, then sharpened as if the words had waited for her to see them:

A rook protects pawns, but even rooks can be toppled.

Her throat tightened. She dragged a trembling hand across her face, smearing away water, trying to anchor herself. Will was coming. She knew him well enough—he'd be cutting through traffic like a man possessed, lights or no lights, to get here.

She let out a shaky exhale, forcing a thread of dry humor into her voice, though her eyes stayed fixed on the note. "Kid... I'll bet your dad's already hitting light speed."

But her gaze didn't waver from the paper on the floor. Not anymore.

The slam of the car door still echoed when another sound cut through the apartment, heavy, determined footsteps on the stones outside, then the sharp rattle of the doorknob.

Emily's phone slipped from her hand. "He's here."

The door swung wide. Will filled the frame, chest heaving from the sprint up, eyes blazing as they swept the room in an instant: Emily pale and shaking, Casey curled on the kitchen floor, naked, dripping, the note at her feet like a brand.

"Jesus, Casey—" He was beside her before the door finished closing, dropping to a crouch, his coat already coming off. He wrapped it around her shoulders, shielding her without hesitation. His jaw was clenched so tight it looked like it might crack.

Casey lifted her head a fraction, her eyes red-rimmed but defiant. She forced a hoarse laugh. "Relax, partner. You don't gotta play knight in shining armor every damn time."

Will ignored the joke. His hand came to rest at the back of her head, grounding her. "They did this here? In your own place?" His voice was low, dangerous.

Emily hovered near the counter, arms wrapped around herself. "She—she was tied in the shower. Drowning. And then I found that—" She pointed at the note, her voice breaking. "And I swear I heard someone leave when I was cutting her free."

Will's eyes flicked to the folded paper on the tile. He reached out, careful, sliding it into an evidence bag from his pocket. His lips pressed into a hard line as he read.

A rook protects pawns, but even rooks can be toppled.

He closed the bag with a snap, his gaze dark. "This wasn't just about scaring you." His hand tightened briefly at Casey's shoulder, grounding himself as much as her. "This was a warning."

Casey tilted her head against his arm, her voice soft but edged. "Then let's send one back."

Will was still crouched at her side, his arm steady around her shoulders, when Emily pulled in a shaky breath.

"I didn't know what to do," she whispered. "I just... I found her like that. And the water—God, the water was almost over her—"

Will's voice cut through, calm but firm. "You did exactly what you needed to do, Emily. You saved her life."

Emily nodded, biting her lip hard, but her eyes kept flicking toward the bathroom like she expected to see the scene replay itself.

Casey let them talk, let the words flow around her like static. She sat with her arms around her knees, chin pressed against her forearms, staring down at the tiles.

Inside, she was unraveling.

She could still feel it—the plastic biting her wrists, the cold water climbing, the gag filling her mouth until she thought she'd choke on her own breath. Her lace. Her underwear drawer. The last break-in. The way her own body had been turned into a joke, a message.

Her shower.

Her space.

No longer hers.

The thought made her tremble so hard her teeth almost clicked. She tried to clamp down, force stillness into her muscles, but the shakes betrayed her.

Breathe, Murphy. Don't let them see it. Don't let them win.

She tilted her head back, a smirk tugging at her lips, though her eyes burned. "Well... guess I'll need to upgrade my home security from deadbolt to lightsaber or move, this is one too many intrusions, somebody using the force to unlock my doors."

Emily's laugh cracked, brittle, and choked, but it was enough to break the tension for a breath. Will's eyes flicked to her, but he didn't call her on it. He knew. He'd seen it before—Casey's quips when she was rattled were armor, not comedy.

Casey gripped her hands tighter around her legs, hiding the tremor in her palm with the curve of her knee. Inside, the terror still clawed at her chest, but her voice came steady.

"Don't worry, kid. Your dad is about to burn rubber like Han hitting hyperspace. We'll get through this."

But in the back of her mind, the water was still rising.

Her gaze slid to the note again, the words crawling under her skin. *A rook protects pawns...*

Emily. Ellie.

Her stomach churned. Whoever wrote this wasn't just in her head; they were watching her pawns, her Em and El.

Watcher Journal

The rook stands tall, but towers fall.

It is not enough to guard the pawns.

Strength without foresight is vanity.

Protection without obedience is failure.

Even stone can be eroded by water, and pride will drown faster than flesh.

The board advances.

Shadows in the Dark

The cartel's presence spreads through Oakhaven like a sickness. Their trucks idle at corners, too shiny, too slow, their tinted glass hiding eyes that never blink. They roam past the Anderson house again and again, circling it as if they own the street. The family inside laughs at a television show, unaware that death lingers just outside their windows.

Kristen Anderson was followed this afternoon. She ran her errands as if the world were still ordinary—coffee, groceries, a quick stop at the pharmacy. She smiled at the clerk, carried her bags, never noticing the black SUV that trailed her from block to block. She did not see how they measured her every pause, how they studied the times she unlocked her door, how long she left the house when she was alone. She did not see the message they tried to send: *We know you. We know where you go. You are a threat to us.*

Casey Murphy's apartment drew the same attention—engines that idled, strangers who lingered. They marked her too. The detectives believe they are hunters, but recently they have been the prey.

And then, the twins. Emily and Ellie left swim practice with towels looped around their shoulders, hair dripping, the smell of chlorine clinging to their skin. They laughed, free and bright, their feet slapping the wet pavement as they walked the trails back to campus from the dorm.

He followed, not in a truck, but on foot. One of the cartel's scavengers, slipping from shadow to shadow, his eyes fixed too long on young women who should never be noticed. His pace was calculated, his hands restless in his jacket pockets. He thought himself invisible.

But I was there.

I walked when he walked, matching his pace and staying in his blind spots. I observed how he leaned forward, noting how his hunger grew each time the girls slowed down to adjust their towels or shift their bags. His breath quickened. He was close enough to reach them – too close.

He will not make that mistake again. He thought the pawns were unprotected, but he hadn't learned the rules of this game. Tonight, he will learn. I will peel him from the shadows he hides in and leave him where no one would think to look. His disappearance will be quiet, absolute, and final. The streets of Oakhaven are deep, and the city forgets the faces of those who vanish.

The innocent pawns are safe because I decide they are safe.

He followed them.

And now he will pay the price.

Pawns Under Siege

A few days later, Ellie frowned at her phone as she crossed the quad, the late afternoon sunlight cutting sharp lines across Ravenwood's red-brick buildings. Notifications buzzed again and again, not from friends or group chats, but from an unknown number.

Be careful who you smile at.

Not everyone deserves your time.

Pawns get taken when they forget the board.

Her chest tightened. She slowed, scanning the students drifting past with backpacks, iced coffees, and earbuds. Some were laughing, some glued to their phones, but every glance over her shoulder felt loaded. Nobody looked back. Everybody looked back.

Her phone buzzed again.

Red isn't your color. Change before tonight.

Ellie froze mid-step. She looked down. Red hoodie. Kansas City Chiefs logo. The blood drained from her face.

"Ellie!"

She jumped, spinning to see Emily jogging toward her, braid bouncing, arms full of sketch pads and supplies. Her sister's grin faded as she took in Ellie's expression. "What's wrong? You look like you saw a ghost."

Ellie shoved the phone into her pocket. "Nothing. Just—my battery's dying."

Emily cocked her head, not buying it. "That's your lying voice."

Before Ellie could reply, someone brushed past them in the crowd. Emily's eyes tracked automatically, and then froze.

Her breath hitched. Same braid. Same jacket. Same earrings

Her. A carbon copy of herself, striding away, earbuds in, not even glancing their way.

Emily's stomach dropped like she'd been shoved off a ledge. "Ellie..."

Ellie blinked. "What?"

"Tell me you saw that." Emily's voice was barely audible, cracking at the edges.

Ellie twisted, searching the tide of students, but the girl was gone, swallowed by the crowd. "Saw what?"

Emily rubbed her arms, suddenly cold though the sun still beat down. "Her. Me. Again. Same braid, same clothes, same everything. I swear to God, it was like looking in a mirror that just... walked away. She looked right, but wrong. Like she was—studying me. Wearing me."

Ellie's skin crawled. She fumbled her phone back out, hand trembling, and showed Emily the messages. The words glared up from the screen like open wounds.

Emily read, her face paling to a bleached white, her fingers tightening on the sketch pads until the cardboard bent. "Ellie... this is—this is stalking. This is..." Her voice cracked. "They're watching us. Right now."

Neither of them spoke for a long moment. The quad moved around them, sunlight flickering off the library windows, laughter and chatter floating like normal life. But to the Anderson twins, the world had shifted. The air pressed heavier, shadows stretched longer. Every laugh was suddenly sharp, aimed. Every eye lingered too long.

Emily grabbed Ellie's hand, squeezing until her knuckles whitened. "We tell Casey. Now. Dads in court all day, I don't care if she's buried in work. She needs to know."

Ellie nodded, but her throat tightened as she shoved the phone back in her pocket. A sour certainty gnawed at her chest.

Whoever was watching didn't just want them afraid.

They wanted them moved, one square at a time, across a board only they could see.

Watcher Journal

Pawns under siege.

They don't see the board. They never do.

One laughs too freely, squandering the strength of silence. The other questions everything, unaware that questions draw attention. They cling to each other as if that is safety. They do not understand that safety is an illusion. Protection is earned, not assumed.

The copy was necessary. A reflection in motion. To show her how fragile her identity is, how easily it can be borrowed, worn, and shed. If she feels unsettled in her skin, then she is learning. Pawns must learn.

And the messages? A warning. Not cruelty. Not yet. Pawns who smile at the wrong pieces invite capture. A careless gesture can cost everything.

They think they are free, wandering squares of their choosing. But every step is already mapped, each path already calculated. They are not lost. They are being moved.

One square at a time.

Call Casey

Ellie's hands were shaking so badly she almost dropped the phone. Emily finally snatched it from her, pressed call, and paced in a tight circle while it rang.

"Come on, come on..." Emily muttered.

On the fourth ring, Casey's voice answered, brisk and a little tired. "Murphy."

"Casey, it's us." Emily's voice cracked. "Ellie and I."

Instant alertness. "What happened? Where are you?"

Ellie leaned in so Casey could hear. "We got messages from an unknown number. They knew what I was wearing. They called us pawns, said I shouldn't smile at people. And–" she swallowed, her throat tight– "they said red isn't my color. I was in a red hoodie, Casey. They saw me. Right there."

There was silence on the other end, just a sharp exhale. Then Casey's voice, low and steady, the one she used when things went bad. "Alright. First things first, you're together?"

"Yes," Emily said quickly. "We're still on campus. But Casey—" She broke off, glancing over her shoulder. "I saw it again. Her. Me. Someone dressed exactly like me. Down to the braid. She walked right past us."

Another pause. Casey's voice tightened. "Okay. Listen to me. You two are going to get to the Student Union. Somewhere with people, cameras, light. Don't split up, don't play hero. You stick together until I get there."

Emily squeezed Ellie's hand, nodding fast even though Casey couldn't see. "Okay. We'll move."

Ellie's voice wavered. "Casey... what does this mean? Why us?"

Casey was quiet for a moment, and when she spoke again, her tone was softer, but hard underneath. "It means someone's trying to rattle you. But here's the thing—nobody rattles my pawns. You're under my protection. You get me?"

Ellie bit her lip. "Got you."

"And for the record," Casey added, her voice sharpening just a hair, "if this creep thinks they can play Star Wars with us, they're about to find out I'm not just the Rook. I'm Chewie with a blaster. And I don't miss."

Despite the fear clawing at her chest, Emily gave a shaky laugh. "Only you would drag Star Wars into this."

"Hey, kid," Casey said. "If it buys me one second of calm before I storm in, I'll quote Jar Jar Binks. Now get to the Union. I'm en route."

The line went dead. The twins looked at each other, fear still sharp in their eyes, but steadied, just a little, by the voice that had promised to come running.

The Student Union buzzed with life when Emily and Ellie slipped inside. Groups of students lounged on couches, the smell of coffee and fried food clinging to the air. Bright lights overhead made it feel safer, but the twins stuck close together, scanning every face.

Ellie kept whispering, "They're here. Watching. I can feel it."

Emily squeezed her hand. "Casey's coming. Just hold on."

Outside, Casey's unmarked sedan screeched into a parking spot. She yanked her phone out even before her boots hit pavement, punching Will's number on instinct. It rang once, twice—then kicked to voicemail.

"Damn it, Will," she muttered, pacing toward the doors. She knew where he was. Court. Which meant his phone was off, sealed away in some leather bag at the metal detectors. Which meant she was on her own for now.

She slipped the phone back into her pocket, jaw tight. "Fine. Rook it is."

The glass doors banged open. Casey strode in, eyes cutting over the room like she was sweeping for hostiles. She spotted the twins immediately, waved them over to a quiet corner table, and sat down opposite them.

"Phones. Both of you. Now."

They slid them across. Casey pulled a slim tool from her pocket, her thumb scrolling with surgical precision. "Encrypted texts. No return number. Could be a clone. Could be a mirror app. Hell, it could be smoke and mirrors with a third-party spoof." She slid them back with a grim set to her jaw. "Point is, someone's inside your digital pockets."

Emily's shoulders hunched. "So they know where we are. Right now?"

Casey glanced around the Union, her voice steady but sharp. "Not necessarily. If they had full access, they'd know I was coming too. And trust me—nobody with half a brain wants to tango with me when I'm pissed off."

Ellie gave a shaky laugh. "That's supposed to make me feel better?"

"Kid," Casey said, leaning in, "I just compared myself to Chewbacca with a blaster. You ever see Chewie miss?"

Emily cracked a tiny smile despite herself. "Nope."

"Exactly. So yeah. You're covered."

But Emily's face stayed pale. She tugged her braid over one shoulder, voice low. "Casey... what about her? The double? It wasn't in my head. It was me. My clothes. My walk. Like she studied me."

Casey leaned back, arms crossing, expression sharpening. "Not fashion. Deliberate. Somebody's watching closely. Which means they're on campus. Which means..." Her jaw flexed. "We don't screw around."

The words landed heavily. The Union chatter muffled, the room suddenly too loud and too quiet all at once.

Ellie's hands twisted in her lap. "So what do we do?"

"You do what you're doing right now. You stay together. No solo missions. No detours. And if anything feels off—I don't care if it's a weird look or someone sneezes wrong—you call me. I'll be here before they finish blinking."

The twins exchanged a look, scared but steadied a little.

Casey forced a grin she didn't quite feel. "Hey—remember, pawns only fall if the rook's asleep on the job. And I don't sleep."

She stood, scanning the Union one last time. Too many faces. Too many eyes.

And with Will out of reach, the certainty hit hard.

This was on her.

Watcher from Above

From the mezzanine above the Union, the view was perfect.

The Watcher leaned against the railing, one elbow propped casually as though just another student killing time between classes. Below, Casey Murphy cut through the crowd like a blade, her presence impossible to miss. The twins sat where she placed them, obedient pawns at their rook's command.

How touching.

Phones passed across the table. Casey's eyes are scanning. The twins were clinging to every word like frightened children.

The Watcher smiled faintly, notebook balanced on one knee. Each movement was cataloged: Emily tugging her braid when nervous, Ellie's restless shifting when lying, Casey's habit of sweeping the exits twice before settling her gaze on the person in front of her. All the tells. All the weaknesses.

The words floated up faintly from below. Not clear, but enough. Rook. Pawns. Protection.

Casey thought she could hold the board. That was her flaw. A rook only moved in lines. Predictable. Straightforward. Easy to anticipate.

The Watcher's fingers brushed the smooth pawn in their pocket, rolling it slowly until the edges pressed against the skin. Pawns didn't need the rook to survive. They only needed the right player. Someone who saw their value. Someone who could move them into power.

Casey looked up then, eyes scanning the second level, but the Watcher had already blended back, posture slack, notebook closed. Just another student, nothing remarkable. Invisible in plain sight.

Below, Casey leaned closer to the twins, all protective warmth and grit, pulling them in like they were hers. The sight twisted something sharp inside the Watcher's chest.

They weren't hers. They were pawns.

And pawns, when guided, could rise.

The Watcher turned and walked away, melting into the current of students changing classes. The Union buzzed on, oblivious.

But the board was shifting.

And the rook didn't even know how close checkmate already was.

Close Enough

The bullpen had thinned out, most detectives gone for the night, supervisors out on patrol. Will stood by the coffee pot, his cup cooling in his hand as he watched Rachel at her desk.

She sat perfectly poised, her blouse tucked neatly, her braid draped forward like an afterthought. Diligent. Focused. Too focused.

"Rachel," Will called. "Walk with me."

She looked up quickly, a small, practiced smile flickering across her lips. "Of course." She rose smoothly, tucking her notebook under her arm. As she passed, she adjusted her blouse just enough to draw the eye, the gesture disguised as absent-minded.

They stepped into the corridor. Will leaned against the wall, arms folded. "Some of the intel you pulled on the Serpents—that wasn't easy to find. Where'd it come from?"

Rachel leaned against the opposite wall, mirroring him. The angle tipped her collar just enough to reveal a line of skin. Her eyes stayed on him, steady, unblinking. "Mostly open socials. People don't hide as much as they think. Backgrounds of photos, receipts, geotags—it's all breadcrumbs if you know how to follow them."

Will's gaze held hers, searching for the crack. Then his eyes dropped briefly to the DHS badge clipped at her waistband, the one that gave her clearance into the task force system. "You're not pulling any of this off the restricted servers, are you?"

Her smile didn't falter. She rolled her pen between her fingers, slow and steady. "No, Detective. I wouldn't risk access to something I've been trusted with. I told you—it's all breadcrumbs if you know how to follow them."

Will didn't look convinced.

Rachel leaned in, just slightly, collapsing the space between them. Not overt. Not reckless. Just close enough for him to register the warmth in her voice when she added softly:

"You don't have to worry, Detective. I know where the lines are."

His jaw tightened. "I worry when people think they're untouchable. Dangerous ground, Rachel."

Her lips curved, not quite a smile, more like a secret. "That's why I'm glad you're the one watching over me. Makes me feel... safer."

It was delivered with just the right amount of naïveté, enough to pass for a rookie's gratitude. But the lingering pause, the deliberate softness in her voice, was not an accident.

Will pushed off the wall, needing the space back. "Remember—it's my job to keep you safe, not yours to test me."

Rachel dropped her gaze as if chastened, biting her lip lightly. "Yes, Detective." She tucked her pen behind her ear, the slight motion drawing attention again as though by chance.

They walked back into the bullpen side by side. She slid into her chair, all business again, fingers moving over the keyboard. The DHS banner flashed across her screen, login credentials accepted without hesitation. Rows of chatter logs, intel feeds, and cross-agency reports bloomed across her monitor.

To anyone passing by, it appeared to be an intern doing busywork. To Will, watching from the corner of his eye, it looked like temptation.

His unease deepened.

Competent. Perfect.

And now, deliberate.

Her mask held, but he knew she wasn't just playing intern.

She was playing him.

Will seeks Casey

The bullpen was quieter still once Rachel slipped out, her bag over her shoulder, announcing cheerfully, "Coffee run. You two want your usual?"

Will waited until the door closed behind her, then let out a breath he hadn't realized he was holding.

Casey was perched on the corner of her desk, boots crossed, scrolling her phone. She glanced up at his expression and smirked. "That's the look of a man who's either constipated or hiding something. Which is it, Obi-Wan?"

Will set his cup down hard enough to slosh coffee onto his fingers. He didn't even flinch. "Something's off about Rachel."

That got her attention. Casey pocketed her phone, leaning forward. "Off how? She's Joe Donovan's kid. Golden-girl intern, bright-eyed, follows orders. What's setting your spidey-sense tingling?"

"She's too perfect," Will said, voice low. "Every answer rehearsed. Every movement is measured. Tonight in the hall—she mirrored me. Matched posture, words, even... tone."

Casey arched a brow. "So she's smart. Maybe she's just trying to impress Daddy's old buddy. Doesn't make her a Sith Lord."

Will didn't smile. "She leaned in. Close. Too close. She knows how to draw attention without making it obvious. Clothes. Posture. Even the way she bit her lip at the right time. It wasn't an accident."

Casey blinked, then let out a short laugh. "You're telling me your mentor's kid is trying to femme fatale you? That's rich."

"I'm telling you she's deliberate," Will countered. His jaw tightened. "She's playing a part, and she's good at it. Too good for a rookie intern."

The grin faded from Casey's face. "You think she's leaking? Feeding somebody info?"

"I don't know yet," Will admitted. "But she's not just wide-eyed and grateful. She's practiced. Like she's rehearsed how to keep me off balance."

Casey whistled low. "Well, damn. Kid's either auditioning for rookie of the year or trying to pull a Jedi mind trick." She tipped her chin toward Rachel's desk. "Hell, she's got more clearance on those DHS terminals than half the detectives in this place. Wouldn't take much to wander a little too far."

Will rubbed the back of his neck, the weight of it sitting heavy. "Joe asked me to look after her. That's what I'm doing. But if she's hiding something..."

Casey finished the thought for him. "Then she's playing in dangerous territory."

Will's gaze flicked to the door Rachel had exited through. A faint trace of perfume still lingered in the air, sharp, floral, too familiar. Worse was the image burned into his mind: her leaning just close enough, mirroring his every move like she'd practiced it.

Casey caught the look and smirked again, though softer this time. "Relax, Skywalker. I'll keep my saber sharp. If your protégé's got a dark side, we'll sniff it out before she blows up Alderaan."

Will didn't answer, but the crease between his brows deepened.

Rachel Returns

The bullpen door swung open with a cheerful jingle of the bell, and Rachel stepped in, balancing a cardboard tray with three steaming cups. The bright logo of Jack'd Up Coffee was scrawled across the sides, foam still frothing at the lids.

"Afternoon fuel delivery," she announced, smiling wide as she crossed the room. "Caramel latte for Casey, black with two sugars for Detective Anderson, and mine's the boring drip."

Casey raised a brow as Rachel slid hers across the desk. "Kid, if you memorized my order already, you're either a genius or a stalker."

Rachel laughed, brushing the braid off her shoulder. "Just paying attention. You don't exactly hide your caffeine habits."

Instead of drifting back to her desk, Rachel lingered, setting her cup down right beside Casey's keyboard. She leaned in, close, too close, her perfume faint but distracting, her gaze fixed on Casey's monitor.

"What are you working on?" she asked, bracing a hand on the desk's edge. "Interview notes? Can I see how you structure them?"

From his corner, Will's pen stilled. Watching.

Casey smirked, sliding her chair back. "You always hover over people like this, Rookie, or am I just special?"

Rachel flushed but leaned closer anyway, and that's when her skirt snagged on the drawer handle. A faint rip, the hem jerking upward, flashing more than she intended.

"Shit!" Rachel yelped, tugging at it, which only made it worse. For one mortifying second, her underwear flashed in full view.

Casey jumped up, crouching by the drawer. "Hold still. You'll shred it if you keep pulling like that." She freed the fabric with a sharp tug and smoothed it down. "There. Clothes intact. Crisis averted."

Rachel's cheeks were crimson. She grabbed her cardigan and wrapped it around her waist, knotting it tight. "Oh my God. That was so embarrassing. Thanks, Casey. I didn't mean for that to happen."

Casey gave her a half-smile. "Hey, it happens. Desk one, Rookie zero."

Will didn't miss the flicker of relief in Rachel's eyes, or how quickly she recovered. Too quick.

Her phone buzzed. A message lit up the screen: *Maya – Old Roomie: Hey! A bunch of us are going out tonight. Come meet us at Barrel House after 9 p.m. First round's on me.*

Casey caught the hesitation. "Roommate from Ravenwood?"

Rachel nodded. "Yeah. We haven't hung out in a long time. I don't know..."

"Maybe you should," Casey said. "Get back in the groove. Blow off some steam. You've been buried in files since day one. Might be good for you."

Rachel chewed her lip. "I don't really... do bars anymore."

"Doesn't have to be wild. Just dip a toe in. If it gets too late, you can crash at my place. Couch with your name on it."

Rachel smiled faintly, sweater still tied at her waist. "Thanks. I'll... think about it."

Casey leaned back, grinning. "That's the spirit, Rookie. Worst case? You get a bad drink and free entertainment from drunk college kids. Best case? You remember you're allowed to have a life."

Rachel finally retreated to her desk, perfectly composed again.

Casey muttered as she passed Will, "Thought she was after your attention, but maybe she's just a walking wardrobe malfunction with stage fright. Might've read her wrong."

Will raised a brow. Casey smirked. "Or..." She winked. "She's Jar Jar Binks. Clumsy on the surface, secretly scheming in the Senate."

Will didn't answer, but his jaw tightened.

Rachel Delivers

The knock came just after nine. Will was halfway through a glass of Buffalo Trace, notes spread across the coffee table, when it came again. He wasn't expecting anyone.

When he opened the door, he froze for a beat.

Rachel stood in the porch light, a folder clutched to her chest. A leather jacket slipped halfway off one shoulder, doing little to hide the short, shimmering dress beneath it. Her legs caught the light as she shifted her weight, heels clicking softly, eyes lifting to his with a look that balanced nerves and intent.

"Rachel," he said carefully. "It's late. Everything alright?"

She tilted the folder up between them like an excuse. "I finished updating the Serpents' social pulls. Thought you'd want it before morning. Didn't want it sitting on my desk."

Will stepped aside. She brushed past him as she entered, the faint drag of her chest grazing his arm.

Will stepped aside, letting her in. "You could've emailed it." "I know," she said, placing the folder neatly on his coffee table. She leaned forward a touch too far, as if testing the boundary, revealing extra skin as her skirt rose higher and the jacket rose to her waist, another exposure. "Dad always said you looked out for rookies. Figured this was the right way, face to face." As she adjusted her skirt instinctively, as if nothing had happened to it.

The mention of Joe Donovan hit him like a punch. For a second, Will could hear his mentor's gravelly laugh, see him leaning across a desk years ago. Then the image was gone, replaced by his daughter's shimmering silken dress, bare legs, perfume hanging in the quiet.

"You're smart," Will said, his voice low, steady. "But your dad was right. I look out for rookies. And that means telling you straight, this?" His gaze flicked to the dress, the exposed shoulder, then back to her eyes. "It paints a target. Not everyone will keep you safe."

Rachel tilted her head, braid sliding forward to brush her collarbone. Her lips curved. "You sound just like him."

"That's not a bad thing," Will said, softer. "Joe wanted you safe. So do I."

She let the silence linger, her eyes fixed on his. Then she chuckled softly, fiddling with the zipper of her jacket. "Relax, Detective. It's just a dress. I'm meeting some Ravenwood girls. Bad music, cheap drinks. I just thought..." She moved closer to him as she spoke, her perfume warm in the air. "...if something happened, at least you'd know where I was."

Will's jaw flexed. He held the line. "If anything happens, you call me. No hesitation. Got it?"

Her smile was bright and obedient, but her eyes lingered a moment too long. "Got it."

At the door, she paused, her hand brushing the frame, nails catching the wood like a whisper. "Thanks for always looking out for me. Dad was right about you."

Then she slipped out, heels striking against the pavement, the sway of her stride deliberate.

Will kept his eyes on the door until it shut. Only then did he notice it: the perfume she left behind, curling through the room like smoke. Sweet, familiar, but wrong. He'd smelled it before, somewhere it didn't belong. A crime scene.

He sank into his chair, staring at the untouched bourbon. Casey's voice echoed in his head, irreverent and sharp: *"Careful, Obi-Wan. She's got the femme-fatale thing cranked up to eleven. Next thing you know, she's twirling around here like Leia in Jabba's palace."*

The corner of his mouth twitched. But the unease in his gut didn't let him smile.

Joe would expect him to protect her.

But Will couldn't shake the fear that Rachel wasn't the one who needed saving.

The Phone Call

Will's phone buzzed against the kitchen counter, the screen lighting up with Rachel Donovan.

He frowned. It was nearly midnight. He thumbed it on.

"Rachel?"

Her voice came through low, shaky, threaded with panic. "Mr. Anderson, Will, I... I think something's wrong."

Will straightened, grip tightening around the phone. "Where are you?"

"The Barrel House," she whispered. "I was with my old roommate, but I can't find her now. I... my drink tastes off. I don't... I don't feel right. Dizzy. Like the room keeps sliding."

Will was already moving, keys in hand. "Rachel, listen to me. Don't drink another sip. Where exactly inside are you?"

She gave a ragged laugh, part nerves, part something else. "In the back corner booth. I thought I'd be fine, but... I don't know. I don't want to call the cops and make a scene."

"You did the right thing calling me," Will said firmly, though unease coiled in his gut. "Stay put. Don't leave the booth. I'll be there in ten minutes."

A pause. Then softer: "Thank you. I didn't know who else to call. I know you're reliable."

Will slid behind the wheel of his Tahoe, engine roaring to life. "You've got me. I'll get you out of there."

Before he could end the call, her voice came again, quieter, trembling just enough to cut through him.

"Please hurry. I don't like the way they're looking at me."

The line went dead.

Will gripped the wheel tighter, headlights cutting through the dark streets of Oakhaven as he floored it toward Barrel House.

Barrel House Bar and Grill

The neon glow of Barrel House bled across the cracked pavement as Will pulled into the lot, tires screeching. Even from the street, the bass thumped through the walls, a steady pulse that rattled his chest.

He shoved through the door and swept the room. Packed. Music hammered from the speakers, bartenders barked orders, students laughed too loud, too long.

Then he saw her.

Rachel.

She sat in the corner booth, just where she'd said she'd be. Her jacket clung to her shoulders, but it did nothing to hide how pale she was under the strobing lights. She slumped low, her body sliding toward the edge as if her muscles no longer listened to her. Her skirt bunched against the vinyl, holding her in place by inches.

A glass sweated on the table, untouched. The condensation ran down in thin streams, pooling beneath it. She didn't so much as glance at it. Her eyes were locked on the door. On him.

Will's chest tightened. Something was wrong—terribly wrong. Her stare wasn't recognition; it was desperation, a plea stretched thin across her fading strength.

He shoved past shoulders, ignoring curses, moving faster.

"Rachel."

Her head snapped up, relief flooding her face like she'd been holding her breath too long.

"Will, thank God."

She slid out of the booth but wavered, steadying herself on the edge of the table.

He caught her elbow instantly, his grip firm. "Easy. You feel lightheaded?"

Rachel nodded, leaning into him, her weight softening against his side. "Like I've had ten shots. And I only had one."

Will's jaw tightened. Classic signs. "Alright. We're leaving. Now."

He guided her toward the door, his body a shield against the crowd. She pressed closer, clutching his sleeve, her voice lower now, blurred at the edges. "It's... it's strange. I feel so warm. Like... waves rolling through me. Feels... good."

Her head tipped against his shoulder for a moment, her lips close enough that he caught the ghost of her breath. "It's like... like I can't stop it. Like something's pulling me under but... it feels too good to fight. Like... like being touched when you didn't know you needed it."

Will tightened his hold on her, his jaw set. "Stay with me, Rachel. Don't give into it."

She gave a shaky laugh that wasn't really laughter at all, her words drifting with dangerous weight. "Feels like... someone's here, holding me up, keeping me close. I don't want it to stop."

Will forced his voice steady, though his pulse hammered. "Focus on me. We're almost out. You're safe."

Outside, the humid night air wrapped around them like a wet blanket, carrying the sour tang of spilled beer and the fading echo of laughter from the bar. The bass thumped dimly through the brick walls, a heartbeat that wouldn't quite let go.

Will kept his arm firm around Rachel's waist as he steered her toward his SUV. Her heels dragged slightly against the pavement, each step uncertain, like she was walking through water.

At the passenger door she swayed, catching herself on the frame. Will guided her up, steadying her until she collapsed into the seat, her legs folding awkwardly beneath her. She clutched the seatbelt like it was the only solid thing left in her spinning world.

"Do you need a hospital?" Will asked, searching her pale face, her pupils wide and glassy under the streetlight.

Rachel shook her head hard, too fast, too desperate. "No... no hospital. Please. I don't want—" Her voice cracked, splintered. "I don't want a report. I don't want people looking at me like... like that." Her hand whitened on the belt. "I just... I just wanted to get out."

Will hesitated, jaw tight. He could see the tremor in her hands, the shallow rise of her chest. But then her eyes fixed on him, wide and pleading, and something in her gaze told him this was more than fear—she wanted him to *see her*, to believe her.

"Alright," he said finally, his voice steady. "I'll get you home. Tomorrow we'll talk it through. Together."

Her shoulders eased, just slightly. "Thank you."

She leaned her head back against the seat, eyes fluttering shut. But when a streetlight slid across her features, Will caught it—a fleeting, fragile smile, gone as quickly as it appeared.

Her lips moved again, soft and dreamlike. "Will..." She paused, as though tasting the name, holding onto it. "Take me to Casey's. She... she said I could crash there tonight."

Will pulled out his phone and dialed. "Murphy, it's me," he said the moment she picked up. "I just pulled Rachel out of the Barrel House. She's not right."

A faint noise stirred beside him. Rachel, slumped against the seat, whispering as if she were inside a dream: "Will... it's like... like I'm floating. So warm. Everything's heavy, but it feels... good. You're here... right?" Her words trailed off, blurring into slurred breaths.

Casey's voice sharpened on the other end. "Not right how?"

Will's grip tightened on the wheel. "She wanted to take you up on that offer to crash at your place. But I think she's been drugged. I need a female's help with her. Now."

Rachel let out a soft, breathy laugh, head rolling toward him, eyes unfocused but fixed on his outline. "Feels like... like I'm dreaming you. Don't go."

Casey didn't hesitate. "Bring her. I'll handle it."

Will hung up and tossed the phone into the console, his focus snapping back to Rachel. Her head lolled against the seat, the streetlights painting her skin in fleeting stripes of gold and shadow as he pulled onto the road.

"Stay with me, Rachel," he said firmly, one hand tight on the wheel. "We're almost there."

Her eyes fluttered half-open, unfocused but searching, as if she were chasing a dream that kept slipping away. "Mmm... your voice..." Her lips curved faintly, dazed. "Feels close. Safe. Like I'm... like I'm lying in it."

Will clenched his jaw, glancing over at her. "Rachel, listen to me. You've been drugged. Just breathe and hold on."

She gave a soft laugh, almost a sigh. "It's... strange. I can't stop it. Feels like... waves rolling through me... like someone's touching me inside my skin. Good... too good." Her hand reached blindly, brushing his sleeve, gripping it like an anchor. "Don't... don't let go. Promise?"

"I'm right here," he said, steady but clipped, every muscle tight.

She leaned her head against the seatbelt, eyes half-lidded, voice dropping lower, thick with warmth she couldn't control. "Feels like you're... carrying me somewhere soft. Like, I don't have to fight. Like I could... fall into you and let it happen."

Will's knuckles whitened on the wheel. "Don't fall asleep. Keep talking to me."

She smiled faintly, eyes slipping shut again. "Then talk back... tell me I'm not dreaming."

Will's throat tightened, but he forced the words out, sharp and grounded. "You're not dreaming. I've got you. You're safe."

Rachel sighed, almost content. "Safe. With you..." Her voice thinned to a whisper, trailing off as the road stretched ahead, headlights carving a narrow path through the dark.

Casey's Apartment – Arrival

Casey had cleared the coffee table of takeout boxes and tossed a blanket across the couch by the time Will guided Rachel through the door. The girl was quiet, too quiet, her pupils blown wide under the dim lamp light.

Rachel moved as if underwater, each step obedient to Will's steadying hand. Her jacket slipped from her shoulders, crumpling on the floor, forgotten.

Casey arched a brow. "Alright, Rookie. Couch is yours tonight. But first—let's get you out of that bar-floor cocktail dress and into something you can actually sleep in."

Rachel turned toward her voice, eyes hazy but intent, as if Casey were the only thing anchoring her. She nodded once, then—without hesitation—reached for the straps of her dress. The fabric slid down her arms in a slow cascade. "Casey, mmm... your voice is so sweet, like it could wrap around me and..." She trailed off, a vague, dreamy smile brushing her lips. "...make me forget everything else."

The dress pooled at her ankles. She stood in little more than barely there sheer lace, tan-lined skin catching the lamplight as if it belonged to someone else's dream.

Casey froze mid-step, her breath hitching. "Whoa, Rachel..." She darted forward, catching her by the shoulders and guiding her quickly toward the couch. "That's not what I meant. Let's get you a t-shirt."

Rachel leaned into her touch without resistance, still smiling faintly. "Mm... anything you say. I like when you... tell me what to do."

The muscle in Will's jaw ticked as he turned aside, his expression caught between frustration and the awkwardness of a man who suddenly felt like an intruder. He bent, scooping the fallen dress from the floor, and laid it carefully folded across the back of a chair as if handling evidence instead of silk.

Rachel let Casey guide her down onto the couch, her movements loose, boneless, like a marionette with cut strings. She leaned back into the cushions, hair spilling over her shoulders, her bra strap slipping as though she couldn't be bothered to fix it.

Her eyes drifted toward the ceiling, then back to Casey, heavy-lidded but focused. "I met a guy tonight," she murmured, her words slurred but unfiltered. "He kissed me... and for a second, I thought... I was happy." Her lips twitched in a fragile smile that dissolved as quickly as it came. "But he wasn't... what I needed."

Casey froze, crouched in front of her with a blanket in hand. "Rachel, don't. Not right now."

But Rachel kept going, her voice low, dreamlike, her honesty sharpened by the drug. "It felt good, but not... not the kind of good that lasts. You know?" Her gaze slid, soft and searching, first toward Casey, then toward the doorway where Will hovered, tense and silent. "The kind of good I want is... here."

Casey's breath caught, but before she could speak, Rachel shifted closer, brushing her shoulder against Casey's arm with unconscious intimacy. "You... you sound so sweet when you talk. Makes me feel... safe. Like if I listen, I could stay right here forever."

Her hand slipped from the blanket to Casey's arm, fingers curling loosely in the fabric. She tilted her head toward Will, eyes glossy with heat and haze. "And you... always come when I call. Always. Makes me feel like I don't have to be alone. Like I could... lean into it. Into you."

Casey shot him a quick, tight look over Rachel's head. "She's not in control," she said sharply, more for him than for her.

Rachel only sighed, sinking back into the couch, compliant, pliant, a faint smile ghosting across her lips. "Mmm. Please don't stop talking to me... either of you. Feels... too good."

Rachel just blinked at Casey, wide-eyed but strangely serene, her body loose, pliant, waiting—as if she were only capable of following the next instruction.

Casey kept her voice steady, calm but firm. "Here you go," she said, holding out an oversized sleep shirt. "One of my favorites. You'll be comfortable in this."

Rachel's sat up on the edge of the cushion, fingers fumbled clumsily at the strap of her bra, tugging it down over her shoulder as if undressing in front of them were the most natural thing in the world. Her lips curved faintly, dreamy. "Oh... I get it. You want me to take everything off first. That's... easier, right?"

Casey's tone cut sharply, immediately. "No. Stop."

Rachel froze, her hands falling still at her sides. Obedient. Mechanical. Like she'd been waiting for the correction.

Casey drew in a slow breath, fighting to keep her composure. She stepped in, gently steering Rachel by the shoulders, turning her away from Will. She caught him in the corner of her eye—stiff, jaw tight, gaze locked anywhere but the exposed skin in front of him—yet hovering close, ready to move if he had to.

"Easy," Casey murmured, crouching to meet Rachel's hazy gaze.

Rachel tilted her head toward her voice, eyes heavy but intent, as if Casey's words alone tethered her to the room. "Mmm... I like when you tell me what to do. Makes me feel like... I belong somewhere. Like I don't have to think." She leaned forward slightly, brushing her forehead against Casey's shoulder in a slow, languid motion. "Feels... nice."

Casey didn't let her unease show. She quickly and efficiently slid the bra straps down, refusing to let her hands linger as she freed Rachel from the garment. As Rachel instinctively stood, she pulled the oversized shirt over her head in practiced motions, Casey softly murmuring reassurances. The fabric fell past Rachel's thighs, providing coverage, though the wide neckline slipped low on one side, exposing a bare shoulder. Casey guided her hands through the sleeves and then smoothed the shirt down into place.

"There," Casey said softly, more to herself than to Rachel. "All set. Safe."

Rachel swayed slightly in the shirt, then smiled vaguely, her voice light and hazy with suggestion. "Safe...

mmm. With you... with him. Feels like maybe I don't need to wake up if this is the dream."

Will's jaw flexed hard, his voice steady but low. "She's not herself. Just keep her grounded until it passes."

Rachel sighed, eyes closing, her head lolling to the side. "Grounded... only if you're both holding me down."

Casey's stomach tightened, but she pulled the blanket over Rachel firmly, tucking her in like a younger sister. "Rest, Rookie. That's all you need to do. Just rest."

Casey glanced at Will. His arms were folded, his face shadowed, but she saw the tension in his jaw, the way his hand flexed like he needed to *do* something.

And for the first time that night, Casey wondered if this was just the haze of a drug.

Rachel jumped up from the couch and shed the blanket, standing as if she were looking into the future.

"Sit," Casey ordered, her voice more forceful than she intended. Rachel obeyed immediately, lowering herself onto the couch.

For a moment, the silence was thick. Casey's eyes flicked to Will, unsettled, then back to Rachel—docile, agreeable, like a robot with her wires cut.

And a cold thought slid through Casey's chest: *This is what the girls on campus must have looked like. The missing time. The blank stares. Hell—this is what I must've looked like that night when he drugged me.*

Casey's fists clenched. She forced her voice softer. "Alright, kid. Drink this water. Then sleep. We'll figure it out in the morning."

Rachel nodded again, sipping obediently, her gaze drifting out of focus.

Will lingered by the door, eyes shadowed. "I'll be back in ten," he muttered. "Need some air."

Casey didn't stop him. She was too busy staring at Rachel, the blanket slipping off one bare shoulder, her movements mechanical, precise.

Like a pawn waiting for someone to move her.

Casey Reacts

Rachel lay curled on her side, the oversized shirt sliding off one shoulder, her breaths shallow but steady. Out cold, or close enough.

Casey stood in the doorway to the living room, arms crossed, watching the rise and fall of her chest. She should have felt relief. Instead, her stomach was a knot.

The way Rachel had dropped her dress. The way she'd started to take off her bra in front of them without a flicker of shame. That wasn't drunkenness. That wasn't just a spiked drink. That was *programmed obedience.*

Casey rubbed her arms, goosebumps rising. She couldn't forget the image of herself on her apartment floor not long ago, chloroform still stinging her throat, her shirt gone, her bra the only barrier between her and humiliation. She remembered waking with a bloody nose, feeling disoriented, knowing someone had touched and posed her like a doll.

And then more recently, worse. The soda in her own fridge was drugged. Sitting on her couch with bourbon and a show before the world went black. Waking naked, hogtied in her shower, her own lace shoved between her teeth, water filling around her ribs. Nearly drowned in her own bathroom while her attacker watched. The memory clenched her chest so hard she nearly doubled over.

She forced herself to breathe and to look back at Rachel again. The campus girls came to mind next—the ones who whispered about "lost time." The ones who insisted they hadn't drunk enough to black out. Casey had chalked it up to trauma, to gaps in memory. But tonight, staring at Rachel, it was like watching a demonstration.

Obedience. Compliance. Skin and bone moved like pieces on a board.

Casey leaned back against the counter, arms crossed, but when Will moved toward the trash can with his empty coffee cup, memory made her stomach drop.

He froze mid-motion.

There, half-buried under crumpled paper towels and the cardboard sleeve from a six-pack, were three pregnancy tests.

His jaw flexed, the cup still in his hand.

Casey's eyes widened. "Don't." Her voice cracked sharper than she meant it to. She crossed the kitchen in two strides, shoving the lid down. "Negative," she said quickly. "All of them. I checked."

Will looked at her then, really looked, at the brittle edge in her voice, at the faint tremor in her hand where it gripped the counter. "Casey..."

She cut him off with a hollow laugh, no humor in it. "I have no clue what the hell happened between the drink I poured for myself and waking up half-drowned in my own shower. None. Just a black hole where the night should be."

The silence stretched, heavy.

Will set his cup gently on the counter, his voice low but steady. "Then we treat it like evidence. Whatever's missing, we'll find it. You don't carry this alone."

Casey pressed her palms flat against the countertop, head bowed for a moment. When she lifted it again, her smirk was back, thinner, brittle, a shield barely holding.

"Don't go getting all knight-in-shining-armor on me, Anderson. I'm not your damsel."

Will didn't rise to the joke. He just held her gaze, quiet, letting the weight of his promise sit between them.

"Go home," she said firmly, no hesitation in her voice. "I've got the Padawan. She's safe now. Go hug those girls and kiss your wife. I've got her back here."

Finally, he nodded once, grabbed his coat from the chair, and moved toward the door.

At the threshold, he paused and looked back at her. "You don't have to fight the dark side alone, Casey. You've got an entire band of rebels who love you, and we've got your back no matter what."

He nodded again, then slowly pulled the door shut behind him.

Alone in the silence, Casey let out a shaky breath she hadn't realized she was holding. Her smirk slipped away, and a single tear traced its way down her cheek.

Confession

Rachel woke to the faint hum of Casey's refrigerator and the smell of strong coffee. Her body felt heavy, her tongue sandpaper-dry. For a moment, she didn't know where she was.

Then she sat up too fast, blinking into the soft light of Casey's living room. The couch cushions were rumpled around her, her legs bare beneath an oversized t-shirt that slid off one shoulder. Not hers. Her dress was folded neatly on a chair, her shoes placed carefully beneath it. Not her doing.

She rose unsteadily, her knees trembling, each step unbalanced.

Casey stepped out of the kitchen, holding a steaming mug. Her T-shirt was wrinkled, and her hair was in a messy bun. She froze in the doorway, noticing Rachel wake up and moving.

Rachel gave a shaky laugh, tugging at her shirt hem. "Well, don't we look like twins."

Casey arched a brow, deadpan. "The galaxy barely tolerates one of me, kid. Two would be overkill."

But Rachel's smile faltered. Her hands smoothed the fabric over her thighs, and her voice lowered. "This... this isn't mine. How did I even get here?"

Casey leaned her hip against the counter, weighing her words. "You called Will last night from the Barrel House.

Said you thought your drink was spiked. He picked you up and brought you here. You were out of it. I helped you change, set you up on the couch."

Rachel blinked, her expression twisting from confusion to alarm. She shook her head, tears brimming. "I don't... I don't remember any of that." Her throat worked. "Casey... this isn't the first time."

Casey set the mug down with a quiet *clink*, all her detective and protective instincts tangling in her chest. "Tell me."

Rachel wrapped her arms around herself, her voice trembling. "Back at Ravenwood... it started at parties. I'd lose time. Hours gone. I'd wake up in my dorm, or sometimes not even know how I got home. At first, I thought maybe I was drinking too much. But then the bruises started. I couldn't explain them."

Her voice cracked. "Friends, I came with said they saw me leave with guys. Guys, I didn't remember even talking to."

Casey's chest tightened, but she kept her face calm, her tone gentle. "And then?"

Rachel wiped angrily at her tears, forcing herself on. "One day on campus, three of them—frat boys—cornered me. They laughed. Said they'd *seen me.* Said the whole school had. I didn't know what they meant until one of them pulled out his phone." Her breath hitched. "There was a video. Me. Out of it, I looked barely conscious, but there. Someone had recorded everything."

Casey stayed silent, letting her vent, but inside her stomach twisted. She had seen it too, the jagged horror of that video buried in Steve's archive, and the memory of it clung like smoke. But Rachel didn't need that truth right now.

Rachel's words tumbled faster, rawer. "I heard the rumors floating around, so I went looking, found the whole thing later, on the dark web. I couldn't walk across campus without hearing whispers, laughter, like everybody knew. So I dropped out. I quit nursing school. I couldn't breathe there anymore."

She was crying openly now, shoulders shaking, fists tight at her sides.

Casey took a slow step forward, her voice softened to the calm she'd use with a victim on the worst night of their life. "That wasn't your fault, Rachel. None of it."

Rachel shook her head violently. "No, it was my fault for trusting them. For going to the parties. For—"

Casey cut in, firm. "Don't you dare. They chose. They planned. They drugged you. They filmed you. That's on them, not you."

Rachel broke then, her face crumpling. "One of them... one of the ones who did it... he's dead now. The one with the pawn in his mouth. I recognized him. I know it was him."

Casey felt her pulse quicken, but forced her expression steady. "Whitmore, you're sure?"

Rachel nodded, clutching herself more tightly. "The assault, that's why I came here. That's why I asked to intern. I wanted to help. I thought... I thought maybe if I worked with you and Will, I could help stop the ones still out there. Help the other girls who don't even realize they're pawns yet, in a sick game."

She wiped at her eyes again, trying to pull herself back together, her voice small. "I look up to you. To both of you. I just want to help. I'll do whatever it takes."

Casey exhaled slowly and carefully, then crouched down to be at Rachel's eye level. Her voice cracked a little despite herself. "You're stronger than you think, kid. Stronger than they ever credited you for. You want to fight? You're not doing it alone. You've got us now."

Rachel gave a wet, shaky laugh. "Rule number one... don't run off like a wannabe Skywalker, right?"

Casey smiled despite the heaviness in her chest. "Damn right. Leave the reckless heroics to me. I've got the lightsaber scars to prove it."

Rachel sniffed, nodding, shoulders sagging with a mixture of exhaustion and fragile relief.

Casey straightened, hiding her unease behind a mask of big-sister sarcasm. But inside, the truth gnawed: Rachel wasn't just venting. She was unraveling.

And Casey couldn't shake the dread that Rachel's confession was only the surface of something much darker.

Getting Back Home

Rachel lingered by the arm of the couch, twisting the hem of Casey's oversized t-shirt between her fingers. Her dress still lay folded on the chair, her heels tucked neatly beneath it.

"Casey," she said softly, almost embarrassed, "do you think I could borrow something? Just until I get home. I don't exactly want to walk out in last night's bar outfit."

Casey gave her a once-over, bare legs, wrinkled tee, and nodded. "Yeah, kid. No problem. Shorts and a shirt should do it. I've got plenty that don't smell like I rolled through a crime scene."

That earned the faintest laugh from Rachel, and Casey ducked into her bedroom. A minute later she came back with a folded set: running shorts and a Ravenwood tee that had seen a hundred laundry cycles.

"Here." Casey dropped them in Rachel's hands. "Not fashion week, but it'll keep you decent."

Rachel quickly changed into the clothes, then slipped into her flats and scooped up her dress and bra, folded the borrowed T-shirt, and laid it on the end table. When she emerged from around the couch, Casey was already grabbing her keys.

"C'mon. I'll run you to your place," Casey said. "You can get a shower, shake off whatever they slipped you last night."

They slid into Casey's SUV. Rachel tucked her clothes on her lap, gazing out the window as they pulled away. Casey drummed her fingers on the steering wheel before pulling out her phone.

She hit Will's number on speaker. "Hey, Anderson. Got the kid. Think we need to let her take a day to recover?"

From the other end, Will's voice carried that low rumble. "Wouldn't blame her if she did."

Rachel shook her head instantly. "No. I want to come in. Please. I'll just shadow, stay quiet, but I want to be there."

Will hesitated. Casey glanced sideways at Rachel, then back at the road. "You heard her, boss. She's stubborn as a Wookiee."

Rachel leaned closer toward the phone. "Will... could you pick me up after I shower? It's right along your way from the house, closer to the Barrel House. Then I can get my car on the way."

There was a pause, then Will exhaled. "Fine. I'll swing by. Be ready."

Rachel nodded, as though he could see it. "I will. Just need a quick shower and fresh threads. I'll be waiting."

Casey smirked, shaking her head. "Alright then. I'll grab breakfast for the three of us and meet you both in the conference room."

"Copy that," Will said. "See you soon."

The line clicked dead. Casey shot Rachel a look, and one corner of her mouth tugged upward. "You really don't make it easy on us, you know that?"

Rachel smiled faintly, hugging the bundle of her clothes closer. "I just don't want to sit this out. Not anymore."

Casey didn't press further, but the weight in the car was thick. The silence that followed wasn't uncomfortable, but it wasn't simple either.

Back at Rachel's Place

Casey's SUV rolled to the curb outside Rachel's small apartment complex. The brick facade looked tired, blinds tilted in different directions, but her windows were neatly shut, curtains drawn.

Rachel shifted the bundle of borrowed clothes in her lap and leaned toward Casey. "See you in a few. Jack'd Up, large iced latte, extra shot, and a blueberry muffin. Thanks."

Casey smirked. "High-maintenance already. Got it."

Rachel smiled faintly, tugged the strap of her bag over her shoulder, and slipped out. She gave a small wave before heading up the stairs, her ponytail swaying. Casey waited just long enough to watch her unlock the door and step inside, the lock clicking behind her, before pulling away toward the precinct.

Inside, Rachel let her bag drop to the counter and immediately pulled out her phone. Her thumbs moved quickly, the words precise:

Rachel to Will -- *Casey just dropped me off. Showering, fresh threads. Will leave the door open—let yourself in. Hair takes forever to dry. Thanks.*

She hit send and tossed the phone onto the bed before disappearing into the bathroom, the roar of the shower filling the small apartment.

Fifteen minutes later, Will's unmarked car slid into a space. He climbed out, scanning the lot with a practiced eye before heading up the steps. He rapped his knuckles against the door.

"Rachel?" he called, voice steady.

From inside came the muffled roar of a hair dryer. No answer.

Will pulled out his phone.

Will to Rachel -- *I'm here.*

He waited, listening. Nothing but the hair dryer whirring. After a long moment, he tried again.

"Rachel? It's Will. I'm coming in."

The door gave under his hand, unlocked, just like she'd said.

Will stepped inside, boots sinking into the low, cream-colored carpet. The place was warm, almost too warm, the air heavy with a faint mix of coffee grounds and something floral that tugged at his memory but refused to resolve.

His eyes adjusted quickly. The apartment was small, but arranged with precision, a bookshelf lined with hardbacks and framed photos, spines turned just so, edges flush as if someone measured them. On the kitchen counter, a French press and a row of ceramic mugs stood drying on a rack, handles aligned like soldiers.

The living room was clean, but not comfortably lived-in, the kind of neat that spoke more of staging than relaxation. A throw blanket was folded perfectly over the arm of the couch. A single candle sat unlit on the coffee table, its label boasting some boutique fragrance, *white tea & peony*.

No clutter. No shoes kicked off in the corner. No open notebooks or laundry baskets or the mess of a young woman juggling work and life. It felt arranged. Controlled.

The hum of the hair dryer carried from behind the closed bathroom door, steady and unnatural in the silence.

"Rachel," he called, his voice carrying low across the tidy space. "It's Will. I'm here."

No answer. Just the drone, like static.

He set his coffee cup down on the counter, the metal canister clinking too loudly in the stillness. Crossing to the couch, he sat but didn't sink back, posture straight, hands resting on his knees. The couch cushions were stiff under him, as if rarely used. From here, he could see a slim laptop on the dining table, lid shut, cord coiled neatly beside it. The scent of perfume hung heavier near it, sweet, sharp, just a note too strong, curling into the air like it was waiting for him to notice.

Will exhaled through his nose. He told himself this was simple: he was here to make sure Joe Donovan's daughter was safe. That was all.

But the unlocked door. The hair dryer running. The faint perfume that stirred some half-memory of a crime scene he couldn't quite place.

Something was off.

The hair dryer cut off with a snap. Silence, then the sound of bare feet on hardwood.

Rachel stepped into the living room wrapped in a towel knotted loosely above her chest. Damp hair clung to her collarbone, water dripping down her skin, darkening the edge of the fabric. The lower end barely covers the top of her thighs. The floral scent of her shampoo filled the air between them.

She froze when she saw Will on the couch. “Oh! Detective—I didn’t... I didn’t know you were already in. Guess it took longer than I thought. Still a little fuzzy.” Her voice carried a laugh, light and embarrassed, but she didn’t move to tighten the towel.

Will stood up immediately, eyes averted. “I called out. You didn’t answer. Didn’t want to intrude further, I just wanted to make sure you were alright.”

Her laugh softened, almost grateful. “Guess I get lost in the noise. I’m fine, really. You don’t have to worry.”

He kept his gaze fixed on the bookshelf, jaw tight. “Get dressed. I’ll wait.”

She adjusted the towel, which dipped deliberately, baring more inches of skin, barely in place, and she didn’t move to fix it. Her gaze didn’t waver. “Stop treating me like I’m made of glass. I can take a hit, Will. Even a hard one. That’s how you find out what someone’s really made of.”Will’s tone was iron. “Rachel. We need to go.”

She nodded obediently, but the glimmer in her eyes betrayed something else. Turning, she padded toward the bathroom, hips swaying slightly, deliberately unhurried, causing the slit in the undersized towel to reveal herself as she walked, each step like a strobe of towel against the flash of bare wet skin.

Just as she reached the doorway, hairbrush in one hand, Will's coffee cup in the other, a corner of the towel slipped from around her, falling down one side. For a brief moment, just long enough to register, her entire backside was exposed in the golden hallway light. The towel drops to the floor, Rachel giggles, and kicks it into the bathroom. Then, the door shuts partway, leaving Will with the image burned into his mind against his better judgment.

He dropped onto the couch, rubbing a hand down his face. His pulse ticked hard at his temple, not from temptation but from anger at himself for even noticing.

This was Joe Donovan's daughter. His mentor's kid.

And yet, beneath the faint trace of steam and soap in the apartment, he caught that perfume again. Familiar. Maddeningly so. A faint, floral-citrus note that clung too long, pricked something deep in his memory—but he couldn't place it. Not from Rachel. From somewhere else.

By the time she returned, she was dressed in a loose sweater and dark jeans, her hair damp and a braid slipping over her shoulder. Soft, casual, almost apologetic.

"Better?" she asked, her voice low, shy.

Will's gaze met hers, steady, controlled. "Rachel, don't mistake me for someone who won't notice when you're playing with fire."

Her lashes lowered, and the smile that followed was too innocent to be real. "That's why I trust you, Detective. Because you'd never let me burn."

She grabbed her bag, swinging it over her shoulder as if nothing had happened. "Ready when you are."

Will rose, following her out, but his thoughts were anything but steady. The towel. The perfume. The way every move felt calculated.

She wasn't just pretending to be an intern.

She was playing a game, but what was the goal?

Oakhaven PD, Conference Room

Casey shouldered the door open, balancing two Jack'd Up bags and a tray of coffees. "Breakfast cavalry reporting for duty. Extra bacon for the rook—don't ever say I don't love you."

Will sat at the far end of the table, already flipping through a case folder. Rachel trailed behind him after they'd swung by to grab her car from the Barrel House lot. Her sweater slouched casually, hair still damp but braided neatly down her back, jeans pressed crisp. Too crisp for someone who'd claimed to be stumbling through last night.

As Rachel slid past Casey toward a chair, a scent drifted after her—bright citrus, threaded with something floral, faintly sweet. Casey's nose twitched.

"Wait," she said, setting down the food. "Is that perfume? Or lotion?"

Rachel blinked, then let out a soft laugh. "Lotion, I think. Clearance rack. Why?"

Casey grinned. "Because it's good. Not the usual drugstore fog. Fresh. Reminds me of spring on Endor." She tore open a bag with a smirk. "You wear it every day?"

Rachel shook her head, just enough pink in her cheeks to sell the innocence. "Not usually. Thought today needed a little extra."

"Careful, Rookie," Casey said. "Keep walking in here smelling like that, and you'll make the rest of us look bad. Especially Will—he's stuck in the Old Spice system, circa Clone Wars."

Will glanced up from his folder, dry. "Appreciate the glowing review, Murphy."

Casey chuckled, busy unwrapping sandwiches, not noticing the way Rachel's gaze flicked toward Will—not at his eyes, but at his quiet. Measuring. Testing whether he bought her blush-and-lotion story.

Will held her glance. For a breath, the mask faltered—calculation gleaming behind the soft edges of her expression. Then she ducked her head, tucking a damp strand behind her ear, posture resetting into shy and grateful.

Casey dropped a sandwich in front of her. "Here. Eat up. Rookie brains need fuel if you're gonna keep up with Jedi."

Rachel smiled warmly, playing the part.

But Will's grip tightened around his coffee cup. Unease prickled sharply under his skin.

Casey thought she was mentoring a kid.

Will had just seen the truth.

The mask wasn't innocence.

It was design.

The Watcher Observes

The news feed bled sound into the café, Kristen Anderson's face caught mid-stride as she dodged reporters outside the courthouse. Subtitles scrolled beneath her:

DA under fire... Mistrials pile up... Lack of evidence erodes public trust.

The microphones pressed in like vultures. Kristen's polished smile faltered; her eyes betrayed her exhaustion. She pushed past, but the silence in her wake was louder than words.

The Watcher stirred their coffee slowly, the pawn in their pocket warm from constant touch. The board was clear enough.

The King—Detective Will Anderson—steady, immovable. He shielded, he endured. Kings were meant to stand until the endgame, no matter how battered.

But queens... queens carried reach, influence, power. They were supposed to guard the pawns, to see farther than the King ever could. Yet this queen betrayed her pawns, again and again, abandoning them to predators, leaving them to bleed. Each mistrial, each collapsed case, was another pawn left unprotected.

A queen who betrayed her pawns was no queen at all.

The crowd's jeers—*weak, useless, corrupt*—were not just noise. They were prophecy.

The Watcher pressed the pawn harder into their palm until the edge cut. Pawns were fragile, yes. But pawns who learned betrayal became dangerous. They grew teeth. They sharpened.

If a queen betrayed *them*—not in court, not in politics, but truly, deeply, intimately—then correction would be swift. Brutal. A toppled queen was more than a lost piece; she was a warning carved into the board.

Memory came, unbidden: My fathers's voice like iron, eyes like stone. *Trust no one. The board lies. A smile is a mask. Assume betrayal until it proves itself otherwise.*

He had been right. He had always been right. And his lesson hummed now in the Watcher's bones.

The King could not save his queen. The King was blinded by duty, chained by blood. But the pawns had seen enough.

And this queen—this betrayer—was already tipping.

All that remained was the hand to finish the move.

Family Dinner

The bullpen was quieter than usual, the late afternoon sun throwing long bars of light across the desks. Casey leaned against the edge of hers, sorting through a folder of names. Rachel sat across from her, scribbling notes, posture neat, hair falling in a tidy braid.

"Alright, Rookie," Casey said, tapping her pen against the list. "We've still got a few possibles. Some of Brock Prescott, Derek Langley, Tyler Brentwood, and Zach Whitmore's classmates. A bartender at Jax's Pub. And the union janitor. We need to run them down. I'd love to take another run at Carter Vance if that slimy lawyer would let us."

Rachel looked up. "I can start compiling social media traces for the classmates tonight—see who posts when, where. People leave more of a trail than they think. Maybe find Carter as well?"

"Not bad," Casey said with a half-smile. "But you also need food. Humans eat, remember?"

Rachel blinked, caught off guard by the change in tone. "Food?"

"Dinner," Casey clarified, dragging the word out. "You know, plates, forks, chewing. Not just vending machine Snickers."

Will walked past with his phone in hand, only half-listening, until Casey tilted her head toward him. "What do you think, Anderson? After everything she's been through, maybe the kid could use a little time around people her own age. Em and El are close enough. They could all meet for dinner at your place. The Anderson homestead. Safe, warm, fewer psychos."

Will frowned slightly. "I was planning on heading to the Barrel House. See if we can pull video, figure out who messed with her drink."

Rachel's voice slipped in, quieter. "You won't find much. My old roommate... she said she saw me with someone. A guy, whose name I don't remember, was talking to him and then didn't feel well. Last time she saw me, I was heading to the bathroom. She got wasted and left with some guy, left me." Her fingers tightened around her pen, knuckles pale, but her face stayed carefully neutral.

The silence that followed was heavier than it had been before. Casey cleared her throat, gentling the air. "All the more reason for a night off duty. Recharge, Rookie. You're no good to us if you burn out."

Will's gaze lingered on Rachel, studying her, then he thumbed out a text. *Kristen—Casey and Rachel are joining us for dinner tonight.*

Casey grinned like she'd won a round of sabacc. "See? Even the King listens to his council sometimes."

Rachel ducked her head, a smile tugging at her mouth that didn't quite reach her eyes.

At the House

The two cars rolled into Will's driveway, engines ticking as they cooled in the twilight. Casey climbed out, stretching her arms overhead with a groan. Rachel followed, hugging her satchel like a shield, then falling into step beside her.

Her voice came quietly, almost hesitant. "You know... you're kind of like the big sister I never had."

Casey smirked, one brow arched. "Big sister? Careful, Rookie, you just called me old without actually saying it."

Rachel laughed, but it was accompanied by a softness that lingered in the air. "No—I mean it. Growing up with my dad... it was just him and me. He's... hard. Straight-laced. Trust no one, always on guard. Never let me date or go out with friends, super overprotective. He's a cop, like Will, but without the... warmth. Without any breathing room." She glanced sideways, studying Casey's reaction. "You're different. You give me that space."

For a beat, Casey just watched her, something soft flickering under her usual sarcasm. Then she bumped Rachel's shoulder lightly. "Kid, you've earned a little space. And hey—just because you're our intern doesn't mean you're off-limits for fun outside the precinct."

Rachel tilted her head, smiling in that way that seemed both shy and calculating. "Fun like what?"

Casey grinned wide. "Like girl things. Nails, bad hair dye choices, spa days. Or, better yet, binge-watching the entire *Star Wars* saga at my place while we binge-drink the night away. Take your pick: soda, wine, or raiding Will's bourbon stash."

She wagged a finger at Rachel, mock-serious. "Or, if you really want in, you could get inducted into the Anderson Women Wine-and-Dash Club. That's where Kristen and I drink too much Moscato, streak through the house like maniacs, and cannonball into the pool. Total chaos. It's practically an initiation rite, so fair warning: you'll have to partake sooner or later."

Rachel's cheeks flushed, her laugh bubbling out despite herself. "That sounds... terrifying."

Casey bumped her shoulder. "Terrifying? Kid, it's liberating. Trust me—you'll thank me once you're feeling the night breeze everywhere, then wet, floating drunk, and laughing so hard your ribs hurt."

Rachel ducked her head, still smiling, but her eyes flicked up at Casey through her lashes. "I don't know if I could ever... do something like that. But maybe that's why I should."

The words hung in the air for a moment, soft and shy on the surface, but with a flicker underneath. It was as if she wasn't just imagining the ridiculous scene Casey described, but also pondering what it meant to be welcomed into something so intimate, so reckless, so completely theirs.

Casey chuckled, brushing it off with an easy grin. "Don't worry, Padiwan. We'll break you in slowly. No streaking until at least the third bottle."

She gave Rachel a teasing sidelong glance. "Hell, we've already survived seeing each other in string bikinis, me saving you from two wardrobe malfunctions, and dressing you after your big Barrel House night. Don't think I forgot you standing in your living room in nothing but panties while I hunted down one of my favorite oversized T-shirts for you."

Rachel flushed, biting her lip, but her laugh came warm. "Oh my gosh, don't remind me."

Casey chuckled. "Point is, we're way past the awkward stage. So yeah, you're stuck with me."

Rachel's laugh bubbled out, light but controlled, her eyes shining. "That actually sounds kind of perfect." She let a pause hang, then added softly, almost like a confession: "I'd like more time like that. With you. Away from... all the rest."

Casey slung an arm briefly around her shoulders before reaching for the porch door. "Then it's a date, Rookie. Just promise if I start doing my Yoda impression after the second glass of wine, you'll cut me off."

Rachel leaned in, close enough for Casey to feel the warmth of her words. "No promises."

That was the moment the porch light snapped on, flooding them both in gold.

Will stood framed in the doorway, keys still in his hand. His eyes caught on the closeness—Rachel leaning just a little too near, Casey's arm still slung around her shoulders. He didn't say anything, but the faint tightening of his jaw spoke volumes.

Casey pulled back naturally, grinning at him. "Relax, Obi-Wan. We're not plotting against you. Just planning movie night. And maybe some girl power bonding time in your pool."

Will's eyes flicked from Casey's easy grin to Rachel's soft, almost grateful expression.

For Casey, it was a simple moment of bonding.

For Will, it was one more crack of unease crawling under his skin.

At Dinner

Will hadn't given Kristen much warning before telling her that her guests were coming. Typical. But she'd learned long ago how to pivot, and she had her ace up her sleeve. Downtown, her friend at Lowcountry Lasagna always had pre-made family meals for nights just like this one.

By the time Will and the others walked through the door, Kristen was sliding foil pans onto the counter: a bubbling chicken parm, a heavy pan of lasagna, mac & cheese with a golden crust, roasted Brussels with bacon, Cajun-spiced vegetables, and, of course, one of the restaurant's homemade banana puddings.

The dining room filled with chatter, plates scraping, the warmth of food carrying over into something lighter than any of them had felt in weeks.

Kristen poured herself a glass of red, then lifted the bottle toward Rachel. "Wine?"

Rachel's face brightened, eager but composed. "Absolutely. Thank you."

Emily and Ellie groaned in unison from across the table. "Not fair!"

Casey jabbed a fork toward the twins with mock sternness. "Not fair? You've still got three years until you can order anything stronger than a Coke, so don't even start. Now shut up and eat your Brussels sprouts."

Ellie pushed hers around with the tip of her fork. "You sound like Mom."

Casey smirked. "Yeah, but when I say it, it comes with the full force of the Dark Side. Don't test me."

That earned a laugh from Will, a roll of the eyes from Kristen, and a snort from Emily that nearly sent mac & cheese across her plate.

Rachel, meanwhile, sipped her wine and smiled into her glass. Her shoulders looked looser than Will had ever seen them. For once, she wasn't just the intern in the bullpen; she looked twenty-two, young, alive, and a little too comfortable under his roof.

Will's unease tugged faintly, but he buried it under another bite of lasagna. Kristen had pulled off the impossible: for one evening, the Anderson table sounded like family, not fallout.

And for Rachel, that was precisely the point.

Kristen Observes

Will rose from the table, reaching for the serving spoon buried in the lasagna. Plates clattered around him, forks scraping, chatter bouncing off the walls. For the first time in weeks, the house almost sounded like it used to.

Kristen slipped up beside him at the counter, topping off her wine. Her voice was low, meant only for him.

"You keep watching her," she murmured.

Will stiffened, scooping another heap onto his plate. "Who?"

Kristen gave him a look, the kind that cut through any dodge. "Rachel. Don't play dumb. Every time she laughs, you look like you're waiting for the other shoe to drop." She softened, her shoulder brushing his. "It wasn't like this the last time she was here. Back then, you let yourself relax around her. Tonight... you can't."

He sighed, staring down at the bubbling cheese. "She's Joe's kid. That alone makes me protective. And... she's been through hell."

Kristen swirled her glass, her expression gentle now. "Protective, sure. But it's more than that. You're carrying something heavier. Just... don't let it close you off so much that you miss the truth, one way or the other. She's either what she says she is... or she isn't. And if she isn't?" She touched his arm lightly. "You'll see it before anyone else."

Before Will could answer, Casey's voice drifted over from behind them. "Wow. You two look like you're plotting against the Emperor over there."

They both turned. Casey leaned on the doorway with her glass of tea, smirking. "Careful, Skywalker. That's how Jedi get in trouble, too busy brooding about the Dark Side to notice what's right in front of 'em."

Kristen raised a brow, amused but grateful for the cut-in. Will shook his head, a wry smile tugging at his mouth despite himself.

Casey jabbed her thumb toward the table. "Now c'mon, Vader, get back before the twins eat all the mac & cheese. You snooze, you lose."

Will exhaled, setting his plate down. For just a moment, the heaviness eased.

But as he walked back to the table, Rachel caught his eye across the room and smiled, warm and easy. And the difference Kristen had named, the way his guard was up now when once he'd let it down, came flooding back with the unease.

After Dinner

Later, as the dishes clattered into the sink and the twins squabbled over who had to load the dishwasher, Will stepped out onto the back patio with a beer in hand. The night was cool, cicadas humming in the trees.

Casey slipped out after him, tugging her hoodie tighter. She leaned against the railing, eyeing him sidelong. "You've got that face again."

Will took a pull from his bourbon. "What face?"

"The brooding-Jedi face. Like you're two steps away from a hood and a dramatic monologue about balance in the Force."

He snorted softly, shaking his head. "You've been watching too many movies with Emily."

"Please. You should thank me. At least I give you metaphors you can't dodge." She jabbed a finger at him. "You're wound up about Rachel."

Will stayed quiet, staring into the dark yard.

Casey sighed. "Look. I get it. She's Joe's kid. You feel responsible. And yeah, she's... a little much sometimes. But don't overthink it. She's twenty-two, Will. A kid. Half the stuff she does, she probably doesn't even realize how it lands."

His jaw worked, silent.

Casey nudged him with her shoulder. "Unless..." Her grin was sly. "...she's a Sith apprentice in disguise. Then, yeah, you're screwed."

That finally drew a low chuckle from him. But it didn't quite reach his eyes.

Casey caught it, her smirk fading. "Hey. All I'm saying is, trust your gut, but don't let it eat you alive. You've carried enough ghosts. Don't make Rachel another one unless she proves she deserves it."

Will exhaled slowly, the glass heavy in his hand. Inside, laughter spilled from the kitchen, Rachel's among them, light and easy.

But all Will could hear was the echo of Kristen's warning.

And Casey's joke, lingering like a shadow: *Sith apprentice in disguise.*

The sliding door creaked, and Rachel came out with two glasses hooked in her fingers and a bottle tucked under her arm. The porch light caught her braid and the faint glint of her earrings.

"Kristen said the adults probably need a bottle or two to unwind," she teased, setting the bottle on the table. "And she told me this one's from *your* Eagle Rare stash, Detective Anderson. Apparently, you two have a whole ritual out here."

Casey's grin was quick. "Ritual? More like therapy with bourbon. He broods, I quote *Star Wars*. Balance to the Force."

Rachel laughed, pouring for Casey first, then herself. As she leaned forward, her braid slipped down, brushing her collarbone. She glanced at Will while filling his glass, her voice softer. "Seems like a good ritual to me. Mind if I join this one?"

Will's eyes held hers a moment too long before he took the glass from her hand. His tone stayed even. "It's not really a club. Just... a place to clear our heads."

Rachel swirled her drink, the amber catching the light. "I could use that. Clearing my head. And I trust yours," she added, almost too casually.

Casey arched a brow but grinned as she raised her glass. "To surving another day without someone trying to drown me in my own shower."

Rachel clinked lightly against Casey's glass, then tapped Will's. "To that. And to good company."

Will took a slow sip, his jaw tight, gaze flicking from Rachel's open smile to Casey's smirk. Casey didn't miss it.

Rachel leaned back in her chair, one leg tucked under the other, her posture open, a touch too relaxed. "I can see why Kristen said this is your spot," she murmured. "Feels safe out here." Her eyes lingered on Will as she added, "Safer with you."

Casey rolled her eyes with a grin. "Careful, Rookie. That's how he gets roped into fixing your car, too."

Rachel laughed, ducking her head, the moment broken. But the warmth of her words hung between them, too deliberate to ignore.

Will tipped back his glass, pretending to focus on the bottle's label. But the unease in his chest only sharpened.

Poolside Bourbon

The bottle of Eagle Rare was dangerously low when the three of them wandered out by the pool, glasses in hand. The turquoise water shimmered against the night sky, and the warm air hummed with that bourbon-heavy looseness that dulled sharp edges.

Rachel had kicked her sweater off earlier and now sat perched on the stone edge, camisole straps sliding with every careless laugh. Her legs dangled into the water, toes stirring ripples.

"See? This beats stale burnt coffee and fluorescent lights," Casey declared, tipping her glass toward the stars. "We oughta move the bullpen out here. Call it Pool Division."

Rachel giggled, tipping back her own glass. "I'd volunteer for that assignment." She leaned to splash Casey, but the movement was too quick, her balance tipped. She caught herself on her elbow with a squeal, but not before her camisole rode up and one strap slipped completely free. For a moment, too much of her was visible in the shimmering pool light.

Casey burst out laughing, nearly spilling her drink. "Jesus, Rookie! Bourbon hazard zone!"

Will had instinctively turned, only to catch a glimpse before yanking his eyes away, jaw tightening. Heat rushed to his face faster than the whiskey burn.

Rachel blinked, looked down, and casually tugged the strap back into place with unbothered ease. Her grin turned sly, eyes flicking toward Will. "It's okay, Detective. I saw you look. We're all adults here. No harm, no foul."

Casey chuckled and slapped her knee. "Oh my God, why Will, you're redder than a Sith lightsaber!"

Will muttered, "Alright, that's enough," and stood, his glass empty but his voice firm. "Time to call it a night."

Rachel leaned back on her hands, unruffled, still grinning as she kicked her feet lazily in the water. "Relax. If I wanted to shock you, I'd cannonball in. Clothes and all."

Casey was doubled over, bourbon tears on her cheeks. "Please, please, somebody write this down. Rookie 1, Will 0."

Will pinched the bridge of his nose, exhaling hard, trying to find his footing between protector and the gnawing unease that Rachel's mask—deliberate or not—was slipping just enough to expose more than skin.

Rachel raised her glass, still grinning. "To Pool Division."

Casey clinked hers with it, laughing. Will, after a beat, tapped his empty glass to theirs.

But his mind wasn't laughing. Not at all.

The Walk Inside

The three of them finally peeled themselves away from the pool, bourbon glow heavy in their limbs. Casey was still laughing as she scooped up the empty bottle.

"Pool Division adjourned," she announced in her best mock-sergeant voice. "We'll reconvene at sunrise. Bring donuts."

Rachel slipped her sweater back over her camisole, but her grin hadn't faded. She lingered a step behind Will as they crossed the patio. "You really don't have to look so mortified, Detective. I've been to frat parties. This is mild."

Will shot her a look over his shoulder. "This isn't a frat party, Rachel. It's my backyard." His voice was calm but edged, more protective than angry.

Casey swung the bottle like a trophy. "Relax, Obi-Wan. Rookie's fine. If she can handle bourbon and a pool, she can handle your disapproving dad glare. At least she wasn't prancing around naked with a pool float."

Rachel smirked, tilting her head. "Disapproving dad glare? I thought it was more of a knight-in-shining-armor thing."

Will exhaled, pushing the sliding door open for them. "It's called making sure you don't end up on a case file, Rachel."

"See?" Rachel said brightly as she brushed past him into the kitchen, citrus-floral perfume trailing in the air again. "Knight in shining armor."

Casey plopped the bottle on the counter and leaned back, arms crossed, watching the two of them with a smirk. "You two are adorable. Like Luke and Leia, if Luke glared more and Leia drank bourbon."

"Casey," Will said warningly.

"What? I'm complimenting." Casey grinned wider.

Rachel leaned against the counter, arms folded, the sweater slipping just enough off her shoulder to look careless—but not careless at all. Her voice softened. "Thank you. For letting me be here tonight. I... haven't felt this safe and relaxed in a long time."

Will's gaze flicked to hers, then away just as quickly. His jaw flexed. "That's the point. Safe."

Casey clapped her hands together. "Alright, feelings circle over. Rookie, you're cut off. Will, you're stuck on water duty. And me?" She pointed at herself with a proud grin. "I'm finishing the banana pudding."

Rachel laughed, shaking her head. "Fine. I'll behave. For now."

Will reached for his keys on the counter, already bracing himself. He knew Rachel's mask was deliberate, her slips too calculated to be clumsy. But tonight—whether it was bourbon or bravado—she was blurring that line again.

And it was becoming increasingly difficult not to see it.

Will walked Rachel out, the gravel crunching under their steps. Her sweater hung loose, sliding down her shoulder as if it had given up fighting her movements. "I'll drive you, pick your car up tomorrow," Will said.

"I'm fine, Officer Anderson, I'm right as rain, can get myself there no problem, I'm not even feeling it was just having fun back there with Casey," Rachel replied.

"Text me when you're home," he said, the command wrapped in his usual protective tone.

Rachel leaned against the car door, smile lazy, eyes bright with just enough bourbon warmth to blur the line between playful and dangerous. "Yes, Detective. Always so serious. You know, if you weren't careful, a girl might start thinking you care about more than just your paperwork."

Will's brow ticked, jaw tightening. "I do care. About keeping people safe. That's all."

"Mmm." She tipped her head, braid spilling forward, gaze locked on him like she was calling his bluff. "Safe is good. But you should know something about pawns..." She stepped closer, just brushing his space with her perfume. In a low whisper, "Sometimes they want their knight to notice *them*. Not just protect them."

Will froze, every muscle wound tight. His mouth opened, but nothing came out.

Rachel grinned at his silence, satisfied, then slid gracefully into the driver's seat. Before shutting the door, she leaned out just long enough to add, voice low and teasing: "Goodnight, Will. Try not to dream about your rook and your pawn at the same time. Might get confusing."

The door shut with a soft thud. Her headlights swept across him as she pulled away, leaving him standing stiff in the driveway, heat rising in his chest that he cursed himself for feeling.

Will pushed back through the sliding door, rubbing a hand over his face. Inside, Casey was parked at the kitchen counter, spoon in hand, banana pudding container practically empty.

She looked up mid-bite, spoon dangling. "If you want some pudding, you'd better get over here before I start licking the bottom of this thing."

Will gave her a look, tired, fond, and exasperated all at once. "I'm going to bed. Long day tomorrow."

Casey smirked. "Mmhmm. Can't believe you let her drive home after serving her bourbon. Real smooth, Detective Dad."

He sighed, shoulders heavy. "She'll text soon. Maybe I should've made her stay."

"Ya think?" Casey said, digging out another scoop. "Don't worry, she'll ping your phone in five minutes with a smiley face and a thank-you for being her knight in shining Kevlar."

Will muttered, "I'm going to bed," again, turning toward the hall.

"Not so fast, flyboy." Casey set the pudding down and pointed her spoon at him like a weapon. "I'm not going anywhere. You take the couch. I'm crashing in the bed with your wife."

He stopped, turned back. "Excuse me?"

Casey shrugged, deadpan. "Didn't pack pajamas. Not sleeping on your couch naked for you to oogle me over your morning coffee. Your wife will say hello, as if it's just another Tuesday. No oogling."

Will dragged a hand down his face. "I am way too old for this shit."

Casey grinned, tossing her shirt at his chest as she headed down the hall. "Goodnight, old man."

The bedroom door clicked shut behind her, leaving Will standing in the living room, shirt in hand, staring at the couch like it had personally betrayed him. His thoughts churned restlessly, long after the house fell quiet.

Then his phone on the coffee table buzzed. Rachel Donavan across the pop-up. Had she even made it to the light?

Thanks for looking out for me tonight. I feel like I can actually breathe when you're around. Guess that's what a good partner does, right?

Will exhales, shoulders sagging. On the surface, harmless. The kind of thing a rookie might text her superior after a rough night.

But the pause before *"partner"* gnaws at him.

She's young. Smart. Damaged. And deliberate.

He tells himself it's nothing, just her way of clinging to stability.

Still, the echo of her words follows him in the dark hall as he sits on the couch and tries to relax so he can sleep.

Shadows Intent

The night was humid, cicadas thrumming in the trees as Rachel had just slipped into her car at the curb. Dinner had been warm, almost too normal for her taste, laughter over casserole, bourbon by the pool with Casey and Will, Casey tossing quips like grenades. For a moment, she'd almost forgotten the shadows waiting outside the Andersons' walls.

She turned the key, told Will goodnight, and hit the street. Headlights swept across the quiet street; she just set her phone down after texting Will. That's when she saw it.

Up the block, parked half in shadow under the oak trees, a black SUV. The same model Casey had mentioned a few days ago. The one that hadn't belonged.

Her chest tightening, she pulled away from the stop, her pulse pounding louder with each look in the mirror. A hundred yards behind, the SUV gradually left the curb.

Rachel's fingers fumbled over her phone. She hit Casey's name.

Casey answered on the second ring, her voice still sharp from banter with Will. "Rookie? You lost already?"

"Not funny," Rachel said, her voice low, tense. "I think I'm being followed. Black SUV, behind me now. Casey... I think it's the same one you saw."

On Casey's side, she was already awake, so she was searching for her clothes to get ready. As she stepped into the hallway, stumbling with clothes in hand, she called Will's name. Will immediately straightened up, his expression turning serious. Casey's smirk disappeared. Switching the phone to speakerphone, "Where are you right now?"

Rachel's grip tightened on the wheel. "Just past the stoplight on Oakridge, heading toward my apartment. They slowed when I slowed. They speed up when I do. It's not nothing."

"Alright, listen to me." Casey's voice snapped into command mode. "Stay on the main roads. Do not lead them to your place. You hearing me?"

"Yes," Rachel whispered, rechecking her mirror. The SUV's headlights glared back, steady.

Will's voice cut in, as Casey stood by him at the couch, calm but edged with steel. "Rachel, you're going to make a right at the next intersection and head toward the PD. Units will meet you en route. We'll intercept if we have to."

"Copy," she said, breath shallow.

Casey, after donning the shirt, Will had just tossed her as he stood up from the couch, was already zipping up her boots and grabbing her keys, motioning for Will. "We're coming to you. Keep talking, Rookie. Don't hang up. You're not alone."

Rachel swallowed, forcing herself to breathe. "Okay. But Casey... if this *is* them..."

"Then you picked the right rook to call," Casey said grimly. "We'll be there in five."

The line stayed open, three voices linked across the dark, as Rachel's taillights cut through the quiet streets and the SUV's shadow followed.

Rachel's fingers cramped on the steering wheel, slick with sweat. In her rearview mirror, the black SUV held steady, headlights unblinking. Not just a vehicle, a hunter's stare, following every move.

Her voice came out thin, higher than she wanted. "Turning onto Main. They're still with me."

Casey's voice snapped sharp in her ear, fast and grounding. "Good. Stay on Main, Rookie. Bright lights, traffic, cameras. Don't give them shadows to work with."

Shadows. Rachel's pulse skipped. That's what it felt like, shadows alive, crawling in her rearview, waiting for her to slow down.

From the speaker, Will's calm baritone pressed in like weight against her ribs. "Patrol units are moving toward your route. Keep steady. Don't panic. We're two minutes out."

Two minutes. Her grip slipped on the wheel. Her throat locked. "Two minutes feels like forever."

"Then make forever work for you," Casey countered. That grit, that defiance, it was like Casey could shove the darkness back just by talking. "Hit a yellow, stretch your turns. Stall 'em. Let us close."

Rachel tried to breathe deeper, but the air wouldn't fill her chest. Her reflection ghosted in the glass, wide eyes, mouth tight, pale. The SUV's glare swallowed the rest of the mirror.

They weren't headlights anymore. They were eyes. Cold. Patient. Shadows given shape.

"They're close," she whispered. "Too close. I can see them in my rear window now."

Will's voice came low, immovable. "You're not alone. We've got you."

But she didn't feel alone. Not yet. Not with the dark pressing against her glass. She wanted to believe him, wanted to sink into that calm and let it hold her, but the SUV was still there. The shadow didn't let go.

Then, headlights cut over the hilltop ahead. Not cold. Familiar. White beams cresting the rise.

Will's Tahoe.

"There!" Casey's voice barked in her ear. "Ten car lengths up, right lane. Rookie's sedan. And behind her—"

Rachel's breath caught, hope and fear crashing at once.

"Do you see them?" she gasped.

Will's reply was flat, solid as iron. "We see them. And they see us now."

Almost as if answering him, the SUV lunged sideways, swerving hard. Tires screamed, shadows peeled off the road and scattered. In an instant, it was gone, cutting down a side street, swallowed back into the dark.

Rachel's knuckles locked on the wheel. "They're running!"

Casey swore, sharp enough to jolt the speaker. "That's no country club couple."

Will's growl came through, steady as pursuit. "Hang on."

But by the time Rachel reached the intersection, the shadow was gone. No taillights. No shape. Just the stink of burned rubber clinging to the night air.

The radio crackled: dispatch reporting negative on all canvass.

Rachel dropped her forehead against the steering wheel, eyes stinging, the weight of the empty mirror pressing down.

Casey's voice cut through, jagged with frustration. "They're good. Too damn good."

Rachel lifted her gaze again, staring at her own pale reflection in the mirror. The shadows were gone, but the truth pressed heavier than ever.

She hadn't been imagining them.

The shadows were real.

Will and Casey idled at the curb as Rachel's sedan rolled into her spot. She killed the engine, jumped out, and jogged over to the Tahoe. Leaning into the passenger window, she forced a tired smile.

"I'm good. Really. I'll head inside, lock up, and try to get some sleep."

Casey's hand shot out, gripping her shoulder before she could pull back. With her other hand, she drew her Springfield Hellcat from under her jacket and pressed it toward Rachel.

"Take this," Casey said, voice flat and firm. "Use it if you see anyone who isn't Will or me."

Rachel's throat bobbed. She curled her fingers around the pistol, its weight both foreign and grounding. "Goodnight. See you tomorrow."

Will gave her a long, unreadable look but said nothing. Casey released her shoulder only after Rachel stepped back toward the stairs.

Her apartment door shut with a heavy click, the deadbolt sliding home beneath her shaking hand. Rachel stood still, chest heaving, forehead pressed to the wood. For a moment, fear throbbed through her like electricity, raw, consuming.

Then it began to change.

She looked down at the pistol in her hand, its matte black surface cold against her palm. Fear bent itself into something else, anger, sharp and deliberate. They thought she'd cower. Thought she'd fold.

Not tonight.

Her hands were still trembling as she strode to the window, but her jaw was locked now, her breath cutting sharper. She yanked the blinds shut with a snap, then pressed her palms flat to the glass, staring into the night where the SUV had been.

They thought she'd cower. Thought she'd fold in on herself, too scared to breathe.

Her reflection in the glass looked pale, eyes wide, but she leaned closer until her breath fogged it. "Not me," she muttered. "Not anymore."

She poured herself a glass of water, hand clenching around it like a weapon, swallowing fast until her throat ached. When she slammed it down on the counter, it rang against the granite, a sharp promise.

Rachel crossed to her desk, tugging her laptop from its case. Fingers still shaky, she powered it on, the blue glow cutting across her face. If the shadows wanted her rattled, fine. She'd use it. Fuel it.

They weren't the only ones who knew how to stalk.

Casey would tell her to back off. Will would order her to stay in her lane. But they weren't the ones with the SUV in their mirror tonight. They hadn't felt the shadows breathing down their neck.

Rachel's lips curled into a faint, fierce smile. "You wanted me on the board?" she whispered. "Then play."

She opened a folder of files she shouldn't have, tags, socials, encrypted chats pulled off the task force drives when no one was looking. Lines she wasn't supposed to cross.

But tonight she wasn't thinking like an intern.

She was thinking like prey that had decided to bare its teeth.

Rachel froze mid-step.

Through the slats of her blinds, the SUV was back. Parked crooked under the sodium light at the far end of the lot. Same dark shape. Same tinted glass. Its engine wasn't running, but she swore she could feel it humming, waiting.

Her pulse hammered as she set the pistol on the counter and reached for her hoodie. She could stay put. Call Will. Call Casey. Wait like a good soldier.

But the thought curdled in her gut. *They're right out there. Watching. Daring me to hide.*

She pulled the hood over her hair, slipped the pistol into her waistband, and killed the apartment light. The glow of her laptop still pulsed on the desk, but she left it—let them think she was home, hunched over a screen, oblivious.

The stairwell smelled faintly of damp concrete as she descended, footsteps careful, controlled. Every echo carried too far. The lot yawned wide when she stepped out, the air sharp in her lungs. Her eyes locked on the SUV.

No movement.

No door cracked.

Just glass like blank eyes staring her down.

She closed the distance slowly, one hand brushing the pistol grip under her sweatshirt, her breath shallow but steady now. The closer she got, the more the dark tint reflected her own face back at her—small, defiant, jaw clenched.

At the rear quarter panel, she crouched, fingers grazing the cold metal. The hood ticked faintly, cooling. *Not long ago. Someone was here.* Her stomach flipped, but she forced herself to circle, crouching low, scanning the tires, the plates. South Carolina tag. Smudged. Numbers memorized in a heartbeat.

Her reflection stretched across the driver's side window. Nothing moved inside. But the faint scent of tobacco drifted out when she leaned close—old smoke clinging to the upholstery. Someone had been sitting here. Watching her door.

Her fingers tightened on the pistol. For a split second, she considered rapping her knuckles against the glass, forcing whoever it was to show themselves. But then she caught the red dot of a dashcam light, glowing faint in the dark. Recording. Cataloguing her face.

Rachel's throat went dry. She eased back, heart jackhammering. They wanted her to come close. Wanted her on tape.

She turned on her heel and walked—slow, deliberate—back toward the stairs, never breaking pace, never running. If they were watching, she wanted them to see her spine straight, head high.

At the top step, she glanced back once more. The SUV hadn't moved, but she felt it, like a predator's eyes tracking the deer that refused to bolt.

Inside her apartment again, she locked the door, chest heaving. She leaned the pistol against the sink, scribbled the plate number on a sticky note, and pressed it to the laptop screen.

"They wanted me to see them," she whispered, voice raw. "Fine. I saw you. But you didn't see me."

Contact with Oblivion

Will stood on the back patio, phone pressed to his ear, the damp night air heavy around him. Mercer's voice was a low growl on the other end, all business.

"I'll make some calls to Rivers and see about doubling the DHS presence at your PD by morning: Plainclothes, long lenses, plate readers. Cartel wants to move in on your people? Fine. We'll flood the board."

"Good," Will said, his voice steady but iron hard. "Because they're already moving pieces."

He ended the call, sliding the phone into his pocket just as the glass door behind him rumbled open.

Casey leaned out, hair mussed, one hand braced on the frame, shirt already slung over her shoulder. "You done playing spymaster out here, Skywalker?" Her smirk tilted wider. "Because I'm about to steal your bed."

Will arched a brow. "Pretty sure that's my wife's bed."

"Exactly." Casey stepped out a little farther, arms folding over her chest. "And since I didn't pack pajamas—and you didn't offer to stop so I could grab some like I asked, I'm not about to wake up in the morning to you doing some bleary-eyed ogling over your first cup of coffee. So, couch duty for you, Obi-Wan. I'm crawling back in beside Kristen. Remember, she's my soul sister. She doesn't care about naked Casey. To her it's just another Tuesday, 'what's up, sister,' and move on."

Will pinched the bridge of his nose, jaw flexing. "You're unbelievable. Twice in one night."

"Damn right." She jabbed her thumb toward the door, grinning. "So back to the couch with you. And technically that was last night and this morning. I'm gonna crawl back into bed and just hope Kristen doesn't mistake me for you in the middle of the night."

Will shook his head, muttering under his breath as Casey slid through the door with a wink. Alone again on the patio, the quiet pressed in, and he thought maybe the couch didn't sound so bad after all.

As Will headed inside and stretched out on the couch, Kristen stirred as Casey slipped back under the covers. Her voice was drowsy, amused. “Quit stealing the blanket, sister.”

Casey smirked into the dark. “See? Told him it was just another Tuesday.”

From the couch, Will muttered into the quiet, half-sigh, half-grumble, “God help me, I live with lunatics.”

Pieces in Play

• The Chevy SUV sat crooked in the far corner of the lot, its paint sun-faded, hood dented, and one headlight hanging loose. The Toys "R" Us sign above the abandoned building still clung to the wall, its pastel letters chipped and broken, a mocking relic of a once-innocent time. Now, the lot reeked of hot asphalt, oil, and old trash, the smell of neglect and violence.

Casey crouched by the driver's side, flashlight sweeping over the blood-spattered interior. "Three of 'em. Ink's cartel, no doubt, Sinaloa break-off. All got carved up before somebody put 'em down."

Will pulled open the back door. The man slumped across the bench seat had a ragged slash up his arm, his shirt was soaked, and his throat was a mess of bruises from where someone had tried choking him out. "Not clean hits. Somebody wanted them to fight first." He shut the door with a dull thud. "This wasn't discipline. This was payback."

Casey straightened, boots crunching gravel, eyes sweeping the yawning black storefronts. "Which means somebody's sending a message. And it wasn't subtle."

Will pulled out his phone and dialed Rivers' number. "Anderson. Toys 'R' Us lot on Franklin. Three dead in an old Chevy, all bearing cartel ink. It looks like another crew worked them over before dropping them. We're not dealing with internal cleanup. This appears to be a turf war."

There was a brief pause, then Rivers' voice, rough as gravel: "On my way. Don't touch a damned thing until I get there."

Twenty minutes later, the low rumble of diesel engines echoed into the lot. A pair of DHS Suburbans pulled under the flickering streetlight, doors swinging open. Tactical vests, rifles slung over shoulders, men spreading out with practiced efficiency.

Evan Rivers stepped out last, his jacket billowing in the night wind, salt-and-pepper hair catching the glow of a streetlight. His eyes flicked from Will to Casey, then focused on the Chevy.

"Christ," he muttered, striding closer. He leaned into the driver's window, eyes narrowing at the tattoos sprawled across lifeless arms and throats. "Cartel, no question. These boys didn't just get hit, they got worked. That's deliberate."

Casey folded her arms. "Somebody wanted them humiliated before they were dead. Somebody wants a new flag planted."

Rivers glanced back at her, jaw tight. "That's not cartel style. This? This has rival crew written all over it."

Will nodded toward the SUV's Texas plates. "They were heading north. Might be crossing boundaries, moving into territory that isn't theirs."

One of the DHS techs leaned into the back seat, glove snapping as he searched. A moment later, he pulled out a heavy plastic sack tucked beneath the rear bench. Inside, dozens of blister packs filled with clear gel capsules.

"Sir," the tech said, voice tight. "We've got product."

Rivers took the bag, held it up to the beam of Casey's flashlight. The capsules glittered faintly in the plastic, clear as water but laced with a blue shimmer when the light caught.

Casey's lip curled. "That the compliance cocktail?"

Rivers's expression hardened, the lines around his mouth deepening. "Yeah. Synthetic. Refined. Clean batch." He looked between them, his voice low and grim. "This isn't just a side hustle anymore. They're moving supply in bulk."

Will's gaze lingered on the SUV, his voice heavy. "And now they're killing to protect it."

Rivers placed the bag into an evidence container, snapping the lid shut with finality. He straightened up, his eyes dark as they scanned the lot. "This isn't just a turf war. This is cartel chess. And Ravenwood?" He nodded toward the dead men. "It's already on the board."

Breakthrough

Encrypted Call — Orin "Oblivion" Mercer

Will's phone buzzed with a single notification on the encrypted app he reserved for one person.

Oblivion: *You alone?*

Will stepped into the evidence room, shut the door, and keyed the deadbolt. *Yeah.*

A secure call connected. Orin Mercer's voice came in low and unhurried, the same calm that made men twice his size nervous.

"Got movement," Orin said. "Cartel chatter spiked again—same cluster tied to Creegan's old routes and a mirror I found of his auction backend. Offshore host. Sloppy clone, but the tags match what DHS pulled from the archive you seized."

Will kept his voice flat. "What tags?"

"Series markers. 'RND' with numerals. Looked like junk until I parsed the bid logs. RND = *Round.* That's how Creegan labeled repeat lots—girls he put up more than once. Round 2. Round 3."

Will felt something cold slide behind his ribs. "Get to it, Mercer."

"I cracked a partial index. One file stuck out. Round 3. Ravenwood geo-stamp in the metadata, forty miles from Oakhaven. Audio picks up a second voice besides

Creegan's—posh, careful diction. I pulled a spectral profile. It's Julien Cain."

Will stared at the steel shelves, his jaw a locked hinge. "You're sure."

"As sure as I've ever been. I'm sending you the index hash and a clean pull I isolated from the mirror. You're not going to like what you see."

A ping hit Will's screen: **RND_03.mp4** plus a still thumbnail—a blurred profile, a familiar braid, a too-thin strap slipping off a shoulder.

Orin's voice softened a shade, which for him meant gravel instead of stone. "One more thing. The victim in Round 3... I think it's your intern."

Silence expanded until Will made it stop. "I'll confirm."

"I figured you'd say that. Call me after." A beat. "And Will? Breathe first."

The line clicked dead.

The File

Will set the laptop on the conference table and log in to the quarantined evidence partition, fingers moving on muscle memory. He entered the hash Orin sent. The file opened.

Grainy video. A cheap mattress. Harsh light that flattened everything into the same sick color.

Rachel.

Her braid. Her nervous half-smile was already failing. A camisole strap slipping, eyes glazed the way drugged eyes never quite find focus.

"Round three," Steve Creegan's voice purred from behind the camera, ugly with pleasure. "Let's see how long you can keep fighting, sweetheart."

Another voice entered, smooth as a knife, Julien Cain. "They'll pay more for this one. She's... different. Very low mileage, practically brand new, rarely driven, if you know what I mean, folks. Still has that new smell to her. Not yet broken in, yours for the right price, Tonight!"

A hand tipped her chin up, presenting her. Cain's ring caught the light. Auction numbers crawled the right margin, bids climbing like a fever chart.

Rachel swayed, tried to pull back, body resisting on reflex even while the drug pulled her under. She blinked. The camera didn't blink back.

Will slammed the laptop shut so hard the room thudded with it. His hands were shaking.

Not frat boys. Not a rumor. **Cain and Creegan.** And Rachel, Joe Donovan's daughter, the intern he'd promised himself he'd protect, had been sold in Creegan's sick marketplace. **Round three,** like she was a product line.

He pressed his palms to his eyes, breath ragged. Memory surfaced uninvited: Rachel sketching crime scenes with surgical precision. Rachel's too-perfect compliance on Casey's couch. Rachel's mask, polite, diligent, uncrackable, the way she looked at him, like she needed saving.

He'd tested her, suspected her. And all along she'd been carrying *this.*

Guilt cut clean through his ribs. Joe's kid. His mentor's blood. He should've seen it. He should've connected the scent, the silence, the steel under her smile, not to be a leak, but to be a survivor.

Was her silence a betrayal?

Or the only way she'd learned to live?

Will opened the laptop again with hands that didn't feel like his own and scrubbed the timeline without sound. Creegan's shadow moved. Cain's hand entered the frame. Rachel blinked. The bid numbers jumped.

He shut it a second time, gently now, like closing a casket.

Across the quiet room, the air felt thinner. The board he thought he knew tipped on its axis.

If Rachel had been their pawn, it explained everything: her armor, her anger, her need to be near the case and in control of the pieces moving on it. It explained the mask.

It didn't tell him whether she'd flip the board.

Will sat back, staring at nothing, and felt the friendship with Joe like a hand on his shoulder and a stone on his chest, both at once.

"I'm sorry," he whispered to a room that didn't answer. "I should've protected you. I wish I had known you were here sooner."

He reached for his phone.

He had to tell Casey.

He had to catch Cain's ghost and finish Creegan's game, for good..

And he had to decide what to do about the intern who was no one's pawn anymore.

Will Updates Casey

Casey was already in the conference room, feet propped on a chair, scrolling through her phone when Will walked in. She glanced up and froze.

"Okay... that's your 'someone just nuked my soul' face. Spill."

Will shut the door, locked it, then dropped into the chair opposite her. For a long moment, he didn't speak, just rubbed his hands over his face like he could scrub the image from his head.

Casey sat up straight. "Will. You're scaring me. What the hell did Mercer drop on you?"

He lowered his hands. His voice came out low, raw. "Round three. That's how Creegan labeled repeat victims. Mercer traced one file. Ravenwood timestamp. Creegan behind the camera. And another voice."

Casey's eyes narrowed. "Don't say it."

"Julien Cain."

She swore, vicious and sharp. "That smug bastard—"

"And the girl." Will's throat worked, like saying it was worse than seeing it. "It was Rachel."

Casey's jaw slackened, words caught somewhere between disbelief and horror. "Rachel... Donovan?"

He nodded once. Couldn't bring himself to repeat it.

Casey leaned back hard, her chair tipping just enough to creak. "Holy shit," she muttered, dragging a hand down her face. "Of course. It's like the Death Star plans were right in front of us and we were too damn busy arguing over who shot first."

Her eyes flicked to Will, wide but sharp. "The way she armors up, the way she watches people like she's running recon for a Rebel assault, hell, even the little rookie blush act. It wasn't just nerves. It was survival training. Every. Single. Move."

She let out a shaky laugh that had no humor. "And here I was, thinking she just wanted to impress you. Turns out, she's been carrying a playbook none of us were allowed to read."

"She was in their auction," Will said flatly. "Cain's hand in frame. Creegan's voice calling it Round Three, like she wasn't a person, just—" He stopped himself, jaw locking.

Casey shook her head slowly. "And we thought she was just some overeager intern playing Nancy Drew. No wonder she's been... testing the waters. No wonder she doesn't trust anyone fully. She's not hiding from us, Will. She's hiding herself."

Silence thickened between them.

Finally, Casey blew out a breath and leaned forward. "So what now? We treat her like a suspect? A victim? Both?"

Will's voice cracked with the weight of it. "She's Joe's kid, Case. My mentor's daughter. And I didn't see it. I tested her, doubted her. Meanwhile, she's been carrying this—alone."

Casey softened, her sarcasm slipping away. "You couldn't have known. Creegan and Cain buried that video deep for a reason. And if Rachel survived that... she's tougher than we gave her credit for."

Will looked down at his hands, knuckles pale. "Or more dangerous."

Casey held his gaze, steady. "Maybe both. But if she's dangerous, she's dangerous to the people who hurt her. Not us."

Will swallowed hard. "I don't know if she can separate the two."

Casey leaned back, her voice firm, grounding him. "Then we keep doing what we've been doing. Watch her. Protect her. But don't underestimate her, Will. Because she sure as hell isn't anyone's pawn anymore."

Will sat back, chest tight. He wanted to believe that. Needed to.

But the image of Rachel's glazed eyes on that screen wouldn't let him.

Journal Insert

I trusted the king.

Trusted him because loyalty was supposed to mean something. Because I thought the board was fixed, safe, guarded.

But kings aren't saviors. Kings are symbols. They stand tall, they move slowly, and they let pawns fall while they cling to their place. He didn't see me go. He didn't even look.

That's when I understood: pawns are never saved. Pawns save themselves.

I will not wait for a king.

I will not wait for anyone.

The game belongs to those willing to take it.

The Date

Rachel's fingers moved steadily over her phone, each tap deliberate, measured. From across the bullpen, she looked like any other intern catching up on texts. Notebook open, pen resting between her fingers, posture neat. But the glow of the screen painted her eyes a shade colder than her smile suggested.

The message waiting for her made bile rise; she hopped up and headed into the bathroom across the hall, though she kept her lips curved faintly as she typed back:

Carter Vance: Still think about you. You were wild that night.

Rachel: Then maybe you'll like what I'm wearing now.

She unbuttoned the blouse she was wearing and slid it off her shoulders, tilting her phone just enough to capture the edge of lace over tan-lined skin, her shoulders bare, her braid pulled tight. Sent. The familiar chime sounded almost like a bell in a ring.

Carter Vance. Julien Cain's cousin. Different last name, but cut from the same poisoned cloth. He was the one who had steered her into Julien's line of sight months ago, the whisper in her ear, the hand on her back, the smirk that sold her off like a drink token. Promise of getting her home safely. That was the first night her face had ended up on Cain's cameras; he was one of the three. That was the night the Watcher had been born.

Her phone buzzed.

Carter: Where?

Rachel's eyes didn't so much as flicker. She typed:

Rachel: Private after-party. Off campus at 10 p.m. Just you and me. Pool's waiting.

The response was instant.

Carter: Send me the address.

She did.

"Something's off with her." Casey's voice was low, pitched just for Will as she leaned against the edge of his desk, arms folded.

Will looked up from the folder in his hands. Rachel sat at her corner desk, braid slung forward, pen moving like she was recording scripture instead of notes. Too focused. Too precise.

"Yeah," Will said quietly. "I see it too."

Casey exhaled sharply, shaking her head. "Day after dinner, she bounced out of there like a kid on a sugar rush—smiles, joking around, cloud-nine happy. This morning?" She jabbed a finger at Rachel without looking. "She's buttoned up like Vader's helmet. No cracks. No grin. Just... surgical. Like she's got some secret game she's running and we're the chumps waiting for kickoff."

Will's gaze stayed steady on the intern, unreadable. "Then we keep watching."

Casey smirked, though her eyes didn't soften. "Feels less like we're watching her and more like she's watching us. And I don't know about you, but I don't like being on the wrong end of the binoculars."

Rachel lowered her phone face down, covering it with her hand as another message came through.

Carter: Got the address, I'll be there. Wear something I like.

Her thumb brushed the pawn in her pocket, grounding her, steady as stone.

"Knights fall sideways. Pawns march forward. Tonight, the cousin bleeds for the king."

She bent her head back over her notes, looking for all the world like the perfect intern.

But the trap was already set.

Casey's Concern

Casey found her by the copy machine, Rachel's braid draped forward as she fed paper into the tray, her motions methodical, too careful.

"Hey," Casey started, trying to keep her tone casual. "You okay?"

Rachel looked up, smile small, controlled. "Of course. Why wouldn't I be?"

Casey crossed her arms, cocked her head. "Because last night at Will's, you were buzzing—laughing, loose. This is the first time I've seen you drop your armor. And now?" She gestured at Rachel's stiff posture. "Now you're wound tight as Beskar steel. So, when are we going to have that movie night? Popcorn, wine, Star Wars marathon, you remember."

Rachel's pen twitched in her fingers. She hesitated. Then, voice calm and deliberate, she said:

"Pawns don't get movie nights."

Casey's breath caught. The words hit her like a live wire, sparking through every note she'd read, every whisper of the Watcher.

Her throat went dry. "What did you just say?"

Rachel blinked, her mask slipping only for a fraction of a second before she recovered. "Nothing. Just meant... students. We don't get breaks. Too much to do."

Casey's heart hammered. "Don't." Her voice cracked sharply, raw. "Don't you dare do that. I know what I heard."

Rachel tilted her head, face softening in a mimic of concern. "Casey... you've been running nonstop. Between the twins, the break-ins, everything, you're exhausted. Maybe you're hearing ghosts where there aren't any."

Casey's fists curled at her sides, fury rising. "I'm not imagining this. Don't—"

Rachel cut her off gently, placing the stack of papers in Casey's hands like a peace offering. "Then let's prove it. Tomorrow night. Movie marathon, your place. I'll even bring the wine and the nail polish. Okay? I need some more downtime. It will be fun."

Casey stared at her, her gut screaming. Rachel's eyes were too steady, her smile too practiced.

But the words were out there, undeniable.

Rachel slid past her, braid brushing Casey's arm as she walked back toward her desk. Calm. Untouchable.

Casey stayed rooted in place, clutching the papers so hard they crumpled, her pulse hammering.

She knew.

And Rachel knew she knew.

Rachel slid back into her chair, posture composed, fingers resting lightly on her notebook. From across the bullpen, she looked like any other intern filing notes. But inside, her pulse was a metronome.

Too close. One word too many.

She replayed it in her mind, Casey's eyes widening, the flare of recognition. The detective wasn't stupid. She'd heard. She'd felt it.

Rachel smoothed her braid forward, masking the heat rising at the back of her neck. She wrote in slow, deliberate strokes on the page, just enough for anyone watching to believe she was focused on the case.

Pawns don't get movie nights.

It had slipped out because it was true. Pawns weren't allowed reprieve. Not until the board was cleared. Not until justice came.

And Casey, The Rook, loud and brash, thought she could corner her. But the rooks are always overextended. Always believed their straight lines gave them strength. They never noticed when the board bent around them.

Rachel pressed the pen harder, almost carving the page.

The rook suspects. Good. Suspicion forces pieces to move. Movement is control. Control is mine.

She glanced at Casey out of the corner of her eye—shoulders taut, papers crushed in her hands, rage trembling through her frame.

Rachel's lips curved faintly. Not a smile. A calculation.

Because now the rook was in play.

And pawns? Pawns only marched where she directed.

Casey shut Will's office door behind her, arms locked across her chest. Her jaw was tight enough to ache.

Will glanced up from the case board. "You look like you've swallowed a grenade."

She didn't waste time. "I asked Rachel if she was okay. Just a normal question. And she..." Casey hesitated, feeling the words crawl back up her throat, hot and electric. "She said pawns don't get movie nights."

Will frowned. "That doesn't sound like her."

"Exactly." Casey's eyes flashed. "It wasn't some slip of a student under stress. It was deliberate. It was... familiar. I've seen that phrasing before. Heard it." Her arms dropped, hands clenching at her sides. "She's got something going on, Will. I don't know what, but it's big. And I think she knows I know."

Will studied her, the weight of her words sinking in. He didn't dismiss her—not with the look in her eyes.

"She recovered quickly," Casey continued, pacing. "Smiled, played it off. Even offered a peace treaty—movie night, wine, nail polish. Like nothing happened, but it did. I'm telling you—she slipped. And it scared her that I caught it."

Will exhaled slowly, dragging a hand across his jaw. "Alright. Let's not guess. Let's find her."

They both pulled out their phones and dialed Rachel's number. Rings. Straight to voicemail. Again. Again. Silence.

Casey's gut twisted. "She's dodging us."

Will was already moving, grabbing the desk phone. "Then we don't play catch-up. We get ahead of it." He dialed Rivers, his tone clipped. "I need your team to be in contact with SouthernLink Wireless tonight. Trace Rachel's phone. I don't care if it's pinging towers or sitting dead in a drawer, I want eyes on it." He paused, voice hardening. "She needs help. Whatever's happening, she's not handling it alone anymore."

Casey leaned on the desk, forcing her voice steady. "This isn't about catching her, Will. It's about getting her the help she's been too proud—or too broken—to ask for. That video..." She swallowed. "Whatever's on it, it's eating her alive."

Will nodded once, the storm outside rattling against the windows as though echoing their urgency. "Then we find her. We talk to her. We get her through this."

The unspoken hung heavy between them: *before she breaks completely.*

Casey leaned on the desk, forcing her voice to stay steady. "This isn't about catching her, Will. It's about getting her the help she's been too proud or too broken to ask for. That video..." She swallowed. "Everything that is on it is eating her alive. To find out that something happened without remembering it is damaging to anyone's psyche. She told me she'd never been in a consensual relationship before. Dad never let her date. Can you imagine what she has been feeling all this time knowing that?"

Will nodded, closed his eyes, and shook his head. The storm outside was rattling against the windows as though echoing their urgency. "Then we find her. We talk to her. We get her through this."

The unspoken hung heavy between them: *before she breaks completely.*

Across town, Rachel's phone buzzed against the table, the glow of the screen cutting across her face as she sat in the rental.

Casey. Will. Voicemail. Again. Again.

Rachel didn't reach for it.

She sat curled in the corner chair, notebook balanced on her knees, pen moving in slow, deliberate strokes. The sound of rain against the window was steady, grounding. Her braid slipped forward as she bent her head, eyes tracing the words as they took shape.

Pawns don't get movie nights.

Pawns don't get to run.

Pawns are tested until they break, or they prove themselves worthy of keeping.

The phone went dark, silent at last. She let the quiet settle, then exhaled, long and measured.

They would come. She knew that.

And when they did, they would see her as she chose to be seen.

Rachel closed the notebook softly, her reflection ghosting in the rain-slicked glass.

Not intern. Not victim.

Not anymore.

Check

The night was split open by thunder. A humid storm crouched low over Oakhaven, lightning spidering across the clouds, the air thick with the smell of rain and ozone.

Will killed the headlights two blocks away, exchanging a grim glance with Casey. The tip had led them here, to an off-campus rental with a pool, where string lights still glowed over the backyard, despite the brewing storm.

"Something's wrong," Casey murmured. Her hand hovered near her holster, eyes sharp. "This is too quiet."

Will nodded, jaw clenched. "It's a trap. But not for us."

They moved through the gate, shoes whispering against wet grass. That's when they saw her braid was tight, face pale but blazing, dressed like a woman looking to get attention. The short, clingy skirt left little to the imagination, riding high enough that every movement teased exposure. Her top was a thin slip of fabric cut low to frame her chest and cling damply against her skin. It belonged in the bedroom, not on the street. She looked like trouble wrapped in temptation, a walking snare baited to make a boy think she dressed for one thing only. The only red flag was a hunting knife gleaming in her hand.

That's when they saw him, Carter Vance, stripped down to a shirt, clinging with sweat, bound at the wrists, a small cut on his arm, forced onto his knees beside the pool. His eyes were wide, terrified, his mouth gagged.

And standing over him was Rachel.

The storm cast shadows across her features, making her look older and harder. Not the eager intern they'd taken under their wing, someone else entirely.

Will caught the scent that had been eluding him since the golf course, since Gerald McBride, murdered at the Lakeview at Rocky Pointe, displayed as a message. It was Rachel, the other person, the elusive enigma, the one watching Ellie from the shadows.

Casey's breath caught. "Jesus, Rachel..."

Rachel didn't turn. Her focus was locked on Carter, voice steady, chilling in its calm.

"You fed me to him. You smiled in my face, called me your friend, and the whole time you were pointing me toward the sharks. Julien. Steve. The others. I thought you were safe. But you were the door that opened, misery, weren't you, Carter?"

Her grip tightened on the knife. Lightning illuminated the scene like a flashbulb, Vance trembling, the blade trembling with him, Rachel standing like an executioner.

Will stepped forward, voice low, deliberate. He held his hands out, palms open. "Rachel. Put it down. You don't need to do this."

Finally, she looked at him, and for a moment her eyes softened, just for him. Then they hardened again.

"Don't tell me what I need, Will. You weren't there. You didn't wake up with gaps in your memory and bruises on your thighs. You didn't take pregnancy test after pregnancy test, wondering if your own body was mocking you. I wasn't careless. I wasn't stupid. I never said yes." Her voice cracked, then rose into a sharp, furious cry. "And they laughed at me. Said I was crazy. Said I was lying."

Casey stepped forward now, hands trembling. "Rachel. I get it. I get the rage. But you've got me now, alright? You've got a sister who understands what it's like to carry that kind of violation. You don't have to burn yourself down just to hurt him."

Rachel shook her head, eyes brimming but fierce.

"The me that could be saved is gone. She died the night the video went live. The real me, the one standing here? She was born from this." She gestured with the knife at Carter, at the pool, at the storm.

Will, slowly, lowered his gun and set it on the wet concrete. His voice dropped, almost a whisper against the rolling thunder.

"Rachel. Listen to me. I want justice, too. I want to end them all, Julien, Steve, the ones pulling the strings. But if you kill him, we lose the chance to blow this open. Vance alive is a thread that leads to all of it. His connection to Cain. The cartel. The club. The drugs. Everything."

Rachel's lip quivered, eyes wide, searching him, begging for something solid to hold on to in the storm.

"Do you love me, Will?"

The question cracked the air sharper than thunder. He didn't flinch.

"I love what you can be, Rachel," Will said, his voice firm but not unkind. "I love the part of you that laughs, that fights, that still wants to belong. But I won't love a monster. Not them. Not what they made you."

He took one step closer, hands still open, voice low enough it felt meant only for her.

"I love the survivor. The one who dragged herself out of hell when no one else believed her. I love the woman who still walks into this bullpen every day, even with scars she thinks no one can see. That's who you are, Rachel. That's who I see standing in front of me, even now."

Her shoulders shook, the knife trembling. For the first time, she didn't look at Carter, but at Will, really looked at him, the stormlight reflecting in her wet eyes.

Casey's breath hitched. She stayed frozen, not daring to break the fragile moment hanging between them.

Will's voice softened, but the steel in it didn't bend.

"If you put that knife in him, Rachel, you'll give them exactly what they wanted: proof that you're nothing but broken and dangerous. You'll bury the part of you I love, the part still worth saving. Don't let them take that from you, too."

For the first time, her mask cracked, a sharp, pained smile, wet with tears. "Then maybe I can't be what you want."

Casey, seizing the moment, edged closer. Will's words held Rachel's attention, but Casey's body coiled, ready to spring.

"You do have a place," Casey said, voice breaking. "With me. With him. You're not alone anymore, Rachel. Don't throw that away. Don't make me lose my sister before I ever got her."

Rachel blinked, chest rising and falling. She loosened her grip on the knife, just for a heartbeat.

And that was all the opening Casey took.

With a sudden lunge, she dove for Rachel-

-and the storm exploded in thunder as the knife flashed, the women crashing to the ground in a tangle of limbs, Rachel's BJJ techniques snapping into place, the fight igniting.

The Fight

The two women hit the wet concrete with a crack. Casey's shoulder slammed down hard, but Rachel moved like water, rolling instantly, knife hand snapping free.

Casey's training kicked in, she trapped Rachel's wrist with both hands, pinning the blade inches from her throat. Rain spattered across their faces, the thunder shaking the sky.

"Dammit, Rachel!" Casey grunted, twisting her hips, trying to buck her off.

Rachel's expression was terrifyingly calm, lips drawn back in something between a smile and a snarl. "You don't understand. You *can't* understand. This isn't about you."

"You're right," Casey spat back, fighting for leverage. "It's about the girls who never made it out. About Emily. Ellie. About *me*. You think you're the only one?"

Rachel twisted like a serpent, using her size against Casey, knee driving down on her ribs. The knife scraped closer. Casey gasped, but clamped down harder, fingers digging into Rachel's wrist.

"You think this makes you strong?" Casey hissed. "You're not punishing them. You're just finishing what they started!"

Rachel's eyes flared, raw and wounded. "They made me a weapon. I won't sit pretty on a shelf and wait for permission to use it!"

With a sudden move, she slipped her wrist, knife slashing down—

"Rachel!" Will's voice thundered across the storm. He was moving, gun abandoned, hands up. But he couldn't fire, not without hitting Casey.

Casey caught Rachel's arm, redirected the blade into the concrete with a screech of metal. She snapped her knee up, cracking Rachel in the side. The younger woman grunted but didn't falter. Instead, she spun them, dropping her weight, snapping into a perfect armbar attempt, trying to hyperextend Casey's elbow.

Casey screamed but rolled with it, rain and grit grinding into her skin. "Son of a bitch—BJJ since you were sixteen, huh?" she growled through clenched teeth.

Rachel's expression flickered at the recognition. "And you still can't stop me."

Casey managed to wedge her boot against the ground, shifting her weight. She slammed her free fist into Rachel's ribs, once, twice, three times. The knife skittered out of Rachel's grip, sliding toward the pool's edge.

Will dove for it, kicking it back with his boot. But Rachel used the moment, twisting her body, mounting Casey again. Her fists came down, wild, controlled fury. Casey blocked what she could, blood seeping from her split lip.

"Stop!" Will bellowed. His voice cut through the downpour and lightning. "Rachel, look at me!"

She froze mid-swing, chest heaving, rain streaming down her face. Casey, pinned, sucked in air, trembling with exhaustion.

Will stepped closer, hands open, voice trembling. "If you kill him, if you kill her, they win. Julien wins. Steve wins. They made you a monster, Rachel, and I'm not going to let you become their masterpiece."

Rachel's knuckles hovered above Casey's face. She was crying now, sobs tearing through her chest. She looked down at Casey, then at Will, then back at Carter Vance—pathetic, whimpering, still bound at the pool's edge.

Her whole body shook. The knife was gone, but the rage burned hotter than the storm above.

Casey's voice came low, ragged, but steady. "You want to finish this game? You've got a team now. Don't play alone. Don't make me lose you before I even get you."

For one heartbeat, Rachel's mask cracked wide open—anger, grief, longing.

Then her body sagged, sliding to one knee sideways off Casey. She buried her face in her hands, sobbing into the rain.

Will crouched instantly, sliding the knife away from reach, his other arm hovering but not touching her. "It's over, Rachel. Let us help you. Please."

Rachel's voice was muffled, broken: "It'll never be over."

Lightning flashed again, painting the scene: Carter Vance bound like a pawn, Casey bruised and bleeding, Rachel shaking in the rain, and Will kneeling between them.

The storm had broken, but the real one was still just beginning.

Checkmate

Rachel trembled as Will knelt in front of her, his hands hovering like he wasn't sure if touching her would comfort or ignite her again. Her face was streaked with tears and rain, her body sagging under the weight of it all.

"Rachel," he said softly. "Come on. Let me help you up."

She let him slide his hand beneath her arm, let him guide her up onto unsteady legs. For a moment, she stood in front of him, tears streaming down her face, inches away, chest heaving. Her wide eyes locked on his, raw, unguarded.

And then she surged forward.

Her lips crashed against his, desperate and searching, tasting of salt and rain. Will froze, heart slamming against his ribs. His instincts screamed to pull back, to stop it, but his body was caught flat-footed, stunned by the suddenness of it.

Rachel pulled back just enough to whisper, her breath trembling against his mouth.

"If you weren't a good man," she said, voice breaking with something like admiration, something like accusation, "you could have had me, all of me."

For one heartbeat, she looked like a shattered twenty-two-year-old girl again.

Then the mask slid back into place.

Casey groaned behind them, pushing herself off the wet pavement, ribs aching, lip bleeding. She didn't see the kiss—just heard Rachel's voice flatten, calm and cold again.

By the time Casey steadied herself, Rachel had already moved.

In one clean motion, Rachel darted forward, hand snapping down to Casey's thigh. She ripped the Sig Sauer 365XL Rose from its holster on Casey's thigh, spinning on her heel with a practiced grace that looked nothing like a rookie intern.

"Rachel!" Will barked, stepping forward.

But she was already pivoting, the gun level in her hands, her braid whipping across her shoulder as she brought it up. Carter Vance whimpered where he knelt by the pool, duct tape slick with rainwater, eyes bulging.

Rachel lifted her foot, planting firmly against Casey's ribs before she could rise. Casey whipped her head around just in time to see Rachel with her gun held up.

Her balance tipped, with the push from Rachel's weight on her and a slight shift in her own weight.

With a splash and a curse, Casey tumbled sideways into the pool, water erupting in a spray that mingled with the rain. She surfaced immediately, sputtering, fury and fear in her eyes.

Rachel stood above her, pistol steady, her expression blank again, the Watcher now fully in control.

"Queens betray pawns," Rachel murmured, her voice eerie in its calm. "But even kings hesitate. The Rook cannot interfere."

Her finger tightened on the trigger.

Will held his hands out, palms up, his voice steady even as the rain sheeted down. "Rachel. Listen to me. You don't want to do this."

Rachel kept the Sig leveled, her finger taut but steady, her braid dripping with rain and sticking to her cheek. Her foot quickly pressed against Casey's shoulder as she approached the side of the pool, pushing her half-submerged back into the pool. Casey spat out water, eyes locked on Rachel's, trying to calculate angles, timing, but she saw the dead certainty in her intern's gaze.

"I like you, Casey," Rachel said flatly. "But don't test me. I will shoot you if I have to."

Will took a step forward, but Rachel barked: "Stay back!" Her eyes cut to him, wild but sharp. "Kings hesitate. That's their flaw."

"Rachel–"

"You want to talk about flaws?" Her voice broke, rising with the storm. "The DA's office said no evidence. Your law enforcement officers took my report, including all the details of who, where, and when. And you know what I got?" Her free hand trembled as she gestured sharply. "They said drinking. They said, *You should know better.*"

Will's jaw clenched. "Rachel–"

"I didn't ask for this!" she screamed, rain mingling with tears on her cheeks. "They knew better. They knew exactly what they were doing when they drugged me, when they violated me. When they laughed, I never consented; they took from me something I can never get back."

Casey, still trapped in the pool under Rachel's aim, coughed from the pouring rain, taking her breath, and snarled through gritted teeth, "Rachel, listen to me—"

But Rachel cut her off, voice low now, almost eerily calm, the gun never wavering. "And what justice do I get, Detective? They get to live. *I died that day.* The day I realized I was used, discarded like nothing. A pawn moved and sacrificed for their game. Sacrificed my virginity for their sick fucking game!" she screamed.

Will's heart hammered, but he forced himself to hold her gaze, steady, unflinching.

Rachel tilted her head, almost like she was listening to a whisper only she could hear. Her voice dropped to a chilling murmur.

"Justice... is removing the pawns from the board."

The thunder cracked above them, rolling across the night sky. The barrel of the pistol glinted in the lightning.

Casey shifted in the water, slow, testing how far she could edge to the side without drawing fire. Rachel's eyes caught the movement instantly.

CRACK!

The gun barked, the muzzle flash stark in the storm-dark, and a round tore into the pool just inches from Casey. The water erupted in spray.

"Stay in the water," Rachel said, voice sharp, commanding. Then, softer, almost sorrowful: "Please. Don't make me change my mind."

Casey froze, teeth bared, chest heaving as she treaded water.

Rachel's expression faltered, and for the first time, she sounded almost... human. "I didn't kill you the last time you were trapped in the water. Remember?" Her lip trembled, but her grip on the pistol was iron. "That was me, Casey. Your soda, your shower... all of it. I put you there."

Casey's breath hitched, fury sparking through the fear. "That was *you*?"

Rachel nodded once, rain running down her face like tears. "But I made sure you survived. You treated me like a person. Like I mattered. You weren't just a cop barking orders; you saw me." She swallowed, her voice cracking just enough to slip through. "I admired that. I still do. I just needed you out of the way. I see I was wrong about you. About Kristen, About Will."

Casey's chest tightened, words caught between rage and disbelief.

Rachel's voice hardened again, mask snapping back into place. "I made sure one of the pawns found you. Messaged her from your phone. Left the trail. And then I gave you more clues, breadcrumbs, about the Serpents, about what they were doing to those girls."

She stepped closer to the pool's edge, gun trained steady on Casey. "But you didn't do anything. Not really. You *watched.* You let them keep playing. So I had to step in." Her tone dropped to a whisper, raw and venomous.

"I had to do your job. Remove the players from the game."

Lightning slashed across the sky, illuminating the entire area like a camera flash: Rachel's braid plastered to her neck, Casey half-submerged, Will standing helpless, his gun still on the ground at his feet.

And Rachel, the Watcher, holding them both in check.

The storm howled around them, the rain hammering so hard it stung the skin and filled every breath with water. Wind lashed at Rachel's braid as she stood over Casey, gun steady, her silhouette flickering in the lightning.

Will's voice rose above the roar, strained but calm. "Rachel. Why Gerald McBride? Why did he have to die?"

Her head snapped toward him, eyes burning with a mix of fury and grief. "Because he was vermin. One of *them*. One of the bidders at Julien's auctions." Her voice wavered, then hardened. "He won me. Do you understand that? *He bought me.* And when the memories came back, when I saw his face again... I made damn sure he knew who I was before I ended him."

Her lips curled, a bitter half-smile that was closer to a sob. "That wasn't murder, Detective. That was reclamation. That was justice."

Lightning forked behind her, a thunderclap rolling through the night.

Will held her gaze, his voice rough. "And the twins? Emily and Ellie? Why mimic them? Why put them through hell?"

For the first time, Rachel hesitated. Her knuckles tightened on the grip, but her eyes flickered, softer for a heartbeat. "Because they're pawns. Innocent. Like I was." Her voice cracked, tears streaking down with the rain. "The Queen wasn't protecting them. Someone had to. So it was me."

Casey stirred in the pool, trying to edge closer to the side, but Rachel didn't even look at her, too caught up in the storm of her own words.

"To protect them, I needed their attention. I had to... guide them. Keep them away from the boys who stare at them like meat, like toys, like... I was." Her voice dropped, thick with pain. "Every time I watched them, I saw what I used to be. Before Julien. Before Steve. Before I was reduced to nothing but a pawn on their board, but this Pawn is now the Queen; this is my board."

She took a shuddering breath, staring past Will as if she were speaking to someone else entirely. "I did them a favor. I didn't want what happened to me to happen to them. Not ever."

Thunder shook the ground, the pool water sloshing against the tiles. Will's heart pounded as he saw her finger twitch against the trigger.

Rachel's eyes snapped back to his, dark, glistening, broken. "They are my reminder, Detective. Of the girl I'll never get to be again."

Rachel's shoulders shook, rain plastering her braid to her neck as the storm howled around them. She turned her gaze from Will to Casey, her voice raw, almost tender.

"I'm sorry for what I did to you, both times. I never wanted to kill you, just scare you," she said, water streaming down her cheeks like tears. "Sorry you had to replace your whole underwear drawer. Thanks for taking care of me when I drugged myself. I needed you two to see, to wake up. I truly am sorry, we'll never get to binge on wine and watch the Star

Wars movies on your couch. I wanted that more than you know. But now I understand what you are. What you gave me. I love you my friend."

Casey, chest heaving as she tried to tread in the pool, froze—because Rachel's apology wasn't hollow. It was *real*.

Rachel's eyes shifted to Will. Her tone softened further, almost reverent. "And thank you... for being my knight in shining armor. For not taking advantage of me. For seeing me. For not being my first consensual encounter, my only one that would have mattered. You are truly the King on this board." She smiled faintly, fragile, then let it fall. "But when this check is done, I'll only have removed one piece. You will still need to clear the board of the predators who move the pawns."

Her jaw trembled. "The twins, I tried. I did my best. I'm sorry."

Then, without hesitation, she pivoted back to Carter Vance, tied and shuddering on his knees by the pool's edge. The barrel of her stolen pistol pressed against his temple, forcing his head sideways and then hitting him with the pistol grip.

"You had fun with me, pretended to help me out, and then you drugged me and raped me, didn't you?" she hissed.

Even in the downpour, the spreading yellow stain between his knees was unmistakable, on the white concrete coating of the pool deck.

"Answer me!" Rachel shoved his head again, steel grinding into his skull. "You had your fun, and that was your death sentence. Signed the night you raped me. More than once, you tricked me, fed me to those sharks, to do what they pleased with me. Time to pay for your crimes."

"Rachel, don't!" Will's voice broke across the thunder, raw desperation. Casey's splashes carried the same plea.

Rachel's expression hardened, her knuckles white on the grip as she looked down on Vance, "Queen takes pawn, Checkmate."

Her finger tightened—

And three green dots bloomed across her rain-slicked torso.

The storm seemed to pause, thunder drowned out by the hum of suppressed rifles. Through the sheets of rain, three men materialized, half-masks covering their faces. Behind them, steady and unflinching, stood Orin Mercer.

"Stand down," his voice carried like iron.

Rachel's eyes went wide. "What the—"

Two faint pops cracked through the storm. Rachel staggered, blinking in shock at the two darts jutting from her bare stomach, the tranquilizer already burning its way through her bloodstream.

Her grip slackened, but she fought to lift the weapon, dragging it toward Vance even as her knees buckled. "No... not yet—"

Her arm trembled violently. She squeezed the trigger as her body gave out, the crack of the gunshot ringing through the storm.

The Fallen Piece

The gunshot echoed against the storm like a final word. Carter Vance jerked forward, a strangled cry ripping from his throat before collapsing onto his side by the pool. Blood began to spill and mingle with the rain, thin streams running toward the water's edge.

"Damn it!" Will lunged forward, sliding across the wet concrete, pressing his hand against Vance's back. "Casey—pressure, now!"

Casey was already moving, splashing out of the pool, her clothes plastered to her body. She dropped to her knees beside them, tearing fabric from her soaked shirt to pack the wound.

Over their shoulders, Rachel lay crumpled, half in the rain, half in shadow. Her eyes fluttered but wouldn't focus, tranquilizer darts still jutting from her stomach. Will made a move toward her—

"Don't."

Orin Mercer stood over her, calm as stone, his masked men lifting Rachel with practiced precision. She didn't fight. Couldn't. Her limbs dragged like dead weight as they hoisted her between them.

Will's jaw locked. "She's our suspect, Mercer."

"She's mine now." Mercer's voice cut through the storm with the finality of a gavel. "You want this cartel operation?

You'll thank me later. She's not going to the county lockup. Not yet."

Will's breath came hard, fury and frustration colliding. He wanted to argue, to draw his gun, to *stop this*. But Casey's voice snapped him back:

"Will! He's fading!"

Vance groaned, barely conscious, blood bubbling at his lips.

Will cursed under his breath and pressed harder on the wound, watching as Mercer and his team disappeared into the storm, Rachel swallowed by the night.

The sound of distant sirens finally broke the silence between thunder. Casey's hands shook as she held the compress. "What do we even tell dispatch?"

"The truth," Will said bitterly, though his voice cracked. "Suspect fled the scene. EMS priority on the victim."

Casey glanced at him, rain dripping from her lashes, her voice low. "She's not just the suspect anymore, Will. She's the Watcher."

Will didn't answer. His hands stayed locked on Vance's back, blood slick between his fingers, but his eyes were still on the dark where Rachel had been.

Hard Day for Carter

The hospital corridors smelled of antiseptic and fatigue. Will and Casey stood outside the surgical unit, their clothes still damp from the storm, their report already filed with Monroe. A clean, clipped version of events.

Suspect was standing over the victim when detectives arrived. Shot fired. Suspect fled. Victim transported.

Every line true. Every detail missing.

Monroe's jaw had worked like a vice during the debrief, but he hadn't pressed. There are too many moving pieces, and his department is already under too much heat. Will had caught Casey's eye across the space between them. Both of them had silently agreed: nobody would believe the truth about Rachel, not yet. Maybe not ever.

The waiting room smelled of antiseptic and burnt coffee, a cocktail of weariness that clung to the skin. Fluorescent lights buzzed faintly overhead, casting a pale glow over the scuffed linoleum and rows of plastic chairs that were too stiff to rest in.

Will leaned against the wall, his jacket slung over one arm, exhaustion carved into the lines of his face. He hadn't shaved in a day, maybe two, and the weight in his shoulders made him look older than he was. Casey sat with her boots kicked out in front of her, spinning the Styrofoam cup between her palms, the dregs of coffee long gone cold. She flicked her eyes toward the hallway every time footsteps echoed, jaw working like she had something to say but thought better of it.

Finally, the surgeon appeared. Clipboard under one arm, surgical cap tucked in his pocket, the man looked as tired as they did.

"Detectives," he said, voice low and even. "Carter Vance survived surgery. The bullet fractured the T10 vertebra, with cord involvement at T11." He glanced at his notes, then back at them, eyes narrowing slightly. "The prognosis..." He hesitated, as though softening it might blunt the impact. "...is permanent paralysis from the waist down."

Casey let out a slow breath, one hand dragging across her face. "So he's not walking out of here."

The surgeon shook his head. "Not walking. Not climbing stairs. Not running. Not..." He stopped himself, lips pressing together. "Function below the waist is gone. He'll wake soon, but he'll never be the same."

Silence hung, punctuated only by the distant beep of monitors and the rattle of a cart being wheeled down the corridor.

Will's jaw locked, the muscles twitching. "Can we talk to him tonight?"

The surgeon shook his head firmly. "Not tonight. He'll be groggy, disoriented. Tomorrow at the earliest. You'll want to tread carefully—he'll be adjusting to a reality he didn't see coming."

The doctor left them, his footsteps fading into the hum of machines and whispers of nurses beyond the ICU doors.

Casey rose, balling her empty cup before tossing it into the bin with a sharp flick. "Guess karma's still on the clock."

Will didn't answer. His eyes had gone distant, staring at nothing. In his head, the storm still raged—the rain, Rachel's trembling voice as she whispered *checkmate*, her gun steady, her eyes haunted.

Casey's hand brushed his arm, a rare moment of softness. "Hey. You good?"

Will blinked, grounding himself. "We'll come back tomorrow. See if he knows who else is on the list."

She nodded, but her eyes lingered on him, as though she could see the gears grinding behind his silence.

Together, they pushed through the double doors into the night. The storm had blown on, leaving the air damp and heavy. Their headlights cut across slick pavement as they pulled away, taillights vanishing into the wet streets.

Behind them, in the high ICU, Carter Vance lay unconscious under the thin glow of monitors—breathing, alive, but broken.

And unknown to them, not alone.

Inside the ICU

The hallways of St. Vincent's ICU were too quiet for midnight. The storm outside had thinned the visitors, and security was lighter than it had any right to be after a shooting. Fluorescent lights flickered overhead, casting long, sterile shadows across polished linoleum.

A figure moved through them like a shadow given weight. Hood up, half-mask obscuring his face, gait precise, deliberate, silent.

Orin Mercer.

He didn't hesitate at the nurse's station, didn't even glance at the cameras angled down the hall. He had already mapped their blind spots. Instead, he slipped through the door marked PRIVATE – NO ENTRY with the ease of a man who belonged everywhere.

Inside, the room was hushed but for the rhythmic beep of monitors and the faint hiss of oxygen. Carter Vance lay pale beneath the thin hospital blanket, IV lines snaking into his arm, pupils still heavy from anesthesia. A sheen of sweat clung to his temples.

Mercer approached the bed and loomed, his shadow swallowing Vance's broken body. He didn't speak at first, letting the machines frame the silence. Then, leaning close, shaking the chest of Vance, his voice was a low rasp:

"If you expose Rachel," he said, each word deliberate, "your family gets the videos. Every single one. Neatly packaged and dropped right on the front porch. Copies for your parents. Your sister. Maybe even the Dean."

Vance stirred, lids fluttering open sluggishly. Confusion swam behind the drugs clouding his gaze. His lips moved, dry, cracked. "...Wh...who...?"

Mercer ignored the question, his voice dropping to a blade's edge. "You're lucky not to have a bullet in your head. Luckier than that girl ever was, you will soon wish she killed you."

Recognition bled through Vance's fog, panic sharpening his eyes. "...Rachel...?"

"You don't speak her name," Mercer snapped. The whisper came sharp as glass.

He leaned in, voice a low growl. "I want the name of your supplier. The cartel contact. Who gives you the poison you pump into those girls? Don't make me ask again—this is your only chance."

Vance's face twisted, sweat running in thin streams. Tears carved clean tracks through it, his voice breaking as the name scraped out.

"Rafael Domínguez... they call him El Gallo."

Mercer stilled. The name wasn't new. A mid-tier broker, loud in South Carolina and Georgia, always crowing on someone else's leash. But if Domínguez was supplying the frat boys directly, the rot ran deeper than anyone wanted to believe.

Behind the mask, Mercer's eyes narrowed. "El Gallo," he repeated, the words hanging like a death sentence. "Of course it's him."

Vance swallowed hard, every muscle trembling. "If they find out I talked... they'll make me wish I'd died on that pool deck. They'll... they'll."

Mercer cut him off, voice flat as ice. "I already told you. They will. You're paralyzed. You can't fight. You can't run. They'll take their time with you. And when they're finished, they'll make sure what's left of you is found. That's how the cartel cleans house."

Vance whimpered, his hands twitching against the sheets, strengthless.

Mercer leaned closer, his whisper colder than the hiss of oxygen in the room. "The only thing standing between you and that fate is me. Remember that. And remember this night every time you close your eyes."

Mercer straightened slowly, tilting his head as though studying him. Then he gave the killing stroke, not with steel, but with memory. His voice hardened to steel.

"'Harder Carter' What a joke."

Vance jolted, eyes wild. Panic consumed what little composure he had left. That nickname was fraternity-only. A secret no outsider should've known.

Mercer bent close once more, the words final and absolute.

"I was never here."

By the time Vance's fingers moved toward the call button, the door was already clicking shut. Only the machinery remained steady and unmoving, indifferent, as Carter Vance lay trembling, haunted not just by the cartel, but by the ghost who had marked him tonight.

The door clicked shut.

For a long time, Carter Vance lay perfectly still, staring at the ceiling, heart hammering so hard it overpowered the beeping of the monitors. The storm rattled against the glass window, rain streaking down like a thousand fingers clawing to get in.

He tried to swallow, but his throat was dry. His hand inched toward the call button—slow, trembling—but halfway there, he froze.

The videos.

His chest seized with a memory. Laughter. Frat brothers chanting his name. "Harder Carter." The secret password whispered in rooms reeking of sweat and spilled liquor, where masks hid faces and girls didn't wake up until it was too late.

He could see them. The girls. Faces blurred, muffled cries under the music. And Rachel. Always Rachel. The one they'd fed to Cain, to Creegan. The one he thought was broken enough to forget.

But she hadn't. She'd come back.

And Mercer—whoever the hell Mercer was—knew *everything.*

Carter squeezed his eyes shut. Panic surged, but it stopped short, like hitting a wall. The numbness below his waist was total, absolute. He couldn't kick, couldn't thrash, couldn't run. He was caged in his own body.

His mind clawed for escape. *Tell the cops. Tell Will. Tell Casey.* But Mercer's words were a vise on his skull. *If you expose Rachel, your family gets the videos.*

He pictured his parents opening their mailbox, pulling out a DVD case. His mother's face, white as death. His father's silence, heavy and final. His little sister—God, his little sister—seeing what he had done.

"No..." His voice cracked, hoarse. "...oh God, no."

The monitor ticked faster, betraying him. He tried to calm down, dragging air into his lungs, but it only made him gag.

And then—beneath the storm outside, beneath the machines inside, he *heard her.*

Rachel. Whispering, the same way she had at the pool. *Checkmate.*

His eyes flew open. Empty room. Just him and the shadows. But he swore he heard her again, closer this time, brushing his ear like a lover.

You had your fun. And that was your death sentence.

Tears burned his eyes, hot and useless. He couldn't even turn onto his side. He was a slab of meat pinned to the mattress, left with nothing but memory and fear.

And worse than the paralysis, worse than Mercer's threats, was the truth sinking in like poison:

Rachel wasn't finished.

She was still on the board.

And Carter Vance knew—whether she stood over him in flesh or as a phantom, he was only one more move away from being removed.

Pawns get taken when they forget the board.

Aftermath

The precinct felt emptier than it should have.

Will stood in the doorway of the bullpen, the hum of fluorescent lights pressing in like static. His gaze drifted to the desk in the far corner—the one that used to be hers. Clean. Bare. Stripped to nothing but faint outlines where a monitor had sat, impressions in the carpet where her chair had rolled. It was as if Rachel Donovan had never been there at all.

But she had.

Her presence lingered in the silence between phones, in the rhythm of the typing that had slowed since she'd left, in the faint shadow that seemed to cling to that corner like a memory burned into the walls. He could almost see her there even now, braid falling over one shoulder, pen scratching notes with that meticulous care, eyes flicking up and watching everything, everyone, while pretending not to.

Casey sat slouched at her own desk, elbows on her knees, her head bowed. In her hand, she clutched something so tightly her knuckles had gone bone-white. She hadn't moved in ten minutes.

Will crossed the bullpen quietly, the way you approach someone standing too close to the edge of a cliff. His jacket whispered as he shifted it over one arm.

"What is it?" he asked, voice low, cautious.

Casey didn't answer right away. Then, with a slow inhale, she turned her palm up. Resting there was a rook—polished marble, cold and heavy, carved with precise detail. Not the cheap plastic kind from a boxed set. This was exquisite. Deliberate. A piece meant to last lifetimes.

"It was in my chair when I came in," she said softly. Her mouth twisted into something halfway between a smile and a grimace. "Guess I got promoted from pawn."

Will let out a breath he hadn't realized he was holding. He lowered himself into the chair beside her, the metal legs creaking in the quiet. "She wanted you to find it."

Casey rolled the rook between her fingers, the marble catching the sterile light, her eyes sharp but shining with tears she refused to let fall. "Hell of a goodbye gift. Cold, precise, like her." She swallowed, then added more quietly, "But also... It's proof. She thought about me."

Will leaned back, staring across the bullpen at the empty desk. His throat tightened unexpectedly. "She thought about all of us."

Casey shifted the rook, thumb brushing the carved crown at the top. "You know what she told me? A couple of nights back, before it all went to hell?"

Will shook his head.

"She said she wished she had a big sister," Casey murmured, voice cracking before she pulled it back under control. "That we'd binge Star Wars, drink too much wine, maybe paint our nails if she could sit still long enough. She wanted that. She wanted to just... be twenty-two. Be normal."

Her grip tightened on the marble until it bit into her skin. "And I told her we would. I promised her. And now all I've got is this."

Will stayed quiet, but a memory rose unbidden, threading through him like smoke. The faint trace of citrus and florals she'd shrugged off as clearance-rack lotion. He'd caught it before.

Not just on her.

At Gerald McBride's body at the golf course.

When Ellie was on the golf course, running.

At frat row, drifting through the crowd.

At scenes where the Watcher had left her mark.

The same scent.

He'd dismissed it then as background noise, a passerby, one of a hundred details lost in the chaos. But now he knew. It had been her. Always her.

Casey noticed his face go distant, unreadable. "What?"

"Her lotion," Will said hoarsely. "I smelled it at McBride's scene. At the golf course. I didn't place it then. Didn't want to. But it was her. She was there."

Casey looked down at the rook, her voice hushed. "So that's how you knew, even then... she was already playing the game."

Will nodded slowly, the weight of it pressing into his chest. "Every move. Every piece. We just weren't ready to see it."

Silence stretched between them, thick with grief and the hollow ache of unfinished business. The rook gleamed cold in Casey's hand, its edges catching the fluorescent glow like it belonged more to shadow than to light.

Rachel wasn't gone.

She was still on the board.

At the Anderson house, the air at dinner was heavier than it had any right to be. Kristen set the plates down harder than she meant to, porcelain clattering against the wood. The sound was too sharp in the quiet dining room. Both twins flinched. Usually, they'd roll their eyes at her mood, maybe pick a fight over who got the last roll. Tonight, they sat in silence.

Emily picked at her napkin, tearing it into strips with nervous fingers. Finally, she whispered, almost afraid of the weight in her own voice:

"She said she was watching us. Protecting us."

The words hung like fog.

Kristen's throat closed. Her instinct was to say what mothers are supposed to say—that they were safe, that it was over. But the words stuck. For months, she had stood in front of microphones, defending the DA's office, swearing justice was being done. All the while, girls like Rachel had been slipping through cracks wide enough to swallow whole lives.

Her fork clinked against her plate as she let it go. "I should have seen it," she murmured, voice breaking. "I should've done more."

Ellie reached across the table, slipping her hand into her mother's, fingers trembling but firm. "It wasn't you, Mom. It was them. They're the ones who did this. Not you."

But guilt settled heavily in Kristen's chest, immovable.

Emily shook her head, eyes wet, voice cracking. "Yeah, she scared us sometimes. The messages, the way she just... appeared. It was creepy." She flicked her gaze to her sister, swallowing. "But deep down... she wasn't trying to hurt us. She was warning us. Remember what she said? That pawns get taken when they forget the board. That's what she thought we were—pawns. And she didn't want us to get taken."

Ellie nodded, her own voice low but steady. "She told me once that pawns could become queens. That if we survived, we could be stronger than her. She believed that, Em. She wanted it for us."

Emily's lips trembled. "And the thing is... I liked her. I really did. When she let herself laugh, she was funny. At the pool and dinner those nights... she felt normal. Like an older sister we didn't know we had. Like she belonged here, with us."

Ellie's eyes filled, but her tone softened into something almost reverent. "She was trying. Even if she used fear, even if she crossed lines... she wanted us safe. She wanted us to learn from her mistakes. She thought if she scared us enough, we'd never let ourselves be played."

Kristen blinked hard, vision blurring. Her daughters were so young, still clinging to innocence even as the world kept chiseling away at it.

She whispered, more to herself than to them, "And who was protecting her? Who helped her cross the board?"

The silence that followed was suffocating. The twins exchanged a glance, but neither spoke. Neither had an answer.

The table sat heavy with the absence of the girl who had both haunted and shielded them. Outside, a dog barked in the night, distant and hollow. Inside, the kitchen clock ticked like a metronome, marking time for a game Rachel had started and left unfinished.

And in the quiet, all three Anderson women realized the same truth: Rachel hadn't been a monster to them. She was a warning. And they missed her.

Epilogue: Hellbound

The storm had broken overnight, but the air still carried the thick, metallic scent of rain-soaked earth. Damp leaves clung to the porch rail, and the yard gleamed dark under the swollen moon. Water still dripped from the gutters, a slow rhythm against the night's hush.

Will leaned on the patio railing, cigar smoke curling into the heavy dark, his bourbon glass warm against his palm. The glow from the kitchen spilled across the lawn, falling across the patches where the girls had played tag when they were small. Through the open window, he could hear them now—Emily and Ellie—laughing faintly as Kristen cleared dishes, their voices weaving together in a fragile echo of normalcy.

Normal sounds. Family sounds.

But his mind wouldn't leave the board.

Knights falling sideways. Pawns marching forward. Queens betraying kings. Every piece Rachel had named, every move she had framed, kept turning in his head like gears. He could still see her braid draped forward, hear the sharp edge of her laugh when she teased Casey, smell the faint citrus-floral trace of lotion she'd shrugged off as nothing special. A mask. A mask that had hidden the girl beneath it, but never entirely erased her.

The glass door slid open with a soft scrape. Casey stepped out, boots thudding lightly against the deck. She carried her own bourbon, a cigar pinched between her fingers, and dropped into the chair beside him as if she belonged there. She swung her boots up onto the opposite chair, kicked them off, sparked the cigar to life, and exhaled a lazy stream of smoke that glowed faintly in the moonlight.

"Alright, old man," she said, smirking sideways at him. "You buying the next round, or am I?"

Will chuckled despite the weight pressing into his chest. "Don't tempt me. You drink half my stash every time you're here."

"Yeah," Casey said, clinking her glass against his, "but my presence, I make it taste better."

For a while, they sat in silence. The cicadas hummed in the trees, steady and relentless. In the distance, thunder rumbled like an echo that hadn't yet learned it was done.

"She wasn't all performance," Casey said finally, her voice low, smoke curling with her words. "There were parts of her that were real. The way she relaxed at dinner, the way she trusted me with that Star Wars night. She wanted to belong. She just didn't know how."

Will stared at the ember of his cigar, watching it pulse and fade. His jaw worked.

"I'll miss her in the office," he said quietly. "God help me, I'll miss her. Joe Donavan's daughter."

His mind drifted back to the first time he'd ever laid eyes on her—years ago, sitting in the passenger seat of Joe's truck when they'd crossed paths by chance. Bright-eyed. All questions and curiosity. He'd teased her about being Joe's daughter, and she'd looked up at him, dead serious, and asked if he hunted bad men too.

She'd grown up after that. Changed. And somehow, despite everything, Will realized he'd never truly known who she was.

He thought of Joe. Of what Joe would think if he saw her now. The thought twisted in his chest, sharp and unwelcome. Will shook it away, clinging instead to the small mercy that he'd been able to help her—that he'd known, even briefly, the woman she'd grown into.

Casey smirked faintly, though her eyes didn't soften. "Even after she flashed you half a dozen times?"

"Don't," Will muttered, though the ghost of a smile tugged at his mouth. His hand tightened around the glass, the bourbon trembling faintly. "I keep thinking about that lotion. The smell. Familiar." He exhaled slowly. "Like it's still here."

Casey leaned back, blowing smoke toward the swollen clouds. "She made sure she'd leave something behind. That's the trick, isn't it? Performance or not, she left fingerprints."

The silence thickened between them until Will's phone buzzed against the table. The vibration rattled the wood, sharp in the quiet. He flipped it over. A number he didn't recognize. Just one line:

The girl is safe. Getting her the best help. Will contact you later. —M

Will stared until the words blurred. Relief. Fear. Both knotted in his chest until he couldn't separate them.

Casey tipped her chin at him, reading his face. "Mercer?"

"Yeah." He will set the phone down slowly, as if it might vanish if he lets go too quickly. His voice dropped to gravel. "She's alive."

Casey raised her glass in a small, solemn toast. "Then I'll drink to that. And to whatever's left of her finding peace."

Through the open window, Kristen's voice carried from inside—soft, steady, explaining carefully to the girls what Rachel had endured, what she had said about them, how their laughter and trust had meant something to her, even when her methods terrified them. The twins' voices murmured back, fragile but sure.

Evidence had already arrived at the DA's office—anonymous, untraceable. Boxes of discs, cataloged sheets with names. A reckoning dropped on the doorstep like a gift and a curse all at once.

But Will knew better than to believe it was over. Somewhere out there, Steve's network still moved pawns. Still played.

He lifted his bourbon, stared into the amber, and let the words taste bitter on his tongue.

The board would never be empty.

The cicadas hummed on. Bourbon burned low in their glasses. The rook gleamed faintly under the porch light, cold and unyielding, a piece carved to outlast the hands that played it.

Will sat back, the weight of it all pressing down, when another echo threaded through his mind, not his own thoughts, not Casey's voice, but hers.

Rachel's Journal Entry

They called me a pawn.
But pawns become queens.
The board is reset.
And I still play.

A moment later, Casey pulled the cork from a new bottle of Buffalo Trace and poured, refreshing Will's glass before topping off her own. She dropped a few ice cubes in each, the sharp clink breaking the heavy quiet. With practiced ease, she clipped the end off another one of her favorite cigars and struck a match, the sulfur tang curling into the air before the rich smoke took over.

On the table, Will's phone buzzed. The name flashing across the screen made his brow crease.

"Mercer."

He picked it up, glass in hand. "Yeah?"

Orin Mercer's voice came over the line, low and clipped. "Anderson, two things. First, we confirmed it was your girl who took out those cartel hitters on the marina boat a few months back. Once we realized it was her, we knew we had to bring her in. She has been digging up connections for months and has access to a lot of intel about their network that could be valuable to us. Word is, they've been hunting her, well, the person they didn't know was her, chatter's been bouncing around the forums for weeks.

"She also claims those two you spotted tailing you the other night? They followed her into the next county. She set a trap. They took the bait. Now they're nothing but food for the wildlife in a field. Didn't do the three at the toy store."

Mercer paused, breath heavy, letting the weight of it land before continuing.

"But here's the big heads-up. *Creegan's dead.* They found him in his cell at the county about an hour ago. And it wasn't suicide. Somebody got to him. No suspects, nothing on camera, just one corpse and a hell of a lot of questions."

Will's jaw flexed. "You're telling me someone Epstein'd Steve Creegan."

"Looks that way," Mercer said grimly. "Thought you'd want to know before it hits the wire. Rivers will probably be breaking the news to you soon."

"Appreciate it," Will said, then ended the call.

He turned back toward Casey, glass still in his hand. "Steve Creegan's dead. Somebody made sure of it."

Casey leaned back, smoke curling from her lips, and set her glass down with a hard thud. Her eyes glittered cold in the low light.

That didn't take long. So Creegan's gone, and the devil has him now, screaming in the dark where he belongs. Hell was always waiting for him, patient and hungry. And now it finally consumes his dark soul.

The room went quiet. Will didn't move, didn't speak, just stared into his glass as the silence thickened. Then, after a long breath, his voice came low and steady. "And still... It's not enough."

Will sat in silence, the weight of it pressing down. Creegan was gone, but the scars he carved still bled through Oakhaven. And Will knew the game was far from over.

Casey's hand came to rest on his arm, steady, grounding him in the silence. When he looked up, their eyes met, calm, yet burning with resolve. The message was clear: *you're not alone, and when the next move comes, we'll strike back together.*

ACKNOWLEDGEMENTS

At the heart of this series are two characters who refuse to stay quiet, Detectives Will Anderson and Casey Murphy. Will is the steady hand, the calm in the storm, the one who carries more than he'll ever admit. Casey is the grit, the laugh, the reckless spark that keeps pushing forward even when the world wants to knock her down. Together, they don't just balance each other; they complement and enhance each other.

I owe them more than a few sleepless nights and half-empty coffee cups, because once they showed up on the page, they never stopped talking. (Casey especially, she'd like it noted that she has the best lines, and Will just broods in the background.)

To everyone who's walked alongside them in these pages—thank you. Writing Will and Casey reminds me that even in the darkest places, loyalty, humor, and sharp-edged banter can still light the way.

Here's to the rook and the knight, holding the line together.

About the Author

W. Mark Harrington draws on more than two decades of law enforcement experience in North and South Carolina, where he's encountered the kinds of cases and characters that linger long after the file is closed. A lifelong fan of the crime and thriller tradition, Mark blends gritty realism with sharp dialogue, messy families, and dangerous secrets to craft page-turners that keep readers hooked late into the night.

When he's not writing about detectives Will Anderson and Casey Murphy, Mark can usually be found with a good bourbon in hand or chasing down new barbecue joints to argue about which region does it best.

He currently lives in South Carolina with his close-knit family of five—each with an "M" name—who good-naturedly accuse him of gaming online when he's actually crafting his next twist-filled chapter. *Pawns in the Shadows* follows Harrington's debut, *Demon of Oakhaven*, and *Devil at Rocky Pointe* in the Anderson & Murphy crime series.

Pawns in the Shadows

Detective Will Anderson has spent his career protecting the city he swore to serve. With his sharp-tongued partner Casey Murphy at his side, he's faced killers, conspiracies, and the shadows left by his late mentor. However, nothing prepares them for what awaits them at Ravenwood University.

Students vanish. Bodies surface. And whispers spread about drugged parties, dark-web assault videos, and a cartel pipeline feeding the violence.

When Joe Donovan's daughter Rachel joins the task force as an eager intern, Will vows to keep her safe. But Rachel has secrets of her own—ones that could either crack the case wide open or put a target on her back as Casey gets cryptic messages from the killer.

In the shadows, a silent Watcher moves pieces across the board. To them, Casey, the Anderson family, and their allies are nothing more than pawns.

And pawns, once cornered, can bleed.

www.ingramcontent.com/pod-product-compliance
Lightning Source LLC
LaVergne TN
LVHW040222110826
845146LV00004B/1248